DEDICATION

I would like to dedicate *Close Obsession* to my family, especially my husband, whose tremendous patience and support made this book possible. (Thank you, sweetie, for putting up with my own obsession and being such a wonderful partner and collaborator in the creation of this work!) As with *Close Liaisons*, most of the credit for plot development, scientific elements, and general editing belongs to him.

I would also like to thank the rest of my family for being so wonderful and for always believing in me. I'm particularly grateful to my niece—the only other person I know who loves romance novels—for reading my first book and letting me know how AWESOME she thought it was.

And again, I would like to give special thanks to my friends T and L for being my beta readers and proofreaders. You girls are the best!

PROLOGUE

The Krinar stared at the image in front of him, his hands clenching into fists.

The three-dimensional hologram showed Korum and the guardians approaching the hut on the beach. One of the guardians raised his arm, and the hut blew into pieces, fragments of wood flying everywhere. The fragile human-built structure was clearly no match for the basic nano-blast weapon all guardians carried with them.

The K raised his hand and the image shifted, the flying recording device approaching the wreckage to take a closer look. He didn't worry that the device would be spotted; it was smaller than a mosquito and had been designed by Korum himself.

No, the device was perfect for this task.

As it hovered over the hut, the K could see the drama playing out in the basement, which had been exposed by the blast. The guardians jumped down there, while Korum appeared to be carefully studying the remnants of the hut above ground.

Of course, the K thought, his nemesis would be thorough. Korum would want to make sure nothing and no one escaped from the scene.

The Keiths—the K had started calling them by that name in his mind as well—were panicking, and Rafor stupidly attacked one of the guardians. A foolish move on his part, the K thought dispassionately, watching as the invisible protective shield surrounding the guardians repelled the attack. Now the black-haired Krinar male was jerking uncontrollably on the floor, his nervous system fried from contact with the deadly shield. Had he been human, he would've died instantly.

The guardians didn't let him suffer for long. At the command from their leader, one of the guardians swiftly knocked Rafor unconscious with the stun weapon embedded in his fingers.

The other Keiths were smart enough to avoid Rafor's fate and simply stood there as the silvery crime-collars were locked into place around their necks. They looked angry and defiant, but there was nothing they could do. They were now prisoners, and they would be judged by the Council for their crime.

After a couple of minutes, Korum jumped down into the basement as well, and the K could see that his enemy was furious. He'd known he would be. The Keiths were as good as gone; Korum would show them no mercy.

Sighing, the K switched off the image. He would watch it in greater detail later. For now, he had to figure out some other way to neutralize Korum and implement his plan.

The future of Earth depended on it.

CHAPTER ONE

"Welcome home, darling," Korum said softly as the green landscape of Lenkarda appeared beneath their feet, and the ship landed as quietly as it had taken off.

Her heart hammering in her chest, Mia slowly got up off the seat that had cradled her body so comfortably. Korum was already up, and he extended his hand to her. She hesitated for a second, and then accepted it, clutching his palm with a death grip. The lover she'd thought of as the enemy for the past month was now her only source of comfort in this strange land.

They exited the aircraft and walked a few steps before Korum stopped. Turning back toward the ship, he made a small gesture with his free hand. All of a sudden, the air around the pod began to shimmer, and Mia again heard the low humming sound that signified nanomachines at work.

"You're building something else?" she asked him, surprised.

He shook his head with a smile. "No, I'm un-building."

And as Mia watched, layers of ivory material appeared to peel off the surface of the ship, dissolving in front of her eyes. Within a minute, the ship was gone in its entirety, all of its components turning back into the individual atoms from which they'd been made back in New York.

Despite her stress and exhaustion, Mia couldn't help but marvel at the miracle she'd just witnessed. The ship that had just brought them thousands of miles in a matter of minutes had completely disintegrated, as though it had never existed in the first place.

"Why did you do that?" she asked Korum. "Why un-build it?"

"Because there's no need for it to exist and take up space right now," he explained. "I can create it again whenever we need to use it."

It was true, he could. Mia had witnessed it herself only a few minutes ago on the rooftop of his Manhattan apartment. And now he had un-created it. The pod that had transported them here no longer existed.

As the full implications of that hit her, her heart rate spiked again, and she suddenly found it hard to breathe.

A wave of panic washed over her.

She was now stranded in Costa Rica, in the main K colony—completely dependent on Korum for everything. He had made the ship that had brought them there, and he had just unmade it. If there was another way out of Lenkarda, Mia didn't know about it.

What if he had lied to her earlier? What if she would never see her family again?

She must've looked as terrified as she felt because Korum squeezed her hand gently. The feel of his large, warm hand was oddly reassuring. "Don't worry," he said softly. "It will be all right, I promise."

Mia focused on taking deep breaths, trying to beat back the panic. She had no choice but to trust him now. Even back in New York, he could do anything he wanted with her. There was no reason for him to make her promises that he didn't intend to keep.

Still, the irrational fear gnawed at her insides, adding to the unsavory brew of emotions boiling in her. The knowledge that Korum had been manipulating her all along, using her to crush the Resistance, was like acid in her stomach, burning her from the inside. Everything he'd done, everything he'd said—it had all been a part of his plan. While she had been agonizing over spying on him, he had probably been secretly laughing at her pathetic attempts to outwit him, to help the cause he'd known was doomed to failure from the very beginning.

She felt like such an idiot now for going along with everything the Resistance had told her. It had seemed to make so much sense at the time; she'd felt so noble helping her kind fight against the invaders who had taken over her planet. And instead, she'd unwittingly participated in a power grab by a small group of Ks.

Why hadn't she stopped to think, to fully analyze the situation?

Korum had told her that the entire Resistance movement had been wrong, completely misguided in their mission. And despite herself, Mia had believed him.

The Ks hadn't killed the freedom fighters who had attacked their Centers—and that simple fact told her a lot about the Krinar and their views on humans. If the Ks had truly been the monsters the Resistance portrayed them to be, none of the fighters would have survived.

At the same time, she didn't fully trust Korum's explanation of what a charl was. When John had spoken about his kidnapped sister, there had been too much pain in his voice for it all to be a lie. And Korum's own actions toward her fit much better with John's explanation than with his own. Her lover had denied that the Ks kept humans as their pleasure slaves, yet he'd given her very little choice about anything in their relationship thus far. He had wanted her, and, just like that, her life was no longer her own. She'd been swept off her feet and into his TriBeCa penthouse—and now here she was, in the K Center in Costa Rica, following him toward some unknown destination.

As much as she dreaded the answer to her question, she had to know. "Is Dana here?" Mia asked carefully, not wanting to provoke his temper. "John's sister? John said she's a charl in Lenkarda . . ."

"No," Korum said, shooting her an unreadable look. "John was misinformed—I'm guessing, deliberately—by the Keiths."

"She's not a charl?"

"No, Mia, she was never a charl in the true sense of the word. She was what you would call a xeno—a human obsessed with all things Krinar. Her family never knew that. When she met Lotmir in Mexico, she begged to go with him, and he agreed to take her for some period of time. The last I heard, she got someone else to take her to Krina. I imagine she's quite happy there, given her preferences. As to why she left without a word to her family, I think it probably has something to do with her father."

"Her father?"

"Dana and John haven't had a very happy childhood," Korum said, and she could feel his hand tightening on hers. "Their father is someone who should've been exterminated long ago. Based on the intelligence we've gathered about your Resistance contact, John's father has a particular fetish that involves very young children—"

"He's a pedophile?" Mia asked quietly, bile rising in her throat at the thought.

Korum nodded. "Indeed. I believe his own children were the primary recipients of his affections."

Sickened and filled with intense pity for John and Dana, Mia looked away. If this was true, then she couldn't blame Dana for wanting to get away, to leave everything connected with her old life behind. Although Mia's own family was normal and loving, she'd had some interactions with victims of domestic and child abuse as part of her internship last summer. She knew about the scars it left on the child's psyche. When they got older, some of these children turned to drugs or alcohol to dull their pain. Dana had apparently turned to sex with Ks.

Of course, this was assuming that Korum wasn't lying to her about the whole thing.

Thinking about it, Mia decided that he probably wasn't. Why would he need to? It's not like she could break up with him even if she found out that Dana was held here against her will.

"And what about John?" she asked. "Is he all right? And Leslie?"

"I assume so," he said, and his voice was noticeably cooler. "Neither one has been captured yet."

Relieved, Mia decided to leave it at that. She had a suspicion that talking to Korum about the Resistance was not the smartest course of action for her right now. Instead, she refocused on their surroundings.

"Where are we going?" she asked, looking around. They were walking through what seemed like an untouched forest. Twigs and branches crunched under her feet, and she could hear nature sounds everywhere—birds, some kind of buzzing insects, rustling leaves. She had no idea what he had in mind for the rest of the day, but she just wanted to bury her head under a blanket and hide for several hours. This morning's events and the resulting emotional upheaval had left her completely drained, and she badly needed some quiet time to come to terms with everything that happened.

"To my house," Korum replied, turning his head toward her. There was a small smile on his face again. "It's only a short walk from here. You'll be able to relax and get some rest once we're there."

Mia shot him a suspicious look. His answer was uncannily close to what she had just been thinking. "Can you read my mind?" she asked, horrified at the possibility.

He grinned, showing the dimple on his left cheek. "That would be nice—but no. I just know you well enough by now to see when you're exhausted."

Relieved, Mia nodded and focused on putting one foot in front of another as they walked through the forest. Despite everything, that dazzling smile of his sent a warm sensation all throughout her body.

You're an idiot, Mia.

How could she still feel like this after what he had put her through, after he had manipulated her like that? What kind of a person was she, to fall in love with an alien who had completely taken over her life?

She felt disgusted with herself, yet she couldn't help it. When he smiled like that, she could almost forget everything that happened in the sheer joy of simply being with him. Underneath all the bitterness, she was fiercely glad that the Resistance had failed—that he was still in her life.

Her thoughts kept turning to what he'd said earlier . . . to his admission that he'd grown to care for her. He hadn't intended for it to happen, he'd said, and Mia realized that she'd been right to fear and resist him in the beginning—that he had indeed regarded her as a plaything at first, as a little human toy he could use and discard at his leisure. Of course, "caring" was far from a declaration of love, but it was more than she'd ever expected to hear from him. Like a balm applied to a festering wound, his words made her feel just a tiny bit better, giving her hope that maybe it would be all right after all, that maybe he would keep his promises and she would see her family again—

A squishy sensation under her foot jerked her out of that thought. Startled, Mia looked down and saw that she had stepped on a large, crunchy bug. "Eww!"

"What's the matter?" Korum asked, surprised.

"I just stepped on something," Mia explained in disgust, trying to wipe her sneaker on the nearest patch of grass.

He looked amused. "Don't tell me . . . Are you afraid of insects?"

"I wouldn't say afraid, necessarily," Mia said cautiously. "It's more that I find them really gross."

He laughed. "Why? They're just another set of living creatures, just like you and me."

Mia shrugged and decided against explaining it to him. She wasn't sure she fully understood it herself. Instead, she resolved to pay closer attention to her surroundings. Despite growing up in Florida, she wasn't really comfortable with tropical nature in its raw form.

She much preferred neatly paved paths in beautifully landscaped parks, where she could sit on a bench and enjoy the fresh air with minimal bug encounters.

"You don't have any roads or sidewalks?" she asked Korum with consternation, jumping over what looked like an ant hill.

He smiled at her indulgently. "No. We like our environment to be as close to its original state as possible."

Mia wrinkled her nose, not liking that at all. Her sneakers were already covered with dirt, and she was thankful that the wet season in Costa Rica had not officially begun yet. Otherwise, she imagined they would be trekking through swampland. Given the highly advanced state of Krinar technology, she found it strange that they chose to live in such primitive conditions.

A minute later, they entered another clearing, a much larger one this time. An unusual cream-colored structure stood in the middle. Shaped like an elongated cube with rounded corners, it had no windows or doors—or any visible openings at all.

"This is your house?"

Mia had seen structures like this one on the three-dimensional map in Korum's office earlier today. They'd looked very strange and alien to her from a distance, and that impression was even stronger now that she was standing next to one. It just looked so incredibly *foreign*, so different from anything she'd ever seen in her life.

Korum nodded, leading her toward the building. "Yes, this is my home—and now it's yours too."

Mia swallowed nervously, her anxiety growing at the last part of his statement. Why did he keep saying that? Did he really intend for her to live here permanently? He'd promised to bring her back to New York to finish her senior year of college, and Mia desperately clung to that thought as she stared at the pale walls of the house looming in front of her.

As they approached, a part of the wall suddenly disintegrated in front of them, creating an opening large enough for them to walk through.

Mia gasped in surprise, and Korum smiled at her reaction. "Don't worry," he said. "This is an intelligent building. It anticipates our needs and creates doorways as needed. It's nothing to be afraid of."

"Will it do that for anyone or just you?" Mia asked, stopping before the opening. She knew it was illogical, her reluctance to go in. If Korum intended to keep her prisoner, there was nothing she could do about it—she was already in an alien colony with no way to escape. Still, she couldn't bring herself to voluntarily enter her new "home" unless she was sure she could leave it on her own.

Apparently intuiting the source of her concern, Korum gave her a reassuring look. "It will do it for you as well. You'll be able to go in and out whenever you want, although it might be best if you stayed close to me for the first few weeks . . . at least until you get used to our way of life and I have a chance to introduce you to others."

Exhaling in relief, Mia looked up at him. "Thanks," she said quietly, some of her panic fading.

Maybe being here wouldn't be so bad after all. If he really did bring her back to New York at the end of summer, then her sojourn in Lenkarda might prove to be exactly that—a couple of months spent at an incredible place that few humans could even imagine, with the extraordinary creature she'd fallen in love with.

Feeling slightly better about the situation, Mia

stepped through the opening, entering a Krinar dwelling for the first time.

The sight that greeted her inside was utterly unexpected.

Mia had been bracing for something alien and high-tech—maybe floating chairs similar to the ones in the ship that had transported them here. Instead, the room looked just like Korum's penthouse back in New York, right down to the plush cream-colored couch. Mia flushed at the memory of what had taken place on that couch just a little while ago. Only the walls were different; they seemed to be made of the same transparent material as the ship, and she could see the greenery outside instead of the Hudson River.

"You have the same furniture here?" she asked in surprise, letting go of his hand and taking a step forward to gape at the strange sight. She couldn't imagine that furniture stores made deliveries to K Centers—but then he could probably just conjure up whatever he wanted using their nanotechnology.

"Not exactly," Korum said, smiling at her. "I set this up ahead of your arrival. I thought it might be easier for you to acclimate if you could relax in familiar surroundings for the first couple of weeks. After you feel more comfortable here, I can show you how I usually live."

Mia blinked at him. "You set it up just for me? When?"

Even with rapid fabrication—or whatever Korum had called the technology that let him make things out of nothing—he probably still needed a little time to do all this. When would he have had a chance to even think about this, given the events of this morning? She tried to picture him making a couch while capturing the Keiths and almost snickered out loud.

"A little while ago," Korum said ambiguously, shrugging a little.

Mia frowned at him. "So . . . not today?" For some reason, the timing of this gesture seemed important.

"No, not today."

Mia stared at him. "You were planning this for a while? Me being here, I mean?"

"Of course," he said casually. "I plan everything."

Mia took a deep breath. "And if I hadn't been in danger from the Resistance? Would you have still brought me here?"

He looked at her, his expression indecipherable. "Does it really matter?" he asked softly.

It mattered to Mia, but she wasn't up to having that discussion right now. So she just shrugged and looked away, studying the room. It *was* somewhat comforting to be someplace that at least looked familiar, and she had to admit that it was a thoughtful thing to do—creating a human-like environment for her in his house.

"Are you hungry?" Korum asked, regarding her with a smile.

Making food for her seemed to be one of his favorite activities; he had even fed her this morning when she'd been afraid he would kill her for helping the Resistance. It was one of the things that had always made her feel so conflicted about him, about their relationship in general. Despite his arrogance, he could be incredibly caring and considerate. It drove Mia nuts, the fact that he'd never truly acted like the villain she'd thought him to be.

She shook her head. "No, thanks. Still full from the sandwich earlier." And she was. All she wanted to do was lie down and try to give her brain a rest.

"Okay then," Korum said. "You can relax here for a bit. I have to go out for an hour or so. Do you think you'll be all right by yourself?"

Mia nodded. "Do you have a bed somewhere?" she asked.

"Of course. Here, come with me."

Mia followed Korum as he walked down a familiar hallway to the bedroom that was identical to the one he had in TriBeCa. She noted the location of the bathroom as well.

"So everything here is stuff I know how to use?" she asked.

"Yes, pretty much," he said, reaching out to briefly stroke her cheek. His fingers felt hot against her skin. "The bed is probably more comfortable than you're used to because it utilizes the same intelligent technology as the chair in the ship and the walls of this house. I figured you wouldn't mind that. Don't be scared if it adjusts to your body, okay?"

Despite the tension squeezing her temples, Mia smiled, remembering how comfortable the seat in the aircraft had been. "Okay, that sounds good. I'm looking forward to trying it."

"I'm sure you'll enjoy it." His eyes gleamed with some unknown emotion. "Take a nap if you want, and I'll be back soon."

Bending down, he gave her a chaste kiss on the forehead and walked out, leaving her alone in an intelligent dwelling inside the alien settlement.

* * *

Less than a mile away, the Krinar watched as his nemesis arrived with his charl.

The gentle way Korum held her hand as he led her toward his house was so out of character that the K almost chuckled to himself. This was an interesting development, the involvement of a human girl. Would it change anything? Somehow, he doubted it.

His enemy would not be swayed from his course, certainly not by some little human.

No, there was only one way to save the human race.

And he was the only one who could do it.

CHAPTER TWO

Mia woke up in total darkness.

She lay there for a moment, trying to figure out the time. She felt incredibly well-rested, every muscle in her body relaxed and her mind completely clear. Right away, she knew she was in Korum's house in Lenkarda, lying on his "intelligent" bed. Stretching with a yawn, she wondered how Korum had managed to sleep on a regular human mattress back in New York. She couldn't imagine wanting to sleep anywhere other than this bed for the rest of her life.

The sheets were wrapped around her body, caressing her bare skin with a light, sensuous touch. She was neither cold nor hot, and the pillow cradled her head and neck in exactly the right way. Whatever tension she'd felt earlier was completely gone.

She had not intended to fall asleep, but the rest had definitely done wonders for her state of mind. After Korum had left, she'd showered and climbed into bed with the goal of resting for a few minutes. As soon as she'd gotten in, the sheets had moved around her, wrapping her in a gentle cocoon, and she'd felt subtle vibrations under the most tense parts of her body. It was as though soft fingers were massaging away the knots in her back and neck. She remembered loving the sensation, and then she must've fallen asleep because she couldn't recall anything else.

Apparently sensing that she was awake, the room gradually got lighter, even though there was no obvious source of artificial light.

It was a clever idea, Mia thought, to have the light turn on so slowly. Bright light after complete darkness was often painful to the eyes, yet that's how most human light fixtures worked, simply on and off—disregarding the fact that light-dark transitions in nature were far more subtle.

Reluctant to leave the comfort of the bed, Mia lay there and tried to figure out what to do next. The sick, panicky feeling of earlier was gone, and she could think more clearly.

It was true that Korum had used and manipulated her.

But, to be fair, he'd done it to protect his own kind—just as she'd thought she was helping all of humanity by spying on him. The sense of betrayal she'd felt yesterday had been irrational, out of place considering the nature of their relationship and her own actions toward him. The fact that he hadn't really done anything to punish her for *her* betrayal spoke volumes about his intentions.

She'd been wrong to paint him with such a dark brush before. If he hadn't hurt her for what she'd done thus far, he probably never would.

However, he clearly had no problem disregarding her wishes. Case in point: she was here in Lenkarda. Yet, if he'd spoken the truth, she would still be able to go visit her parents soon, and even come back to New York to finish college.

All in all, her situation was much better than she'd feared this morning, when she'd thought he might kill her for helping the Resistance.

Still, the circumstances she found herself in were unsettling. She was in a K Center, where she didn't speak the language, didn't know anyone except Korum, and had no idea how to use even the most basic Krinar technology. As a human, she was the ultimate outsider here. Would the Ks think she was dumb because of what she was? Because she couldn't understand the Krinar language or read ten books in a couple of hours, the way Korum could? Would they make fun of her ignorance and her technological illiteracy? She wasn't exactly tech-savvy even by human standards. In general, was Korum's arrogance simply a part of his personality, or was it typical of his species and their overall attitude toward humans?

Of course, agonizing about all this didn't change the facts. Whether she liked it or not, she was in Lenkarda for at least the next couple of months, and she had to make the best of it. And in the meantime, there was so much she could learn here—

The bedroom door opened quietly, and Korum walked in, interrupting her thoughts. "Hey there, sleepyhead, how are you feeling?"

Mia couldn't help smiling at him, forgetting her concerns for the moment. For the first time since she'd known him, Korum was dressed in Krinar clothing: a sleeveless shirt made of some soft-looking white material and a pair of loose grey shorts that ended just above his knees. It was a simple outfit, but it did wonders for his physique, accentuating his powerfully muscled build. He looked mouthwateringly gorgeous, his smooth bronze skin glowing with health and those amber eyes shining as he looked at her lying on his bed.

"The bed is awesome," Mia confided. "I don't know how you slept on anything else."

He grinned, sitting down next to her and picking up a strand of her hair to play with. "I know. It was a real sacrifice—but your presence made it quite tolerable."

Mia laughed and rolled over onto her stomach, feeling absurdly happy. "So what now? Do I get to meet other intelligent objects? I have to say, your technology is very cool."

"Oh, you have no idea just how cool our technology is," Korum said, looking at her with a mysterious smile. "But you'll learn soon."

Bending down, he kissed her exposed shoulder and then lightly nibbled on her neck, his mouth warm and soft on her skin. Closing her eyes, Mia shivered from the pleasant sensation. Her body immediately responded to his touch, and she moaned softly, feeling a surge of warm moisture between her legs.

He stopped and sat up straight.

Surprised, Mia opened her eyes and looked at him. "You don't want me?" she asked quietly, trying to keep the hurt note out of her voice.

"What? No, my darling, I very much want you." And it was true; she could see the warm golden flecks in his expressive eyes, and the soft material of his shorts did little to hide his erection.

"Then why did you stop?" asked Mia, trying very hard not to sound like a child deprived of candy.

He sighed, looking frustrated. "A friend of mine is coming over to meet you. He'll be here in a few minutes."

Mia looked at him in surprise. "Your friend wants to

meet me? Why?"

Korum smiled. "Because he's heard a lot about you from me. And also because he's one of our top mind experts and can help you with the adjustment process."

Mia frowned slightly. "A mind expert? You want me to see a shrink?"

Korum shook his head, grinning. "No, he's not a shrink. In our society, a mind expert is someone who deals with all aspects of the brain. He's like a neurosurgeon, psychiatrist, and therapist combined—literally an expert on all matters having to do with the mind."

That was interesting, but didn't really answer her question. "So why does he want to see me?"

"Because I think there's something he can do to make you feel more at home here," Korum said, his fingers trailing down her arm, rubbing it softly.

He liked to do that, Mia had noticed, to just randomly touch her during their conversations, as though craving constant physical contact. Mia didn't mind. It was that chemistry he had talked about before; their bodies gravitated toward each other like two objects in space.

She forced her attention back to the conversation. "Like what?" she asked, feeling slightly wary.

"Well, for instance, would you like to be able to understand and speak our language?"

Mia's eyes widened, and she nodded eagerly. "Of course!"

"Have you ever wondered how I'm able to speak English so well? And every other human language? How all of us speak like this?"

"I didn't know you spoke other languages besides English," Mia confessed, staring at him in amazement. She had briefly wondered how he knew such perfect

American English, but she'd always assumed the Ks had simply studied everything before coming to Earth. Korum was incredibly smart, so she'd never really questioned the fact that he knew her language and was able to speak it without any accent. And now he was telling her that he spoke a bunch of other languages as well?

"So you speak French?" she asked. At his nod, she continued, "Spanish? Russian? Polish? Mandarin?" He made an affirmative gesture each time.

"Okay . . . What about Swahili?" asked Mia, sure that she had caught him this time.

"That too," he said, smiling at her astounded expression.

"Okay," said Mia slowly. "I gather you're about to tell me that it's not just pure smarts on your part."

He grinned. "Exactly. I could've learned the languages on my own given enough time, but there's a more efficient way—and that's what Saret can do for you."

Mia stared at him. "He can teach me how to speak Krinar?"

"Better than that. He can give you the same abilities that I have—instant comprehension and knowledge of any language, be it human or Krinar."

Mia gasped in shock, her heart beating faster from excitement. "How?"

"By giving you a tiny implant that will influence a specific region of your brain and act as a highly advanced translation device."

"A brain implant?" Her excitement immediately turned to dread as everything inside Mia violently rejected the idea. He had already embedded tracking devices in her palms; the last thing she needed was alien technology influencing her brain. The ability he had described was incredible, and she desperately wanted it—

but not at that price.

"The device is not really what you're picturing," Korum said. "It's going to be tiny, the size of a cell, and you will not feel discomfort at any point—either during insertion or afterwards."

"And if I say no, that I don't want it?" Mia asked quietly, alarmed at the idea that Korum already had the mind expert on the way here.

"Why not?" He looked at her with a small frown.

"Do you really need to ask?" she said incredulously. "You *shined* me—you put tracking devices in me under the pretext of healing my palms. Did you really think I would be okay with you putting something in my brain?"

Korum's frown deepened. "This doesn't have any extra functionality, Mia." He didn't seem the least bit repentant about shining her in the first place.

"Really?" she asked him acerbically. "It doesn't do anything extra? Doesn't influence my thoughts or feelings in any way?"

"No, my darling, it doesn't." He looked vaguely amused at the thought.

"I don't want a brain implant," Mia said firmly, looking at him with a mutinous expression on her face.

He stared back at her. "Mia," he said softly, "if I had truly wanted to put something nefarious in your brain, I could've done it in a million different ways. I can implant anything in your body at any time, and you wouldn't have a clue. The only reason why I'm offering you this ability is because I want you to be comfortable here, to be able to communicate with everyone on your own. If you don't want this, then that's your choice. I won't force it on you. But very few humans get this opportunity, so I would advise you to think really hard before you turn it down."

Mia looked away, struck by the realization that he was right. He didn't need to inform her or get her consent for anything he wanted to do to her. The panic that she thought she had under control threatened to bubble up again, and she squelched it with effort.

Something didn't quite make sense to her. Taking a deep breath, Mia turned her gaze to his face again, studying his inscrutable expression. It bothered her that she still understood him so little, that the person who had so much power over her was still such a big unknown.

"Korum . . ." She wasn't sure if she should bring this up, but she couldn't resist. The question had tormented her for weeks. "Why did you shine me? I hadn't even met the Resistance at that point, so it's not like you needed to keep tabs on me for your big plan . . ."

"Because I wanted to make sure I can always find you," he said, and there was a possessive note in his voice that frightened her. "I held you in my arms that day, and I knew I wanted more. I wanted everything, Mia. You were mine from that moment on, and I had no intention of losing you, not even for a moment."

Not even for a moment? Did he realize how crazy that sounded? He had seen a girl he wanted, and he'd made sure her location would always be known to him.

The fact that he thought he had the right to do this was terrifying. How could she deal with someone like that? He had no concept of boundaries when it came to her, no respect for her freedom of will. He had just casually admitted to a horrible and high-handed act, and she had no idea what she could say to him now.

At her silence, Korum took a deep breath and got up. "You should get dressed," he said quietly. "Saret will be here in a minute."

Mia nodded and sat up, holding the sheets to her

chest. Now was not the time to analyze the complexities of their relationship. Taking a deep breath of her own, she pushed aside her fear. There was no way she could change her situation right now, and focusing on the negative would only make things worse. She needed to find a way to get along with her lover and figure out how to better manage his domineering nature.

"What should I wear?" Mia asked. "I didn't bring any clothes . . ."

"Do you want your usual jeans and T-shirts, or do you want to dress like everyone else here?" Korum asked, a smile appearing on his face. Some of the tension in the room dissipated.

"Um, like everyone else, I guess." She didn't want to stick out like a sore thumb.

"Okay, then." Korum made a small gesture with his hand and handed her a light-colored piece of material that hadn't been there only a second ago.

Wide-eyed, Mia stared at the piece of clothing he just gave her. "More instant fabrication?" she asked, trying to act like it wasn't still a huge shock to her to see things materializing out of nothing.

He grinned. "That's right. If you don't like this, I can get you something else. Go ahead, try it on."

Mia let go of the sheet and climbed out of bed, feeling comfortable with her nakedness. For all his faults, Korum had done wonders for her body image and self-confidence. Because he repeatedly told her how beautiful he found her to be, she no longer worried about being too skinny or having frizzy hair and pale skin. He would've been a boon during her insecure teenage years.

No, scratch that thought. No teenager should be subjected to someone so overwhelming.

Taking the dress, she put it on, making sure that the

low-cut portion was in the back. "What do you think?" she asked, doing a small twirl.

He smiled with a warm glow in his eyes. "It looks perfect on you."

His shorts now had a bulge in them, and Mia smiled to herself in satisfaction. Despite everything, it was nice to know that she had that kind of effect on him, that his need was as strong as hers. At least in this, they were equals.

Curious to see how the dress looked, she walked over to the mirror on the other side of the bedroom.

Korum was right; the outfit was very pretty. Similar in style to the ones she'd seen the female Keiths wear, it was a beautiful shade of ivory with peach undertones, and draped over her body in exactly the right way. Her back and shoulders were mostly exposed, while her front was modestly covered, with strategic pleats around her chest area concealing her nipples. The length was exactly right for her too, with the floaty skirt stopping a couple of inches above her knees.

When she turned around, he handed her a pair of flat ivory sandals, made of some unusually soft material. Mia tried them on. They fit her feet perfectly and were surprisingly comfortable.

"Nice, thanks," she said. Then, remembering one last crucial item, she asked, "What about underwear?"

"We don't really wear it," Korum said. "I can make it for you if you insist, but you might want to try wearing just our clothes."

No underwear? "What if the dress rides up or something?"

"It won't. The material is intelligent as well. It's designed to adhere to your body in exactly the right way. If you move or bend in a certain direction, it will move with you so that you will always be covered."

That was handy. Mia thought of the countless wardrobe malfunctions in Hollywood that could've been prevented with K clothing. "Okay, then I'm ready, I guess," she said. "I have to use the restroom, and then I'm good to go."

"Excellent," Korum said, smiling. "I'll see you in the living room."

And with a quick kiss on her forehead, he exited the room.

* * *

"I like what you've done with the place. Very twenty-first-century American."

Korum's friend had just walked in and was looking around with a smile. An inch or two shorter than Korum, he was just as powerfully built, and had the darker coloring typical of the Ks. His face was rounder, however, and his cheekbones sharper, reminding her a bit of someone with Asian ancestry.

"What can I say? You know I have good taste," said Korum, getting up from the couch where he had been sitting with Mia to greet the newcomer. Approaching him, Korum lightly touched his shoulder with his palm, and the other K reciprocated his gesture.

Mia wondered if that was the K version of a handshake.

Turning toward her, Korum said, "Mia, this is my friend Saret. Saret, this is Mia, my charl."

Saret smiled, his brown eyes twinkling. He seemed genuinely pleased to see her. "Hello, Mia. Welcome to our Center. I hope you've been finding it to your liking so far?"

Mia got up and smiled in return. It was strange to be meeting another K. With the exception of a couple of brief encounters with Korum's colleagues, her lover was the only Krinar she'd interacted with thus far.

"It's been very nice, thank you."

Should she offer to shake his hand? Or do that shoulder thing Korum had just done? As soon as the thought occurred to her, she decided against it. She had no idea what the K rules on physical contact were, and she didn't want to accidentally cause offense.

"Have you had a chance to go anywhere in Lenkarda so far? Korum told me you arrived only this morning."

Mia shook her head regretfully. "No, I haven't. I'm afraid I spent most of the day sleeping." What time was it, anyway? Through the transparent walls of the house, she could see that it was dark outside. It had to be late in the evening, or maybe even the middle of the night.

"Mia was jet-lagged and exhausted from what happened earlier," Korum explained, walking back toward her and placing a proprietary hand around her back. He pulled her down on the couch next to him, and Saret sat down on one of the plush armchairs across from them.

"Of course," Saret said, "I completely understand. It had to be very traumatic for you, learning the truth that way."

Mia stared at him in surprise. How much did he know? Had Korum told him everything, including her role in the Resistance attack on their Centers? She had no idea how her actions would be viewed by the Krinar. Would she be punished somehow for aiding the Resistance earlier?

"Well, the good thing is that it's over," Korum said, taking one of Mia's hands into his and softly rubbing her palm with his thumb. Turning toward her, he promised, "You don't have to worry about any of this again."

"Actually," Saret said with a regretful look on his handsome face, "I'm afraid there might be one more thing that Mia has to do."

Korum's face darkened. "I already told them no. She's been through enough."

Saret sighed. "There was a formal request from the United Nations—"

"Fuck the Unites Nations. They don't get to request anything after this fiasco. They're damn lucky we didn't retaliate—"

"Be that as it may, the majority of the Council believes it's important to extend this gesture of goodwill to them."

Mia listened to them arguing with a cold feeling in the pit of her stomach. The United Nations? The Council? What did any of this have to do with her?

"The Council can go fuck itself too," Korum said in an uncompromising tone. "There's absolutely no need for this, and they know it. She's my charl, and they don't get to tell me what to do."

"She's not just your charl, Korum, and you know it. She's one of the witnesses in what will be the biggest trial of the last ten thousand years, not to mention the human proceedings—"

Mia wanted to throw up as she began to understand where the conversation was leading. "Excuse me," she said quietly, "what exactly is needed from me?"

"It doesn't matter," Korum said flatly. "They can't make you do anything without my permission."

Saret sighed again. "Look, the Council wants her testimony as well. It really would be for the best if you just let her do it—"

Staring at them, Mia began to feel angry. They were

talking about her like she was a child or a pet of some sort. Whatever it was they wanted from her, it should be her decision, not Korum's.

"She doesn't need this right now," Korum said firmly. "They have plenty of evidence, and I'm not putting her through any additional stress—"

"Excuse me," Mia said coldly. "I want to know what the fuck you're talking about."

Clearly startled, Saret laughed, and Korum gave her a disapproving look.

"I think your charl is gutsier than you give her credit for," Saret said to Korum, still chuckling. Turning toward Mia, he explained, "You see, Mia, the traitors that you helped us catch—the Keiths, as your Resistance friends called them—will be tried according to our laws. While our judicial process is fairly different from what you're used to, we do require all available evidence to be presented—and testimony from all the witnesses. Since you were involved throughout, your testimony could play a role in whether they get convicted and how serious their punishment will be."

"You want me to testify in a Krinar trial?" Mia asked incredulously.

"Yes, exactly, and we've also received a formal request for your presence from the United Nations Ambassador—"

"She's not doing it, Saret. Forget it. You can go back to Arus and tell him it's not happening."

"Look, Korum, are you sure you want to do this? We're so close to getting the approval . . . You know this is not going to be viewed favorably—"

"I know," Korum said. "I'm willing to take that chance. It won't be the first time they were pissed at me."

Saret looked frustrated. "Okay, but I think you're

making a big mistake. All she has to do is get up there and talk—"

"You know as well as I do that if she gets up there, the Protector will try to take her apart. I will not put her through that. And I don't want her anywhere near the United Nations right now—that's far too dangerous. Besides, human media might sniff out the story, and Mia doesn't need the whole world watching her testimony at the UN. Her family doesn't even know anything yet."

Her anger forgotten, Mia squeezed Korum's hand in gratitude. She couldn't help but be touched by his protectiveness. It was hard to say what appealed to her less—the idea of appearing in front of the Krinar Council or at the United Nations with the whole world watching.

"Arus said they can make other arrangements for her. The UN hearing can take place behind closed doors, with nothing leaked to the media. And the Council has agreed to accept her recorded testimony for the trial."

"Tell Arus that he can talk to me himself if he's so determined to make this happen," Korum said quietly, his eyes narrowed with anger. "She's my charl. If he wants her to do something, he needs to ask me very, very nicely. And then, if Mia says she's okay with it, I will maybe consider it."

Saret smiled ruefully. "Sure. You know I hate to be in the middle like this. You and Arus can talk it out. I was asked to deliver a message, and that's where my responsibility ends."

Korum nodded. "Understood."

The expression on his face was still harsh, and Mia shifted in her seat, feeling uncomfortable about the role she had inadvertently played in this disagreement. She needed to learn more about this trial and what it all meant, but she didn't want to ask more questions in front of Saret. Instead, wanting to lighten the tension in the room, she asked cautiously, "So how do you two know each other?"

Saret smiled at her, understanding what she was doing. "Oh, we go way back. We've known each other since we were children."

Mia's eyes widened. If they had been children together, then she was in the presence of two aliens who measured their age in thousands of years. "Were you classmates or something?" she asked in fascination.

Korum shook his head, his lips curving slightly. "Not exactly. We were playmates. Our children are educated very differently than humans—we don't have schools like you do."

"No? Then how do your children learn?"

Saret grinned at her, apparently pleased by her curiosity. "A lot of it is play-based. We let them develop most of the key skills they need through socialization and interaction with others, be it children or adults. Later on, they do apprenticeships in various fields with the goal of honing their problem-solving and critical-thinking abilities."

Mia looked at him in fascination. "But how do they learn things like math and history and writing?"

Saret waved his hand dismissively. "Oh, those are easy. I don't know if Korum has talked to you about this before—"

"I haven't yet," Korum said. "You got here as soon as Mia woke up. All I had time to do was mention the language implant."

"Oh, good." Saret sounded excited. "Would you like to get that done tonight, Mia?"

Mia hesitated. If Korum wasn't lying to her, then she would be an idiot to pass on this opportunity. "Can you please explain to me again what exactly this implant is and what it does?" she asked, looking at Saret.

Korum sighed, looking exasperated. "Yes, Saret, please tell Mia exactly what the implant is. She doesn't seem to trust my explanation."

"Can you blame me?" she asked Korum, trying to keep the bitterness out of her tone.

Saret's eyebrows rose, and he grinned again. "Still some unresolved issues, I see."

Korum shot him a warning look, and Saret's grin promptly disappeared. "Never mind," he said hastily. "I don't know what Korum told you, Mia, but the language implant is a very simple, very straightforward device that many Krinar get upon maturity—once our brain is fully developed. It's a microscopic computer made of special biological material that essentially acts as a highly advanced translator. Its function is to convert data from one form into another—thought pattern to language and vice versa. It acts on one area of the brain only and has absolutely no harmful side effects."

"Does it ever malfunction?" asked Mia. "Or can it do something else to me?"

"Like what?" Saret looked perplexed. "And no, this technology has been in existence for over ten thousand years, so it's been fully perfected. It doesn't malfunction, ever."

"Can it make me think something that I don't want? Or broadcast my thoughts?" Now that she'd said it out loud, Mia could hear how ridiculous that sounded.

Saret shook his head with a smile. "No, nothing like that. It's a very basic device. What you're talking about is far more advanced science. Mind control and thought reading are still in theoretical stages of development."

"But it is theoretically possible?" Mia asked in

amazement, the psych major in her suddenly salivating at the prospect of learning even a tiny sliver of what the Krinar knew about the brain. Now that she wasn't so nervous, it occurred to Mia that the K sitting across from her was probably a veritable treasure trove of knowledge about her field of study.

Saret nodded. "Theoretically, yes. Practically, not yet."

Mia opened her mouth to ask another question, and Korum interrupted, looking amused at her unabashed interest, "So does this make you feel more comfortable about getting the implant?"

Mia considered it for a second. How much should she trust them? Korum had already proven himself to be a master manipulator, and she had no idea what Saret was like. But then again, like Korum said, they didn't really need her permission to do this. The fact that they were giving her a choice is what ultimately convinced her.

"I think so," she said slowly.

"Okay then, Saret, can you please do the honors?"

"Um, wait," Mia said, her heart starting to beat faster, "you mean I can get it right now? Is there an anesthetic or anything?"

Saret smiled. "No, nothing like that. It's very easy—you won't even feel it."

"Okay . . ."

Korum got up, still holding Mia's hand. Saret stood up also and approached them. "May I?" he asked Korum, reaching for Mia.

Korum nodded, and Saret extended his right hand, brushing Mia's hair back behind her left ear. She shuddered a little at the unfamiliar touch. Her nails dug into Korum's hand, and she fought the urge to flinch. Even though they'd told her it wouldn't hurt, she couldn't help her primal reaction.

"That's it." Saret stepped back.

"What?" Mia blinked at him in shock.

"It's done. You have the implant. We'll give it about a minute to sync with your neural pathways, and then we'll test it out."

"But how? Where did it go in?"

"It went in through the skin," Korum explained, smiling at her. "You didn't feel it, right?"

"No, I didn't feel anything." Were they playing a joke on her?

Saret laughed, enjoying her reaction. "Good, you weren't supposed to. The device itself has analgesic properties, so you shouldn't have felt the tiny cut it made in the thin skin behind your ear."

Mia raised her left hand, feeling for the wound, but there was nothing.

"So tell me, Mia, do you feel any different? Are you thinking any thoughts you shouldn't be thinking?" Korum asked her with a mocking gleam in his eyes.

Mia shook her head, frowning at him slightly. She didn't appreciate his making fun of her ignorance.

And then her breath caught in her throat.

Korum had just spoken to her in Krinar—and she had understood his every word.

"Wait a second," she said, and the words that came out of her mouth were strange and unfamiliar. Yet she knew exactly what they meant, and her facial muscles seemed to have no problem forming the sounds. "You just spoke in Krinar!"

Korum smiled. "And so did you. How does it feel?"

Mia blinked at him. It felt strange, yet effortless. "It seems to be okay," she said again in Krinar. "I just don't understand how it works. What if I want to say something in English?"

"If you want to say something in English, you just have to think English, and you'll switch languages," Saret explained. "Right now, your brain's natural response is to speak in Krinar because that's the language in which we're addressing you. You have to actively think that you want to speak in English in order to do so when confronted with Krinar speech. However, later on, when you get used to the implant, switching back and forth will be automatic and won't require any extra thought on your part. This is really not all that different from being multilingual. I'm sure you know people who speak several languages fluently—and now you have that same ability, just taken to a different level."

Mia listened to his explanation, the reality of it seeping in. "Wow," she breathed softly, "so I can really, truly speak any known language now? Just like that?"

She wanted to jump up and run around the room, screaming with glee, and she controlled herself with effort, not wanting to appear like a silly kid in front of Korum's friend. It was just so unbelievably amazing. She had always been good with languages in school, studying Spanish and French throughout high school, but she'd never managed to become fluent. And now she could speak whatever language she wanted? Her earlier reluctance forgotten, Mia could now only think of the mind-blowing possibilities.

"Just like that," Korum confirmed, looking down at her with a smile, and Saret nodded as well.

Struggling to appear dignified, Mia fought back the huge grin that threatened to split her face. "Thank you," she told Saret. "I really appreciate it."

"You're welcome, Mia. I hope to see you soon." And with that, he touched Korum's shoulder again and left, the wall to their right disintegrating to grant him passage.

CHAPTER THREE

Once Saret was gone, Mia couldn't contain her elation any longer. She felt like she would choke from the sheer delight that filled her from within, and she knew that she was grinning now, probably looking like an idiot. But she couldn't bring herself to care anymore, her excitement too strong to be restrained.

She was now a polyglot!

She tried to picture herself speaking Cantonese, and the words suddenly came to her. Opening her mouth, she heard the harsh tonal sounds coming out as she told Korum, "I can't believe this is real." Promptly switching to Russian, she continued, "I can't believe I can do this!" And then again in German, nearly jumping from excitement, "Oh my God, I can speak them all!"

He grinned at her, his face glowing with pleasure. Letting go of her hand, he brought his palm up to her face, curving it around her cheek. Looking down at her, he said in English, "I'm glad you're excited. There's so much I want to show you, darling . . ."

Mia stared up at him, her excitement over her newfound ability suddenly transforming into something else. He was so beautiful, and the warm expression on his face as he gazed down at her made her heart squeeze. "Korum," she said softly, "I . . ."

She didn't know what she could say, how she could express what she was feeling. There was still so much unresolved between them, but in this moment, she couldn't bring herself to care about the way their relationship had started, about all the mutual lies and betrayals. In this moment, she knew only that she loved him, that every part of her longed to be with him.

Reaching up, she wrapped her hand around the back of his neck and tentatively brought his face down toward her. Rising up on her toes, she kissed him on the mouth, her lips soft and uncertain on his. She rarely made the first move—he was usually the one to initiate sex in their relationship—and she could feel the sudden tension gripping his body at her touch.

He kissed her back, his mouth hot and eager, and she found herself lifted up into his arms and carried somewhere. The destination turned out to be the bedroom, and they ended up on the bed, his powerful body covering her own, pressing her into the mattress with its weight. Mia's hands frantically tore at his shirt, trying to find a way to get it off him, to feel his nakedness against her own. She felt like she was burning, her skin too sensitive, and the barrier of clothing between them was simply unbearable. Wanting more, she kissed him harder, catching his lower lip between her teeth and biting on it lightly.

Korum sucked in his breath, and she felt him abruptly pull away. Before she could do more than blink, he reared up on the bed and swiftly pulled off his shirt and shorts, revealing his large erection. Mia's mouth watered at the sight of his naked body, all toned muscle covered with that smooth golden skin, his chest lightly dusted with dark hair—and then he was on her, tearing off her dress and leaving her lying there, spread out and exposed before his eyes.

Crawling on top of her, he kissed her again, more aggressively this time, and his hand found its way down her body and toward the junction between her legs. Mia moaned into his mouth, arching her hips toward his hand, and his fingers stroked her folds softly before one finger found its way inside her opening and pressed deep, causing her inner muscles to tighten with the sudden rush of pleasure. "I love how wet you are," he murmured, penetrating her first with one finger and then two, stretching her, preparing her for his possession. Mia cried out, her head falling back, and felt the moist heat of his mouth on her neck, licking and nibbling the sensitive area.

There was something else too, a strange but pleasant sensation that registered somewhere in the back of her brain, a warm vibration that felt like massaging fingers sliding over the back of her body, stroking and caressing her shoulders, the curve of her spine, gently squeezing her buttocks and the backs of her thighs.

The bed, she realized dimly, it had to be the intelligent bed, and then she forgot about it, too immersed in what Korum was doing to pay attention to anything else. His fingers had found a rhythm, two thrusts shallow, one thrust deep, and his thumb was now circling her clitoris in a way that drove her insane. Her nails dug into his back, her entire body shaking with need, and then his thumb pressed on her clit directly and she came apart, convulsing in his arms, waves of pleasure radiating all the way down to her toes.

After the last aftershock was over, Mia opened her eyes and looked at him. He was staring at her with such burning hunger on his face that her breath caught in her throat and her stomach clenched again with answering desire. His fingers were still inside her, and he took them out slowly, causing her to shiver with pleasure.

Bringing his hand up to his face, Korum licked the fingers slowly, clearly savoring her taste. Mia stared at him, mesmerized, unable to look away even as she felt his knee parting her thighs and the hardness of his cock pressing against her vulnerable folds.

He began to enter her, still looking into her eyes, and Mia gasped from the sensation. Even though they'd had sex only a few hours earlier and he had prepared her with his fingers, her body still needed a moment to accommodate him, to stretch around the organ penetrating her so relentlessly. There was something incredibly intimate about being with him like that, feeling his bare skin against her breasts and his shaft inside her, while meeting his gaze with her own. It was as if he wanted to possess more than just her body, Mia thought vaguely, as if he wanted something more than just the sex.

Still looking at her, he began to move his hips, slowly at first and then at a faster pace, each stroke adding to the tension that had again begun to coil inside her. Giving in to the sensations, Mia moaned and closed her eyes, feeling each thrust deep within her belly. He lowered his head, and she felt the warmth of his breath against her ear as he tongued it lightly, making her shiver again. And then his pace picked up again, his hips now driving into her with such force that she was pushed into the mattress, barely able to catch her breath between each powerful stroke.

Her entire body tightened, and Mia screamed as another orgasm hit, her inner muscles squeezing him tightly. As her pulsations eased, she could feel his cock swelling up inside her, and then he came with a hoarse yell, grinding against her until his contractions were fully over.

Breathing hard in the aftermath, Mia lay there, his body feeling heavy on top of her. Apparently realizing it, he rolled off her and pulled her against him, hugging her from the back. His hand found its way to her breast, and he just held her like that, pressed up against his body. As her galloping heartbeat slowed, she felt languid, relaxed . . . and incredibly contented.

"Are you sleepy?" Korum whispered into her hair, stroking her nipple lightly with his thumb, causing it to peak against his palm.

"No," she whispered back. She felt like every muscle in her body had turned to mush, but she wasn't sleepy. Her lengthy nap earlier had taken care of that. "What time is it, anyway?"

"It's about eleven in the evening."

"I slept the entire day?" No wonder she felt so refreshed.

"You must've been exhausted," he murmured, raising his hand to move her hair to the side. The curls were probably tickling his face, Mia realized with some amusement.

"So Saret makes house calls this late?" she asked, her thoughts returning to her new and amazing ability. A huge grin appeared on her face as she imagined demonstrating her skills to her family and friends. They would be so envious . . .

"It's not that late for us," Korum explained, turning her around in his arms so that she was facing him. "You know we don't sleep as much as humans. Any time before one in the morning and after 5 a.m. are considered regular working and visiting hours."

Mia blinked at him, her grin fading. It made sense, of course, but this was yet another way she would be an outsider here. If she tried to keep their "regular" hours, she would quickly find herself sleep-deprived.

"You must've been bored in New York," she said quietly, "with me sleeping all the time, and few places open in the wee hours of the night."

He smiled and shook his head. "No, not at all. That's when I would usually get my work done, when you slept so sweetly in my bed."

"What kind of work? The designs?" Mia inquired with curiosity. There was still so much she didn't know about him, about how he spent his days—and nights—when he wasn't with her. It had been enlightening, observing his interactions with Saret today. She had caught a small glimpse of who Korum was outside of their relationship, and she was hungry to know more.

"Yes, I often work on the designs—that's my passion, that's what I really love to do," he answered readily, regarding her with a warm look in his eyes. "I also have to run my company, which takes up a big chunk of my time. I have a number of talented designers working for me, both here and on Krina, and there's always something that requires my attention—"

"You have people working for you on Krina?" Mia asked in surprise. "How do you communicate with them or oversee them?"

"We have faster-than-light communication," Korum explained, "so it's not that much more difficult to communicate with Krina than with, say, China from here. Of course, I can't see them easily in person, but we do have what you would call 'virtual reality,' where we can have meetings that very closely simulate the real thing. You experienced it a little bit with the virtual map—"

Mia nodded, staring at him attentively. She suspected very few humans knew what he was telling her right now.

"Well, the map is a very basic version of that technology. What we use to conduct cross-planetary meetings is far more advanced."

"Is that also your design? The virtual reality, I mean?" Mia asked, wondering how far his technological reach extended.

"Some of the latest versions, yes. The basic technology has been around for a very long time; it far predates both me and my company."

Mia's stomach suddenly growled. She flushed, feeling embarrassed, and he grinned in response, handing her a tissue for clean-up.

"Of course, you must be hungry after sleeping all day. Why don't we eat and continue our conversation over dinner?"

"That sounds good," Mia said, realizing that she was starving.

He got up, pulling her out of bed as well. Before she could even ask for it, he handed her a brand-new outfit that he'd managed to create in a matter of seconds. It was another dress, similar in style to the one that was now lying torn on the bed. This one was pale yellow in color, and Mia gladly put it on, loving the feel of the soft material against her skin. Korum pulled on his shorts and shirt from earlier, which had somehow survived their sex session.

"Ready?" he asked, and Mia nodded. Taking her hand, he led her toward the kitchen.

Like the living room and bedroom, the kitchen was similar in appearance to the one in his TriBeCa apartment. Further evidence of Korum's attempt to make her feel comfortable here, thought Mia. Walking over to one of the chairs, she sat down and looked at Korum eagerly. He was an amazing cook—part of his passion for making things—and even his most basic creations were more delicious than anything Mia could come up with herself.

"What would you like?" he asked her, walking toward the refrigerator.

Mia shrugged, uncertain how to answer that. "I don't know. What do you have?"

He smiled. "Pretty much everything. Do you want to try some foods native to Krina or would you rather stick with familiar tastes for now?"

Her eyes widened. "You have foods from Krina here?"

"Well, they're not imported from Krina—they're grown right here, in Lenkarda and our other Centers—but we did bring the seeds from our planet."

"I'd love to try them," Mia said earnestly. She was an adventurous eater and loved to taste new things. Thanks to her Polish heritage, Mia had grown up eating foods that were not normally part of the standard American diet, and she now had an open mind when it came to enjoying different cuisines.

Korum grinned, looking pleased by her enthusiasm. Taking a few things out of the refrigerator, he quickly chopped up some strange-looking plants and roots and put everything in a pot to cook.

"How do you usually cook here?" she asked him, watching his actions with fascination. "I can't imagine you use all these appliances normally . . ."

"You're right, we don't. In fact, we usually don't cook," Korum said, taking out some red leafy plants that vaguely resembled lettuce. "Remember when I told you that our homes are intelligent?"

Mia nodded.

"Well, one of their functions is to always keep us supplied with food and to prepare it in whichever way we like it."

Mia gasped, unable to contain her excitement. "Seriously? Your house makes food for you whenever you want?"

He smiled, amused at her reaction. "I can see how that would be appealing to you." Mia's cooking abilities were nonexistent—a fact that her mom frequently lamented—but she loved to eat.

"Appealing? It's amazing!" Why would anyone bother cooking when they could just have their house make food for them?

"It's all right," he said with a slight shrug. "It's convenient and it definitely saves a lot of time, but sometimes I get the urge to make something on my own, to see if I can improve on the recipes the house has in its database."

"Is that how you learned to cook so well? By tinkering with those recipes?"

Korum nodded, his hands now massaging the red leafy vegetables in a way that made an orange substance emerge from the leaves. "More or less. Cooking is a fairly recent hobby of mine—I've only gotten into it since coming to Earth. And it's really only in the last few months that I've learned to use the human appliances instead of just programming the house to tweak the recipes it uses."

Mia stared at her lover in disbelief. He had an

intelligent house that could make whatever food he wanted, and he was wasting time learning how to use the oven? Chopping vegetables using knives instead of utilizing their fancy technology? That was something she would never understand, Mia thought to herself. Not that she minded, of course; it was only because he had this strange hobby that she'd enjoyed so many delicious dishes back in New York.

He finished squeezing the orange liquid out of the red leaves, washed his hands, and took out a long yellow plant that looked a little like a zucchini with a shiny skin. Quickly cutting it up, he added it to the bowl where the red leaves were now swimming in the orange liquid, and then sprinkled some greenish powder over the entire dish. Placing the bowl in the middle of the table, he put a few spoonfuls of the bright-colored salad on Mia's plate and a larger helping on his. The utensils that he used were unusual, resembling some type of tongs with one flat side and one curved side.

"Try it," he invited, watching her expectantly.

A smaller version of the same utensils were lying next to Mia's bowl. Mimicking his earlier actions, Mia grabbed some of the leaves with her tongs and took a bite. The flavor exploded on her tongue, a perfect combination of sweetness, saltiness, and a tangy bite of spiciness underneath. "Oh my God, this is so good. What is it?" she managed to say once she'd swallowed. Her mouth was almost tingling from the overabundance of sensations.

He smiled. "It's a traditional dish from Rolert—the region of Krina where my family is from. It's very easy to make, as you saw, but the trick is to squeeze the *shari* well—that's the red plant—so it releases all the flavors and nutrients."

Mia listened to his explanation while gobbling down

the rest of her portion. As soon as she finished, she immediately reached for a second helping. He grinned and polished off the salad on his own plate.

"That was amazing. Thank you," Mia said when the salad was completely gone.

"I'm glad you liked it," Korum said, carrying away the dishes. Instead of putting them in the dishwasher, he simply held them near a wall. An opening appeared, and he placed them there. And just like that, the dirty dishes were gone.

Seeing the surprised look on Mia's face, Korum explained, "I don't like to clean up, so I *am* using some of our technology to take care of that part."

"So the dishwasher is strictly decorative?"

"More or less. You can use it if you like, but you saw what I just did, right?"

Mia nodded.

"You can do the same thing if you're here on your own. Or just leave the dishes on the table, and the house will take care of them after a few minutes." Walking back to the table, he sat down across from her and smiled. "The main dish will be ready in a couple of minutes."

"I can't wait to try it," Mia told him, smiling back in anticipation.

So far, being in Lenkarda was proving to be a fantastic experience in every way, and she felt an intense wave of happiness washing over her as she stared at Korum's beautiful face. It was hard to believe that only this morning she thought he would be deported to Krina, and now she was sitting in his house in Costa Rica, conversing with him in Krinar language, and enjoying the food he'd prepared for her again.

As her mind drifted to the earlier events, her smile slowly faded. She could've lost him today, she realized again. If Korum was right about the Keiths' intentions, then he could've been killed if the Resistance had succeeded. A sickening cold spread through her veins at the thought.

It hadn't happened, she told herself, trying to focus on the present, but her mind kept wandering. Even though the rebels had failed, the fact was that she'd participated in the attack on the K colonies. And now they wanted her to testify, she remembered with a chill going down her spine, to go in front of their Council and the United Nations and talk about her involvement. Korum seemed to think that he had the power to protect her from the Council, but she didn't understand how something like that worked.

"What's the matter?" Korum asked, apparently puzzled by the suddenly serious expression on her face.

Mia took a deep breath. "Can we talk about what happened this morning?" she asked cautiously. "And about what happens now?"

His expression cooled slightly, the smile leaving his face. "Why?" he asked. "It's over. I want us to move past it, Mia."

She stared at him. "But—"

"But what?" he asked softly, his eyes narrowing. "Do you really want to talk again about how you betrayed me? How you nearly sent me to my death? I'm willing to let it go because I know you were scared and confused . . . but it's really not in your best interests to keep bringing this up, my sweet."

Mia inhaled sharply, trying to hold on to her temper. "I only did what I thought was best," she said evenly. "And you knew everything all along—and you *used* me. And now it seems like your Council wants to use me too, so excuse me if I'm not quite ready to 'move past it'."

"The Council doesn't have any say where you're concerned, Mia," Korum said, looking at her with an inscrutable amber gaze. "They can't tell you what to do."

"And why is that?" Mia asked, her heart beginning to beat faster. "Because I'm your charl?"

"Exactly."

She stared at him in frustration. "And what does that mean? That I'm your charl?"

He regarded her levelly. "It means that you belong to me and they don't have any jurisdiction over you."

Before Mia could say anything else, he got up and walked over to the pot on the stove. Lifting the lid, he stirred the contents slightly, and an unusual but pleasant aroma filled the kitchen. "It's almost ready," he said, coming back to the table.

The two-second pause helped Mia gather her composure. "Korum," she said softly, "I need to understand. You, me—I feel like I'm part of some game where I don't know the rules. What exactly is a charl in your society?"

He sighed. "I told you, it's our term for the humans that we're in a relationship with."

"So why doesn't your Council have jurisdiction over charl? It's like your government, right?"

"Yes, exactly," Korum said, answering the second part of her question. "The Council is our governing body."

"And you're part of it?" Mia remembered John telling her something along those lines once.

"When I choose to be. I'm not a big fan of politics, but it's unavoidable sometimes."

"How can you choose something like that?" Mia asked, staring at him in astonishment. "Are you an elected official or does it work differently on Krina?"

"It's very different for us." Korum got up and walked

over to the stove again. "We don't have democracy the way you do. Who gets to be on the Council is determined based on our overall standing in society."

Mia's eyebrows rose. "What do you mean? Like you're born into the upper class or something?"

He shook his head. "No, not born. Our standing is earned over time. It's based largely on our achievements and how much we contribute to society. Our government is almost like an oligarchy of sorts—but based on meritocracy."

This was fascinating and somewhat intimidating. Korum must've contributed to the K society quite a bit, to have as much influence as he did.

"So how many of you are on the Council?" Mia asked, watching him ladle the stew-like dish into bowls for both of them. It didn't look as exotic as the shari salad, although she could see something purple among the reddish-brown vegetables.

"Currently, there are fifteen Council members. The number fluctuates over time—it's been as high as twenty-three and as low as seven. About a third of us are here on Earth, and the others are still on Krina."

Bringing the bowls back to the table, he sat down and moved one bowl toward her. "Go ahead," he said, "I'm curious if you'll like this also."

Temporarily shelving her questions, Mia tried a spoonful of the stew. To her surprise, it tasted rich and savory, as though it contained some kind of meat products. "This is all plant-based?" she asked, and Korum nodded, observing her reaction with a smile. His expression was warm again.

Mia tried another bite. The texture was soft and a little mushy, almost as if she were eating potatoes, but the flavor was completely different. It reminded her a bit of

Japanese food with its subtle seaweed-like undertones, just much more nuanced. After the second bite, Mia suddenly felt ravenous, her tastebuds craving more of the rich flavor, and she quickly downed the rest of the food on her plate. "This is really good," she mumbled between the bites, and Korum nodded, finishing his own portion.

After they were finished, he repeated the process with the dishes, bringing them toward the wall and letting the house take care of cleaning them. Mia observed him carefully, taking note of his exact actions. It didn't seem difficult, the technology even more intuitive than some of the newer iPads, and she hoped she remembered how to do it if she ever needed to clean the dishes herself.

"Thank you—that was delicious," she said when Korum was done.

"You're welcome," he replied casually, sitting back down at the table. The look on his face was amused and slightly mocking, as if he suspected exactly what she was going to say next.

Mia's temper began to simmer again, and she decided not to disappoint him. "So why are charl not within the Council's jurisdiction?" she asked stubbornly.

"Because that's the way it's always been, Mia," he replied softly. "Because humans are only accepted in Krinar society on those terms—as belonging to one of us. The only exception are those like Dana, who choose to leave their former life behind in order to become pleasure givers on Krina. So you see, my sweet, the Council cannot go to you directly. They have to go through me because, under Krinar law, you're mine."

Mia sucked in her breath, feeling like there was insufficient air in the room. "So I was right," she said quietly. "The Resistance didn't lie to me—you did."

He leaned toward her, his eyes turning a deeper shade

of gold. "They did lie to you. A charl is not a pleasure slave, or whatever it was they told you. It's very rare for us to have a charl, and when we do—these are genuine and caring relationships."

"How can a genuine and caring relationship exist when the two people are not considered equals in your society?" she asked bitterly.

He laughed, looking genuinely amused. "Those types of relationships exist all the time, Mia. Just look at your human society. Are you going to tell me that you don't care for your children, your teenagers, or even your pets? Not to mention that your so-called developed nations have only recently accepted the idea of women's rights, while many regions of Earth still don't—"

"Is that what I am to you? A pet?" Her stomach churned as she waited for his answer.

He shook his head, looking at her intently. "No, Mia, you're not a pet. You're a twenty-one-year-old human girl who still has quite a bit of growing up to do. I wish I could leave you alone, so you could meet someone like that pretty boy from the club—"

He was talking about Peter, Mia realized, surprised.

"—but I can't."

Getting up, he walked around the table and sat down on a chair next to her. Raising his hand, he gently stroked her cheek while Mia stared at him, unable to look away from the golden heat in his eyes. "You've gotten under my skin," he said softly, "and now I want you, in ways that I never thought were possible. I know you still have a lot to learn about me, about your new home here, and I will do my best to make things easier for you, to help you with your adjustment. But you need to stop worrying so much and fighting me at every turn. It can be very good between us, Mia . . . especially if you give it a chance."

CHAPTER FOUR

That night—her first night in Lenkarda—Mia had strange and disturbing dreams. She was flying somewhere again, only this time Korum held her on his lap for the duration of the trip. Her body felt unusually heavy and languid, and she couldn't move—could only lie helplessly in his arms as he carried her somewhere after they landed. In her dream, he brought her into a strange white building where everything seemed to float and walls dissolved on a regular basis. Suddenly, she was lying on one of these floating objects, and it felt incredibly comfortable, as though it had been made for her body and her body alone. There was a mellow light illuminating everything, and a beautiful woman spoke to her softly, gently touching her face with elegant hands. Mia dreamed that she spoke to the woman too, told her how beautiful she was, and the woman laughed, telling Korum that his charl was charming.

And then there was only darkness and Mia slept

deeply for the rest of the night, the dream fading from her memory.

As soon as she woke up the next morning, her mind immediately began replaying the conversation from yesterday and she groaned, burying her face in the pillow. Right away, the bed began a soft massage regimen designed to relax her suddenly tense muscles.

Sighing with pleasure, Mia let it do its thing while she lay there, trying to make sense of Korum and their relationship.

After his little speech last night, he had carried her to the bedroom and spent the next few hours showing her exactly how good it could be between them. Her sex still throbbed delicately when she thought of everything he'd done to her, the many ways he'd made her scream in mindless ecstasy.

She still didn't understand what Korum really wanted from her. Did he truly think she could just calmly go along with everything? From what she'd learned thus far, being a charl in Krinar society was not all that different from being a slave. As far as their law was concerned, she was Korum's possession—something that belonged to him. How could a genuine and caring relationship arise from that? He held all the power; he could do anything he wanted with her, and nobody would interfere.

And even if she were willing to accept that kind of dynamic, there were so many other issues to overcome. As he'd said, she was a twenty-one-year-old human girl—immature and inexperienced compared to a K who'd lived for two thousand years. How could he ever regard her as anything but naive and ignorant? Not only did his species have far more advanced science and technology, but Korum himself must've also gathered tremendous knowledge over his centuries of existence. How could a human ever come close to that over a mere eighty- or ninety-year lifespan? Not that he would even want her when she got older; however strong their attraction was now, he would definitely lose interest in her when she started getting wrinkles and grey hair—if not much sooner.

Closing her eyes at that painful thought, Mia tried to think about something else, to distract herself from such depressing reflections.

On the plus side, physically, she felt amazing. Despite the dreams she vaguely recalled, she must've gotten great sleep because she was filled with energy, and her body was completely free of the soreness that usually accompanied their long sex sessions. Korum must've used some healing thingy on her again, she decided.

It was difficult to believe it was only Saturday. Was it only last week that she was frantically writing her papers? It now seemed like a lifetime ago, with everything that had happened in the last couple of days.

On Monday, she was supposed to start her internship in Orlando, working as a counselor at a camp for troubled children, and instead . . . Well, Mia had no idea what she would be doing instead—or what the future held for her, in general. Her life had taken such an unexpected turn that any kind of planning was impossible.

She was also supposed to be packed and out of her room on Monday, she suddenly remembered with a sinking feeling in her stomach. Mia had made the arrangements to sublet her room out for the summer several months ago, and the subletter—a very nice girl named Rita—was supposed to move in at the beginning of next week. However, given Mia's sudden departure from New York, all of her stuff was still there.

Jumping out of bed, Mia ran to the small table where

her purse was sitting. She'd brought it with her from New York, and it contained something extremely valuable: her cell phone. She needed to call Jessie as soon as possible. Her roommate was probably already getting worried since she hadn't heard from Mia yesterday, and she would definitely freak out if all of Mia's belongings were still in her room when Rita moved in. Jessie would never believe her to be so irresponsible as to forget about the sublet.

Pulling out her cell phone, Mia held her breath, praying that she had reception. But, of course, her hopes were in vain—there were zero bars. Not only was she in a foreign country, Mia realized, but the Ks' shielding technology likely blocked all cell tower signals.

Sighing, she put on a robe and went to brush her teeth before looking for Korum. If she didn't contact Jessie this weekend, her roommate could easily have the police at Korum's TriBeCa apartment by Monday.

Entering the living room, Mia saw Korum sitting on the couch with his eyes closed. Surprised, she stopped and stared at him. Was he sleeping? Hesitant to disturb him, she just stood there, using this rare opportunity to study her alien lover with his guard down.

With his eyes closed, the bronzed perfection of his face was even more striking. High cheekbones blended synergistically with a strong nose and a firm jaw, forming a face that was as masculine as it was beautiful. His eyebrows were dark and thick, slanting straight above his eyes, and his eyelashes looked incredibly long, spread out like dark fans above his cheeks. His hair had grown in the month that she'd known him—he'd probably been too busy chasing after the Keiths to get a haircut, Mia thought wryly—and it was starting to brush against his ears.

As though sensing her gaze on him, he opened his eyes and smiled when he saw her standing there. "Come here," he murmured, patting the couch next to him. "How are you feeling?"

Mia blushed slightly. "I'm fine," she told him.

He just continued looking at her with a mysterious expression on his face, almost as if studying her for some reason. Feeling a little uncertain about where they stood after yesterday's conversation, Mia cautiously approached him. Even though she'd spent most of last night writhing in pleasure in his arms, there was still so much unresolved between them. Pausing a couple of feet away, she asked, "Were you sleeping just now? I'm sorry to interrupt if you were . . ."

"Sleeping? No." He looked surprised by her assumption. "I was just taking care of some business."

"Virtually?" Mia guessed, and Korum nodded, patting the couch again.

Mia came closer, and he reached out with his hand, pulling her onto his lap. Burying his hand in the dark mass of curls, he tilted her head toward him and kissed her, his mouth hot and demanding, his tongue stroking hers until she forgot everything but the incredible sensations he was provoking in her. Barely able to breathe, Mia moaned, melting helplessly against him, her core filling with liquid heat despite the fact that she should be wrung out after the excesses of last night.

Apparently satisfied with her response, Korum raised his head and looked down at her with a half-smile, releasing her hair but still holding her tightly in his arms. "You see, Mia," he said softly, "it really doesn't matter what labels are placed on our relationship. It doesn't change anything between us."

Mia licked her lips. They felt soft and swollen after his

kiss. "No, you're right. It doesn't change anything," she agreed quietly. Learning more about her role in K society didn't lessen her attraction to him one bit. Her body didn't care that, as a charl, she had no say in her own life.

Korum smiled and got up, placing her on her feet. "I have to leave in about thirty minutes for the trial. Would you like to watch it from here?"

Mia's eyes widened. "Like on TV?"

"Through virtual reality," he told her. "I don't want you there in person in case the Council tries to pressure you to testify."

"What would happen if I did? Testify, I mean?" Mia was suddenly curious why Korum was so determined to protect her from that. She wasn't exactly eager to go in front of the Krinar Council, but he did seem unduly worried about it.

"The traitors will have a Protector," Korum explained. "It's a bit like your lawyer, but different. The Protector is someone who genuinely believes in the innocence of the accused—it could be their family member or a friend. When you act as a Protector, you stake everything on the line—your reputation, your standing in society. If you don't succeed in proving the innocence of those you're protecting, then you lose almost as much as they do."

"And do the accused always have this Protector?" Mia asked, trying to wrap her mind around such a strange system.

Korum shook his head. "No. But these traitors do, unfortunately. One of them, Rafor, is the son of Loris—one of the oldest Council members—and Loris took it upon himself to be the Protector in this case. He's one of the most ruthless individuals I know, and he would stop at nothing to protect his son. He also hates me. If I let you go up there as a witness, he's going to do everything he can to make your testimony seem like it's coming from an irrational, hysterical human that I've manipulated for my own purposes. He's going to publicly humiliate you, make you break down in front of everyone, and I won't let that happen."

Mia swallowed, beginning to understand a little. "You don't have some kind of rules about the types of questions that can be asked of the witnesses?"

"No," Korum said. "With so much on the line, all is fair game. The only thing the Protector is not allowed to do is physically hurt you. But there wouldn't be anything to prevent him from verbally destroying you—and believe me, Loris is really good at that."

"I see," Mia said slowly, her stomach tying into knots at the thought of going up against a ruthless Krinar Council member determined to protect his son.

"But don't worry," Korum reassured her. "It's not going to happen. At best, they will get a recorded testimony from you—and that's only if Arus really begs for it."

"Who's Arus?" Mia remembered that name mentioned earlier, during Saret's visit.

"He's another Council member and, among other things, he's our ambassador to the human leaders."

"You don't like him either?" Mia guessed.

Korum's lips curved into a grim, humorless smile. "Let's just say we've had our share of political differences." The look in his eyes was cold and distant, and Mia shivered slightly, glad that it wasn't directed at her.

"I see," she said again. She didn't really, but she didn't think it would be wise to pursue this topic further. Taking a deep breath, she remembered the original reason why she'd wanted to talk to him. "Um, Korum, I wanted to ask you something . . ."

His expression softened a little. "Sure, what is it?"

Mia looked at him imploringly. "I have to call Jessie. My cell phone doesn't seem to have reception here . . ."

His eyebrows rose. "Call your roommate? Why?"

"Because she's going to be worried if she doesn't hear from me for a couple of days," Mia explained, "and because I have to ask her for a big favor. All my stuff is still in my room, and the girl who's subletting it will be moving in on Monday. I should've been packed and out of there yesterday, but . . ."

"But you ended up here instead," Korum said, immediately understanding. "All right, you can contact Jessie and let her know where you are. Maybe she can pack your things for you. If she does, I'll have my driver pick them up and bring them to my New York apartment."

"That would be great, thanks," Mia said, smiling in relief. "And if I could do a quick call to my parents too, that would be really awesome."

He smiled at her. "Sure. I just wouldn't tell *them* where you are."

"No, definitely not," Mia readily agreed. She tried to imagine her parents' reaction to the news that she was in an alien colony in Costa Rica, and it wasn't a pleasant picture. Thinking ahead, she asked, "What about when I go to Florida? What am I going to tell them then?"

Korum shrugged. "The truth, I imagine. I'll be with you, so they can ask me whatever questions they want to reassure themselves of your safety."

Mia's jaw dropped. "You're going to meet my parents?"

"Of course, why not?"

"Um . . ." Mia could think of a dozen reasons why not.

She settled on the first one. "Well, I'm not sure how they would react to, you know, what you are . . ."

He looked amused. "A Krinar? They'll have to get used to the idea if they want to keep seeing you."

Mia stared at him. "What do you mean, if they want to keep seeing me?"

"I mean, Mia," he said softly, "that you're with me now, and your family will need to come to terms with it." At the anxious look on her face, he added, "And don't worry, I'll be patient with them. I know they care about you, and I'll do my best to set their mind at ease."

* * *

A few minutes later, with Mia still in shock at the thought of her parents meeting her alien lover, Korum gave her a thin, silvery bracelet that resembled a wristwatch.

"This is something I just created for you," he explained, placing it around her left wrist. "This will be your personal computing device while you're in Lenkarda. I made it so that it's capable of connecting with human cell phones and computers, and you can use it to call or video-chat with your family. I programmed it with all your connections—"

Surprised, Mia studied the pretty object on her arm. It looked very much like a stylish piece of jewelry, and she vaguely remembered seeing some Ks on TV wearing something similar. "How does it work?" she asked, not seeing any obvious buttons on it.

"It will respond to your verbal commands—that will be the easiest way for you to operate our technology right now."

"So it will understand me if I just say the instructions in natural speech?"

Korum nodded. "It will understand you perfectly in any language because I designed it specifically for you."

Mia blinked. She wasn't sure, but she suspected that Korum was one of the very few Ks who could do something like that—create a unique piece of technology solely for the use of his charl. "Thank you," she said gratefully. "I'll call Jessie right now."

Seeking a little privacy, Mia went into the bedroom. Sitting down on the bed, she lifted her left wrist closer to her mouth and spoke to the bracelet. "Call Jessie, please." Two seconds later, she heard what sounded like dial tones signifying that the call was connecting.

"Hello?" It was Jessie's voice, and it emanated from the little device on Mia's wrist. Unlike with the speakerphones that Mia was familiar with, she could hear Jessie with crystal-clear precision, as though she was in the room with her.

Hoping that Jessie could hear her just as well, Mia said, "Hey Jessie, how's it going? It's Mia."

"Mia? Where are you calling from?" Jessie sounded surprised. "It shows up as an unknown number."

"Uh, yeah, about that . . . I'm actually out of town right now—"

"What? Where?"

"Um . . . in Costa Rica."

"WHAT?" Jessie's shriek was earsplitting.

Mia rubbed her ears. "Yeah, it was kind of an unplanned trip, but everything's fine. I'm with Korum and—"

"Oh my God, what the fuck are you doing in Costa Rica? Did that bastard make you go there? Because if he did—"

"No, Jessie, everything's fine! Look, I just wanted to call you and let you know where I was—"

"Mia, what are you doing in Costa Rica?" Jessie sounded marginally calmer, though Mia could still hear the panicked undertone in her roommate's voice. "And where exactly in Costa Rica are you?"

Mia paused for a second, trying to think how to best explain everything. "Well, I'm actually in Lenkarda—that's the Costa Rican K Center—"

"Oh my God, Mia, he brought you there? Did he find out?" There was sheer terror in Jessie's voice now. "Does he know about . . . you know?"

Mia sighed. "Yeah. He knew all along actually. Don't worry—it's all cool now . . ."

"What do you mean, he knew all along?"

"Look, Jessie, I don't want to go into the whole story right now, but just believe me when I tell you that I'm not in any kind of danger, okay?" Mia spoke quickly, knowing that she probably only had minutes before Jessie did something drastic—like contacting the Resistance again. "We've talked about everything, and there was a misunderstanding on my part—and now everything's fine. I'm just here for the summer. We're going to go to Florida in a couple of weeks to visit my parents, and then I'll be back in New York for the next school year. It's really nothing to worry about, I promise you . . ."

There was silence for a few seconds, and then Jessie said quietly, "Mia, I just don't understand. You're telling me that the alien you've been spying on brought you to a K Center, and you expect me to believe that everything's okay?"

Mia took a deep breath. "Everything *is* okay. Honestly. I made a mistake becoming involved with the Resistance. Korum explained everything, and I just didn't understand the situation before—"

"And now you do? How do you know you can believe

anything he says?"

"Look, I have to trust him, Jessie. He has no reason to lie to me now." At least, Mia hoped so.

"And he's letting you call me?"

Mia smiled. "Yes, of course, so you see—it's really not what you think." She could almost hear the wheels turning in Jessie's head.

"So you're honestly telling me that you're in a K Center and you're totally fine? You're going to come back for school and everything?"

"Absolutely," Mia said, relieved that Jessie was coming around. "It just turned out that instead of going to Florida for the summer, I went to Costa Rica, that's all."

"What about your internship in Orlando?"

"That I haven't quite figured out yet," Mia reluctantly admitted. "I'll have to call them and explain that I won't be able to do it anymore."

"So you're not going to do an internship the summer before your senior year? That's a really bad career move, Mia . . ."

"Yes, I know," said Mia, not needing her roommate to remind her of that. "Maybe I'll be able to get something during the school year with the career placement office . . . I'll figure something out. But I'll be going to Florida for a few days soon, so that'll be nice."

"Going with him?"

"Yep." Mia grinned, imagining her roommate's reaction to what she was about to tell her next. "He wants to meet my parents."

"WHAT? Are you kidding me?"

Mia laughed. "I know, right?"

"What, does he want to marry you or something?" Jessie sounded as incredulous as Mia still felt.

"No, of course not," Mia said, her mind boggling at

the thought. "I think he's just being nice. Maybe. I have no idea if meeting parents is a significant thing in K culture or not. Besides, he's way older than my parents, so it's not like he's going to be intimidated by them . . ."

"Wow, Mia," Jessie said slowly. "I don't even know what to tell you—"

"You don't have to say anything, Jessie. I know the whole thing is crazy, but I'm totally fine. Look, I actually wanted to ask you for a humongous favor . . ."

"Let me guess," Jessie said dryly. "Rita is moving in on Monday, and all your wonderful new clothes are everywhere."

"Yes, precisely." Mia injected a pleading note into her voice. "Jessie, if you do this for me, I'll be so grateful . . ."

She could hear Jessie sighing. "Of course. I'll do it for you. But where should I put everything? In storage?"

"No, Korum's driver in New York can pick it up and bring it to his place."

"Oh . . . I see," Jessie said, sounding oddly hesitant. "So does this mean you're officially moving in with him?"

"No, of course not! It's just for the summer, instead of storage, you know."

"I don't know, Mia." Jessie sounded upset again. "Somehow, I don't see you living here again . . ."

"Jessie. . ." Mia didn't really know what to say. She couldn't promise anything because so much was still uncertain. Would Korum want her to live with him in TriBeCa when they came back to New York? And would it be a bad thing if he did? She'd only known him for a month at this point, and it was difficult for Mia to imagine what their relationship would be like in another two months.

"It's okay, you don't have to say anything," Jessie said, sounding falsely upbeat. "We couldn't stay as roommates forever, you know. This was bound to happen. Granted, it happened under some pretty strange circumstances, but I'm sure his penthouse is much nicer than our roach-infested building."

"Jessie, please . . . It's too soon to talk about that—"

"I don't know," Jessie said, a teasing note entering her voice. "You guys seem to be moving along pretty fast—already meeting parents and everything . . ."

Mia laughed, shaking her head in reproach even though her roommate couldn't see it. "Oh, please, now you're just being silly."

They chatted some more, with Jessie asking about Mia's experience thus far in Lenkarda. Mia gladly told her about the food and bragged about the intelligent technology she'd encountered, describing the bed in minute detail. As expected, Jessie agreed that there were some definite perks to having an affair with a K. She was also blown away by Mia's newly acquired language abilities.

"Do you really understand me?" Jessie asked in Mandarin, a language she'd picked up from her immigrant parents.

"Yes, Jessie, I really do understand you. Isn't that amazing?" Mia answered in the same language, and rubbed her ears again when Jessie shrieked with excitement.

Finally, promising to call Jessie again in a few days, Mia told the little device to hang up and disconnected.

Her parents were next on the list.

Her mom was happy to hear from her, even though she seemed concerned that Mia was not calling from her usual phone.

"Don't worry, mom," Mia explained. "My cell is malfunctioning, and I just got this temporary phone to use and haven't figured out all the settings yet." That was mostly true. Her cell phone was indeed malfunctioning in the K Center, and she hadn't yet explored all the capabilities of Korum's device.

"All right, honey," her mom said. "Just don't forget to call or text us, please."

"I won't," Mia promised. "I'll be busy for the next few days with the volunteering project, but I'll definitely call you on Wednesday."

"How is that going, by the way?" her mom asked, sounding a little irritated. Mia had told her parents she was staying in New York for an extra couple of weeks to help out her professor with a special program for disadvantaged high school kids. Naturally, her mom hadn't been pleased with the delay in seeing their youngest daughter.

"It's great," Mia lied. "I'm learning a lot, and it'll be phenomenal for my resume." She mentally cringed at having to lie to her parents like this, but she couldn't tell them the truth, not yet. Korum was right: it would be best if they learned about him in person and had a chance to talk to him to alleviate their concerns. If Mia told them where she was right now, her parents would be beside themselves.

Trying to redirect the conversation, she asked, "How is dad doing? Has he had any headaches recently?"

"Yeah, he had one a few days ago," her mom said, sighing. "It was not one of his worst ones, thankfully."

"Tell dad to stop stressing and take it easy with the computer. And take regular walks, okay?"

"Of course, honey, we're trying."

"Take care of yourselves, all right?"

Her mom promised to do so, they chatted some more, and then Mia said goodbye and went to find Korum before he left for the trial.

He'd offered her the opportunity to observe the proceedings, and Mia intended to take him up on that offer.

CHAPTER FIVE

Mia entered the tall white dome without hesitation, a chunk of the wall disintegrating to grant her passage. Korum had assured her that nobody could see, hear, or feel her in this particular version of his virtual world, and she could get the full experience of attending the trial without any stress or unpleasant encounters with the Protector. There were interactive versions of virtual reality too, he'd explained, but those were not appropriate for this situation. He himself would attend in person; it was his responsibility as a Council member and one of the chief accusers in this case.

Stepping inside the dome, Mia gasped in amazement. The place was teeming with Krinar, both male and female, all dressed in the light-colored clothes that their race seemed to favor. It was an incredible sight, with thousands of tall, gorgeous, golden-skinned aliens occupying the giant building from floor to ceiling. The spectators—at least that's what Mia assumed they were—

were literally stacked one on top of another, each occupying the floating seats that Mia was beginning to learn were a staple here in Lenkarda. The seats were arranged in circles around the center of the dome, with each circle floating directly on top of the next. It was a neat arrangement, Mia realized, like an arena of sorts, but with floating seats.

At the center, there were about a dozen podium-like places, with roughly a third of them occupied by Krinar. The rest were empty.

Carefully making her way toward the center, Mia tried to avoid bumping into anyone, but it was unavoidable. The place was simply too tightly packed. The attendees couldn't feel *her*, but Mia could definitely feel *them* when she would get rammed by someone's elbow or have her foot stepped on. How this virtual reality business worked, she had no idea, but it was annoying and rather painful to be the invisible girl in a crowd. Finally, she succeeded in getting through to the center, where a large circular area was completely empty.

Standing safely in that area, Mia looked around with awe.

From the inside, the walls of the dome were transparent, and bright sunlight poured in from all directions, reflecting off the white color of the seats and the light-colored clothing of the Krinar. Unlike the loose, floaty outfits she'd seen them wear before, their clothes today seemed less casual, with more structured lines and fitted shapes for both males and females. Most of the Ks seemed to have dark hair and eyes, although here and there she could see a few with lighter brown and chestnut-colored hair. Korum was of average height here, Mia realized, observing the tall aliens all around her. Someone like her—5'3" tall and weighing a hundred pounds—would probably be considered a midget.

Turning her attention to the podium-like structures, Mia saw Korum sitting behind one of them. Grinning at the thought of observing him while he couldn't see her, Mia walked over to him. He seemed occupied with something in his palm—probably the computer he had embedded there—and paid no attention to her virtual presence. Smiling wickedly, Mia approached him from behind and touched him, running her hands over his broad back. There was no reaction from him, of course, and Mia laughed out loud, imagining the possibilities. She could do anything she wanted to him, and he wouldn't have a clue.

Testing out a theory, she licked the back of his neck. No reaction from him again, but *she* could taste the faint saltiness of his skin, smell the familiar warm scent of his body. Predictably, Mia could feel herself getting turned on, and she pressed against him, rubbing her breasts on the soft material of his ivory shirt. They were surrounded by thousands of spectators, and it didn't matter because no one—not even Korum himself—knew what she was doing.

Grinning hugely, Mia lightly bit his neck and reached for his crotch, stroking the area through his clothes. She felt incredibly naughty, like she was doing something forbidden, even though she knew the entire thing was more or less taking place inside her head. Before she could continue further, however, the noise from the crowd suddenly dropped in volume, and Mia pulled away, realizing that the trial was beginning.

The time for games was over.

The podium-like table in front of which Korum was sitting was low enough that Mia could climb on top of it, and she did so, making herself comfortable. It seemed like a good spot from which to observe the upcoming drama.

Carefully examining her surroundings, she came to the conclusion that the other podium areas were occupied by the other Council members. A third of them were there in person, while the other seats—the empty ones—were now filled with holographic images of both male and female Krinar. She assumed the holographs were for those who couldn't be there in person—perhaps because they were on Krina. She spotted Saret sitting across from them, but she had no idea who the other Krinar were. Mia counted fifteen podiums standing all around the empty circle, but only fourteen were occupied. It was probably the Protector's seat, Mia thought; it made sense that he wouldn't be judging the trial, given his son's role as one of the accused.

A chime-like sound echoed through the dome, and the crowd went completely silent. All of a sudden, the floor in the center of the circle dissolved, and seven large silvery cylinders floated out.

The floor solidified again, and the cylinders landed on it. As Mia watched with bated breath, the walls of the cylinders disintegrated, leaving only the circular tops and bottoms intact. And inside each one, Mia saw the Keiths—the seven Ks who had risked all to help humanity achieve a brighter future.

Or, according to Korum, to try to rule the Earth themselves.

* * *

The Keiths stood there, each within his or her own circle, their expressions bitter and defiant. Silvery collars encircled their necks—the same collars Mia had seen the guards put on them when they were captured. She guessed they were the K version of handcuffs. There were five males and two females, all tall and beautiful as befitting of their species.

Curious to see Korum's reaction, Mia glanced behind her and nearly recoiled at the icy contempt on his face as he looked at the traitors. She could see the dangerous yellow flecks in his eyes, and his mouth was drawn into a flat, cruel line.

He truly hated and despised the Keiths for what they'd done, Mia realized with a shiver, and she wondered again how he'd managed to forgive *her* for her actions.

The arena was still deathly silent. There were no jeers or boos, as one might have expected from such a large crowd. It was the biggest trial of the last ten thousand years, Saret had said, and Mia could see that reflected in the grave mood of the spectators.

A portion of the floor dissolved again, and another Krinar male came up. He was sitting on a broad floating seat, and he got up as soon as the floor solidified again. Unlike every other Krinar there, he was wearing clothes that were black in color. Probably the Protector, Mia thought.

Another chime echoed through the building, and all the Council members got up from behind their podiums. One of them stepped forward and approached the new arrival. Touching his shoulder, the Council member said, "Welcome, Loris."

The Protector smiled and reciprocated the shoulder-touching gesture. "Thank you, Arus." Then, turning his attention to the rest of the Council, he acknowledged their presence with a few curt nods.

So these were Korum's opponents, Mia thought, observing them with a great deal of interest. Loris's hair was jet-black, and his eyes were the color of onyx. He reminded her of a hawk, with his sharply handsome features and a faintly predatory expression on his face. In contrast, Arus seemed much more approachable. With olive skin, black hair, and dark brown eyes, he was very typical of his kind, and there was a certain genuineness in his smile that made Mia think he might not be all that bad as a person.

After the greeting was complete, Arus returned to his podium, leaving Loris standing there.

Hearing movement behind her, Mia turned around and saw that Korum had risen to his feet. He walked around the podium toward the center of the arena, his movements slow and deliberate. Smiling coldly at Loris, he asked, "Is the Protector ready for the presentation?"

Loris nodded, a look of barely contained anger on his face. It seemed that Korum hadn't exaggerated when he said that Loris hated him.

With a flick of his wrist, Korum brought up a three-dimensional image that hovered in mid-air, easily available for everyone to see.

"My fellow Earth inhabitants and all who are watching us on Krina right now," Korum said, his voice echoing throughout the dome, "I would like to show you proof of a crime so heinous that the likes of it haven't been seen in Krinar history for over a hundred thousand years. A crime in which a handful of traitors unhappy with their standing tried to send fifty thousand fellow citizens to their death in a pathetic grab for power. These traitors—the seven individuals you see before you right now—had no desire to advance us as a species, as a society. No, they simply wanted power, and they didn't care what they had to do to achieve it. They lied, they betrayed our people, they manipulated humans susceptible to their empty promises . . . and they would have killed each and every single one of you in their quest to rule this particular planet, to be worshipped by the gullible humans as their saviors—"

"That's a lie," interrupted Loris, speaking through clenched teeth. Red spots of color appeared underneath his swarthy skin, and Mia could almost feel the effort it took him to control himself. "You set them up—"

"It's not your turn to speak right now, Protector," Korum told him, his lips curving in a contemptuous smile. "It's my turn to present the evidence." And with that, he made a small gesture with his hand, and the three-dimensional recording came to life.

The scene was a familiar one for Mia—she had been there in a virtual setting only yesterday. As the recording played, she again saw the old hut where the traitors had taken shelter during the Resistance attack and heard their communication with the mysterious human general. She witnessed the Resistance forces' attempt to storm Lenkarda with their K weapons and relived their crushing defeat. And even though she was seeing this for the second time and knew that most of the human fighters had survived, Mia still felt sick to her stomach by the time the film was over.

Another movement of Korum's hand, and the next recording began to play—this one of a phone conversation between one of the Keiths and some Resistance leaders. They were clearly coordinating their actions prior to the attack. And there were more: three-dimensional videos of the Resistance meetings where they had talked about the Keiths, interactions between human government officials discussing the potential for Earth's liberation, and even a video of John telling Mia about their change in plans and how she had to steal Korum's designs.

Watching all this, Mia again realized just how thoroughly Korum had manipulated her. While she'd thought she was spying on him, he had been tracking her every move; there had never been an opportunity for her to help the Resistance—she had always been his pawn. Her stomach twisted unpleasantly at the thought.

By the time all the recordings had been shown, at least four hours had passed. Mia was hungry and thirsty, and she had a pounding headache, but she couldn't bring herself to leave her spot on top of Korum's podium, morbidly fascinated by the proceedings.

Finally, Korum's presentations appeared to be over.

In the deathly silence that gripped the arena, Korum said in a ringing tone, "And that, fellow Krinar citizens and Earth inhabitants, is why I propose the ultimate punishment for these traitors: complete rehabilitation."

A murmur ran through the crowd, and Mia could almost feel the shock emanating from some of the spectators. Whatever complete rehabilitation meant, it was clearly not something that was commonly used.

The Keiths looked shocked as well, and Mia could see the fear on some of their faces. Whatever punishment they'd been expecting was obviously different from what Korum had just proposed.

The Protector stepped forward. Like Korum, he had been standing in the center for the entire time that the recordings had been playing. His black eyes were filled with fury. "That's unthinkable, and you know it," he gritted out. "Even if they were guilty, what you're proposing is out of the question."

"Are you admitting their guilt then?" Korum asked, his tone dangerously soft.

Loris's brows snapped together. "Far from it. You know they haven't done anything wrong—"

"We'll let the Council and the Elders decide that, won't we?" Korum replied, staring at the other Krinar with a mocking look on his face. "Your turn to present is tomorrow, and I, for once, am very eager to hear how these traitors could possibly be innocent."

"Oh, you will see," Loris said, giving him a look of sheer hatred. "And so will everyone else."

And on that note, a chime sounded again. The trial proceedings were over for the day.

* * *

The Krinar drew in a deep breath, glad that the first day of the trial was over. It had gone exactly as he'd expected.

Korum had demanded the ultimate punishment for the ones he regarded as traitors. If the K hadn't taken precautions, he could have easily been the eighth figure standing there, being judged by the Council.

He had distanced himself from the Keiths just in time. Now nobody would suspect his involvement in the attack on the Centers.

He had made sure of that.

CHAPTER SIX

Starving and mentally exhausted, Mia exited the virtual reality setting by telling her wristwatch-bracelet device to bring her back home. Her breakfast this morning had been light, just a mango-avocado smoothie, and she felt almost faint with hunger at this point. Opening her eyes, she got up from the couch where she had been sitting and went in search of food.

Approaching the refrigerator, she opened it decisively and stared at the various plant foods that occupied it. Some were familiar—she saw a couple of tomatoes and sweet peppers—but others were completely foreign. Mia wished that Korum were here, so he could make one of his delicious and filling concoctions. However, since he'd been at the trial in person, she figured he might be delayed for at least a while longer.

Suddenly, she got an idea. Korum had mentioned that one of the house's functions was to prepare foods. Would it do it for her as well?

"Hey, house," Mia said tentatively, feeling like an idiot, "can you please prepare me something to eat?"

For a second, nothing happened, and then a melodious female voice asked, "What would you like, Mia?"

Mia nearly jumped in excitement. "Oh my God, you talk! That's great! Um . . . I'd like the same thing Korum made yesterday, especially if it can be prepared quickly."

"Yes, Mia," the female voice responded softly. "The shari salad will be ready in two minutes, and the kalfani stew will be done six minutes later."

Grinning in amazement, Mia walked over to the sink to wash her hands. By the time she finished and sat down at the table, a part of the wall had opened and a bowl of salad emerged, floating calmly toward the table.

Mia watched in open-mouthed shock as the salad landed neatly in front of her. It was the perfect portion size for her, and the tong-like utensil was already inside the bowl. The dish was completely ready for her consumption.

"Um, thank you," she said, trying to look around to see where the voice had been coming from. Was there a computer embedded somewhere in the ceiling?

"You're welcome, Mia," the female voice said again. "Please enjoy, and I will have the next dish ready for you within minutes."

Grinning again, Mia dug into the food. So far, she was loving Krinar technology. It was everything that people had been fantasizing about in science fiction, yet it was entirely real—and had an almost magical twist to it that Mia found very appealing. She particularly appreciated how easy it was to operate everything. Natural language voice commands, simple hand gestures—it all seemed so intuitive.

By the time she finished the salad, the stew-like dish from yesterday had floated to the table as well. Mia greedily consumed it, feeling much of the earlier tiredness leaving her as her blood sugar levels stabilized. The food was as delicious as it had been yesterday, and Mia wondered again why Korum bothered learning how to cook when he had access to such remarkable technology in his house.

Finally replete, she cleaned up by bringing the dishes toward the wall—which opened up to accept them, just as it had for Korum—and went into the living room.

It seemed like as good a time as any to call the camp director in Orlando and let him know that she wouldn't be starting on Monday.

* * *

By the time Korum arrived home an hour later, Mia had managed to get bored.

She'd spoken with the camp director and explained that unforeseen circumstances were preventing her from coming to Florida this summer. He had been disappointed, but surprisingly nice about the whole thing, which was a tremendous relief for Mia. Afterwards, she explored the house a bit and even tried talking to it, but the melodious female voice didn't seem all that interested in carrying on a conversation. It did ask whether Mia was warm and comfortable (which she was) and if she desired anything to eat or drink (which she didn't), but that was the extent of their interaction. There didn't seem to be any books around or anything else for her to amuse herself with, either.

Sighing, Mia plopped down on the couch in the living room and stared at the greenery outside. She wished she were brave enough to venture out, but the thought of getting lost in a Costa Rican forest didn't appeal to her. Studying the bracelet-like device on her wrist, Mia wondered if it would work like an actual computer, enabling her to get on the internet. She thought about trying it, but decided to wait for Korum to demonstrate more of its capabilities to her.

Finally, Korum walked in. He looked tense and a little tired, and Mia guessed that more politics had gone on behind the scenes after the trial had formally adjourned. Nevertheless, he smiled when he saw her sitting there.

"Hi," she said, ridiculously glad to see him. Despite everything that had happened between them, despite the fact that she had just seen him treat his opponents almost cruelly, she couldn't help the warm sensation that spread through her in his presence.

His smile widened. Walking over to join her on the couch, he kissed her softly and pulled her closer to him for a hug. Mia hugged him back, surprised, and mumbled into his shirt, "Is everything okay? Did anything happen?"

He shook his head and simply held her, burying his face in her hair and inhaling her scent. "No," he murmured, "everything is good now."

After a few more seconds, he pulled back and looked at her. "I hope you got something to eat? I programmed the house to respond to your verbal commands, to make sure you wouldn't have any difficulties here."

Mia smiled. "Yeah, I figured it out. Thanks for that."

"Good," he said softly, "I want you to feel comfortable here."

Mia nodded slowly. "I'm starting to, a bit. But I actually wanted to ask you something . . ."

"Of course, what is it?"

"I'm bored," Mia told him bluntly. "I don't really have anything to do when you're not here. At home, I have school, work, friends, books, TV—"

"Ah, I see," Korum said, smiling. "I haven't shown you everything that your little computer can do. Tell it that you would like to read something."

"Okay," Mia said dubiously, looking at her bracelet, "I would like to read something . . ."

Almost immediately, one of the walls parted, revealing a section hidden inside—a shelf of some kind. And as Mia watched, an object that looked like a thick sheet of paper floated out toward her.

"How does all this stuff float?" Mia asked in amazement, plucking the object out of thin air. "Plates, chairs, now this . . ."

"The premise is similar to the shields we use to protect our settlements," Korum explained. "It's a type of force-field technology, just applied on a much smaller scale."

"Oh, I see," Mia said, as if that told her anything. A technology whizz she definitely wasn't. Studying the sheet in her hands, she saw that it was actually made of some plastic-like material.

"This is something you can entertain yourself with," he said, sitting down next to her. "It's a little like your computer tablets. You can read any book—human or Krinar—that's ever been written, and you can watch any kind of film you want. This will also work with verbal commands, so you can just tell it what you want to see or read."

"Can I use it to learn more about the Krinar? To read some history books or something?" asked Mia, staring at the object with excitement.

"Sure. You can use it for whatever purpose you want."

Mia grinned. "That's great, thanks!"

He smiled back at her. "Of course. I don't want you to be bored here."

Something suddenly occurred to Mia. "Wait, you said it works by verbal commands, but I've never seen or heard you using verbal commands on anything. How do *you* control all your technology?"

"I have a very powerful computer that essentially allows me to control everything through a specific type of thinking," Korum explained, holding up his palm. "It's a type of highly advanced brain-computer interface. I use some gestures too, but that's just out of habit."

Mia stared at him. "So you control electronics with your mind?"

"Krinar electronics, yes. Human technology is not designed for that."

"What about the others? Is that how they do it too?"

Korum nodded. "Many of them, yes. Some still prefer the old-fashioned way, which is voice commands and gestures, but most have switched over. The majority of our technology is designed to accommodate both ways of doing things because our children and young ones only use the first method."

"Why?" Mia asked, looking at him in fascination.

"Because their brains aren't fully formed and developed, and because there's a learning curve involved with using brain-computer interfaces. That's why I'm setting up everything with voice capabilities for you for now—it's much easier for a beginner to master. Later on, when you understand our technology and society better, I can set you up with the new interface."

Mia's eyes widened. He would give her the ability to control Krinar technology with her mind? The possibilities were simply unimaginable. "That sounds . . ."

"Like a little too much right now?" Korum guessed,

and Mia nodded.

"Hence the voice commands for now," he said. "Your society has advanced far enough that you can easily understand that type of interface, and it's very intuitive."

"So for now, I'll be like one of your children?" Mia asked wryly.

His lips curved into a smile. "If you were Krinar, you would actually be considered an adolescent, age-wise."

"I see." Mia gave him a small frown. "And at what age do you become adults?"

"Well, physically, we attain our adult characteristics right around the same age as humans, somewhere in the late teens or early twenties. However, it's only around a couple of hundred years of age that a Krinar is considered mature enough to be a fully functioning member of our society—although it could be sooner if they make some type of extraordinary contribution."

For some reason, that upset her. Mia didn't know why it mattered to her that she would not be considered a fully functioning member of Krinar society at any point within her lifetime. It's not like they would ever view a human as such anyway. And besides, she had no idea how long her relationship with Korum would last. Still, it rankled her somewhat, the fact that Ks would always consider her little more than a child.

Not wanting to dwell on that topic, she asked, "So did the trial today go as you expected?"

Korum shrugged. "Just about. Loris will try to twist everything, to make it seem like I made the whole thing up. But there's too much evidence of their betrayal, and I don't think anything can save them at this point."

"What does complete rehabilitation mean?" Mia asked, unbearably curious. "Everyone seemed shocked when you suggested it."

"It's our most extreme form of punishment for criminals," Korum said, his eyes narrowing slightly. "It's used in cases when an individual poses a severe danger to society—as these traitors clearly do."

"Okay . . . but what is it?"

"Saret can do a better job of explaining it to you," Korum said. "The exact mechanics of it fall within his area of expertise. But essentially, whatever it was that made them act that way—that personality trait will be thoroughly eradicated."

Mia's eyes widened. "How?"

Korum sighed. "Like I said, it's not my area of expertise. But from what I know as a layman, it involves wiping out a lot of their memories and creating a new personality for them. It's only done when there's no other choice because it's very invasive for the mind. The rehabilitated are never the same afterwards—which is exactly the point in this case."

"So they wouldn't remember who they are?" That did seem pretty horrible to Mia.

"They might remember bits and pieces, so they wouldn't be completely blank slates, but the essence of their personality—and that part that made them commit the crime—would be gone."

Mia swallowed. "That does seem harsh . . ."

His eyes narrowed again. "It's better than what your kind does to criminals. At least we don't have capital punishment."

"You don't?" Mia wasn't sure why she was so surprised to hear that. Perhaps it had to do with the popular image of the Ks as a violent species, arising primarily from the bloody fights during the Great Panic.

"No, Mia, we don't," Korum told her sardonically. "We're really not the monsters you've imagined us to be."

"I never said your people were," Mia protested, and he laughed.

"No, just me, right?"

Mia lowered her eyes, unable to bear the mockery in his gaze. "I don't think you're a monster," she told him quietly. "But I do think it's wrong for you to treat me like a possession just because I'm human. I'm a person with feelings and desires, and I did have a life before you came into it—"

"And now you don't?" Korum asked, tilting her chin up until she had no choice but to look him in the eyes. Noticing the deeper gold surrounding his irises, Mia nervously moistened her suddenly dry lips. "You think that I mistreat you? That I keep you from the fascinating life you enjoyed before?"

"I liked the life I had before," Mia told him defiantly. "It was exactly what I wanted. It might've seemed boring to you, but I was happy with it—"

"Happy with what?" he asked her softly. "Studying day and night? Hiding behind baggy clothes because you were too scared to actually try living? Being a virgin at the age of twenty-one?"

Mia flushed with anger and embarrassment. "That's right," she told him bitterly. "Happy with my family and my friends, happy living in New York and going to school there, happy with the internship I had planned for this summer—"

His expression darkened. "I already promised that you will see your family soon," he said, his tone dangerously flat. "And I told you that I will bring you back to New York for the school year. You don't trust me to keep my word?"

Mia took a deep breath, trying to control herself. It

probably wasn't the wisest move on her part, arguing with him like that in her circumstances, but she couldn't help it. Some reckless demon inside her had awoken and wouldn't be denied. "You've lied to me before," she said, unable to hide the resentment in her voice.

"Oh really?" he said, his words practically dripping with sarcasm. "*I* lied to you?"

Mia swallowed again. "You manipulated me into doing exactly what you wanted," she said stubbornly. "I didn't want any part of it—all I wanted was to be left alone . . ."

He regarded her with an inscrutable expression on his face. "And do you still?" he asked softly. "Want to be left alone?"

Mia stared at him, caught completely by surprise. Her mouth opened, but no words came out.

"And don't lie to me, Mia," he added quietly. "I always know when you're lying."

Mia blinked furiously, trying to hold back a sudden rush of tears. With that one simple question, he had stripped her bare, laid out all of her vulnerabilities for him to exploit. She didn't want him to know the depth of her feelings for him, didn't want her emotions exposed for him to toy with. What kind of an idiot was she, to want to be with someone like him? To hate and love him so intensely at the same time?

His lips curved into a half-smile. "I see." Leaning toward her, he kissed her on the mouth softly, his lips strangely gentle on hers.

"I'll see what I can do about getting you an internship," he said, pulling away from her and getting up. "And I'll introduce you to some other human girls in this Center—maybe you'll meet some new friends."

And as Mia looked at him in shock, he smiled at her

again and went into his office, leaving her to digest everything that had just happened.

CHAPTER SEVEN

Three hours later, Mia was lying on the bed, completely absorbed in the story of the early evolution of the Krinar, when Korum walked into the bedroom.

"We're going to dinner in twenty minutes," he told her, "so you might want to get ready."

Startled, Mia looked up at him. "To dinner where?"

"Arman is an acquaintance of mine," Korum explained, sitting down on the bed next to her and placing his hand on her leg. "He invited us over to his house when I told him about you. He also has a charl, a Costa Rican girl who's been with him for a couple of years now. She's very eager to meet you."

Mia grinned, suddenly very excited. "Oh, I'd love to meet her as well!" She couldn't wait to talk to another girl in her situation and learn about Ks from the perspective of a human who also knew them intimately—and much longer.

Korum smiled back. "I figured you would. How's your

reading going so far?"

"It's fascinating," she told him earnestly. "I had no idea you had also evolved from an ape-like species."

He nodded. "We did. There were many parallels in our evolution and yours, except there ultimately ended up being two different species on Krina: us and the *lonar*—that's the primates I told you about before. We were bigger, stronger, faster, longer-lived, and much more intelligent than the lonar, but we were tied to them because we needed their blood to survive."

Mia stared at him. She'd just learned all that as well, and she couldn't get the images of the early Krinar out of her head. The book had gone into some very vivid descriptions of how the ancient Ks had hunted their prey, with each male Krinar staking out his territory around a small group of the lonar and fighting off the other Ks to preserve the blood supply for himself and his mate. Once inside a K's "territory," the lonar had very little chance of survival, as they would be constantly weakened by material blood loss and traumatized by the experience of being preyed upon. Ultimately, their numbers had dwindled, and the Krinar were forced to adapt, to learn new strategies of feeding.

At that point, the Krinar were still a primitive species, little more than hunters-gatherers. However, the rapid reduction in the lonar population meant that the Ks had to evolve beyond their territorial roots, to learn to collaborate with one another in order to preserve what remained of their critical blood supply. The next hundred thousand years were a time of rapid progress for the Krinar, marking the birth of science, technology, medicine, culture, and the arts. Instead of hunting the lonar, the Ks began to farm them, creating favorable conditions for them to live and reproduce and doing their best to feed only on those who were deemed to be past their prime reproductive age.

These efforts managed to temporarily arrest the decline in the lonar population, and the Krinar society began to prosper. Even with the low birth rate, their numbers began to grow as fewer Ks perished in violent fights to defend their territories. Innovation began to be highly valued, and the Ks invented space travel shortly thereafter. It was the first Golden Age in Krinar history, a time of tremendous scientific achievement and relatively peaceful coexistence among the different Krinar tribes and regions.

"I just got to the point where the plague began," Mia told him. It was apparently the event that ended the first Golden Age, nearly wiping out the entire lonar population and plunging the Krinar society into panic and bloody turmoil.

Korum smiled. "You're making good progress on our history then. What do you think so far?"

"I think it's very interesting," Mia answered honestly. It was also a little scary, how savage they had been in the past, but she didn't want to tell him that. She tried to picture Korum as one of the Krinar primitives, hunting down his prey, and it was a surprisingly easy feat, requiring very little imagination on her part. She could see many of the predatory characteristics still present in his species, from the sinuous way they moved to the territorial traits she'd seen Korum display in regard to her.

"You can continue later," he said, absentmindedly stroking her thigh. As usual, his touch sent a shiver of pleasure through her body. "We shouldn't be late to dinner—it's considered highly insulting to the host."

"Of course," Mia said, getting up immediately. The

last thing she wanted was to offend someone. "Should I dress up somehow?" She was lounging in the jeans and T-shirt that she'd been wearing when she arrived in Lenkarda yesterday. Somehow, the house had already managed to clean them because she'd found them fresh and folded on the dresser in the bedroom.

Korum was apparently two steps ahead of her because he was already opening the door to the walk-in closet. "I created a wardrobe for you," he explained, "so you don't have to rely on me for every outfit. Here, let me show you."

Curious, Mia walked over to take a look, and her jaw nearly dropped. The closet was filled with beautiful light-colored dresses, shoes ranging from barely-there sandals to soft-looking boots, and various accessories. "You made all of this?"

Korum nodded. "I had Leeta send me all of her fashion designs. Aside from working in my company, she dabbles with clothing creation."

Leeta was Korum's distant cousin, and Mia had briefly met her a few times back in New York. She wasn't the warmest and friendliest individual, in Mia's opinion, but her clothing designs seemed quite nice.

"You mean you're not a fashion expert?" Mia pretended to be shocked, comically widening her eyes. He'd certainly been eager to get rid of her entire former wardrobe back in New York.

He laughed. "Far from it. I do know when clothes are being used as a shield, though," he said pointedly, referring to her tendency to wear ugly but comfortable clothes when left to her own devices.

Mia fought a childish urge to stick out her tongue at him. "Yeah, whatever," she muttered.

"For tonight, you can wear this," Korum said, pulling

out a delicate-looking light-pink dress.

Mia put it on, secretly pleased by the heat in Korum's eyes as she changed in front of him, and walked over to look in the mirror. Like all Krinar clothes so far, the dress fit her perfectly, ending just above her knees, and didn't require any kind of bra underneath. There were no sleeves, and her back was left entirely exposed. However, her shoulders were covered with wide ruffled straps, and the square neckline at the front was surprisingly modest. The color was beautiful, giving her pale cheeks the illusion of a rosy glow.

"I've noticed you don't wear any kind of bright or dark clothing," Mia commented, wondering about that peculiar fact. "In general, you seem to favor light colors in everything. Is there a particular reason for that?"

Korum smiled, looking at her with a warm glow in his eyes. "There is. Bright or dark colors have historically been associated with violence and vengeance in our culture, and we prefer not to have them around in the normal course of daily life. Of course, when we leave our Centers and interact with humans, we usually wear human clothes—and we don't care about the colors as much for that. In fact, some of us enjoy clothing that we'd never normally wear here or on Krina—like the bright red dress you saw Leeta wear in New York. If she were to dress like that among the Krinar, everyone would think she'd gone crazy and was planning a vendetta of some kind."

Something clicked for Mia. "Is that why the Protector was wearing black at the trial? Because he's on a warpath?"

"Exactly," Korum said. "He's making a statement that he believes he's been wronged and that he intends to seek revenge."

"Seek revenge how?" Mia wondered, and Korum shrugged, apparently not in the mood to discuss politics right now. Since they didn't have much time, Mia decided to let it go for now and focus instead on the upcoming dinner.

"Here, you can wear these shoes," Korum said, handing her a pair of soft ivory booties. Like all K footwear, these seemed to have a flat sole. Apparently, the concept of high-heeled shoes was not as popular among Krinar females as it was among human women.

Mia pulled on the boots—which immediately conformed to her feet and became comfortable—and tried to tame her hair a bit with her fingers. After lounging for hours, she had a serious bedhead look going on, with her long curls tangled and sticking out in all directions. After a couple of minutes, she gave up on the hopeless cause. Even with the regular use of Korum's wonder shampoo, her hair would never be as straight and sleek as she'd like.

"It looks beautiful, Mia. Leave it," Korum said, observing her efforts with quiet amusement.

Mia couldn't help smiling at him. It was one of the things she found peculiar about him: he actually seemed to have a thing for her hair, often touching it and playing with the curls. Since she'd never seen a curly-haired K, she assumed he simply liked it because of the novelty factor. "Okay, then I'm ready, I guess . . ."

"One more thing," Korum said, coming up behind her and fastening an unusual iridescent necklace around her neck, his warm fingers brushing against her throat. It was a deceptively simple design, just a tear-shaped pendant on a thin chain, but the shimmery material made it indescribably beautiful. It was as if all colors of the rainbow were gathered around her neck, competing with each other for attention.

"Wow," Mia breathed, touching the pendant with reverence. "What is it?"

"It's a genuine shimmer-stone necklace," Korum explained. "Shimmer-stone occurs naturally only in my region of Krina, and this one has been passed down through generations in my family. It's just shy of a million years old."

Mia turned around to stare at him in shock. "And you're putting it on me? What if I lose or damage it?"

"You won't," Korum reassured her, smiling faintly. And offering her his arm, he asked, "Shall we go?"

Speechless, Mia looped her arm through the crook of his elbow and followed him out—with a million-year-old Krinar family heirloom sparkling merrily around her throat.

* * *

Five minutes later, they stood before a cream-colored house that looked a lot like Korum's. The ride to the other end of the colony took less than a minute in the small aircraft Korum had created explicitly for that purpose.

As they approached, the wall of the house disintegrated in front of them, and they walked in.

A tall, lean Krinar male stood in the middle of the room, dressed in the usual light-colored garb. His hair was the lightest shade of brown Mia had ever seen on a K, almost sandy-colored, and his hazel eyes had a greenish undertone that looked particularly exotic with his golden skin. The smile on his narrow, ascetic-looking face was broad and welcoming.

Walking up to Korum, he touched his shoulder with

his open palm. "Korum, it's such an honor to have you here," he said. His manner was somewhat deferential, and Mia realized that it was probably a big deal for him—having a member of the Council in his house.

Korum smiled back and reciprocated the gesture. "I'm glad to see you too, Arman. Thank you for the invitation."

While the two Ks were greeting each other, Mia examined her surroundings with a great deal of curiosity. This was the first fully Krinar dwelling she had been to—with the exception of the arena—and she was fascinated by its almost Zen-like aesthetic. There was absolutely no clutter anywhere; in fact, there didn't seem to be any furniture with the exception of two large floating planks. Mia guessed those were meant to serve as places for the guests to sit. The outside walls were fully transparent, while the rest of the interior was a beautiful shade of cream.

"And you must be Mia," Arman said, turning and addressing her directly.

Mia smiled at him. "Yes, hi. It's nice to meet you."

To her surprise, Mia realized that she liked this K. There was a kind look in his eyes, and something almost gentle in the way he spoke that made her feel very much at ease in his presence.

"Oh, it's very nice to meet you as well," Arman said, his smile getting wider. "Maria has been looking forward to meeting you ever since we learned about you yesterday."

At that moment, a human girl walked into the room. Dressed in a beautiful halter-style white dress that showed off her slim, curvy figure to perfection, she was strikingly pretty and bore a strong resemblance to a young Jennifer Lopez.

Smiling hugely, she swiftly came up to Mia and warmly embraced her, brushing her lips against Mia's left cheek. Some kind of exotic perfume tickled Mia's nose. Slightly startled, Mia awkwardly hugged her back.

"Oh my dear, how are you?" she exclaimed in Spanish, pulling back to look at Mia. "I'm Maria, and I'm so glad to see you! What a lovely necklace! How are your first couple of days here? Did Korum show you around already? You poor thing, you must be so overwhelmed with everything right now! I remember I didn't even know how to use the toilet at first!"

Mia blinked, overwhelmed only by the girl's enthusiasm. She was like a pretty tornado, sweeping along everything in her path. "I'm good, thanks," Mia answered in Spanish, inwardly still marveling at her new language abilities. "I haven't really seen much of the Center yet—I only arrived yesterday."

"Oh, you haven't gone to the beach yet? It's so nice, you really should!" Turning to Korum, she frowned at him, her smooth brow furrowing slightly.

Korum laughed. "Hint taken. I'll show Mia the beach tomorrow."

"Maria!" their host exclaimed. "Please be nice to our guests!"

"I'm always nice," Maria retorted, grinning. "That's why you love me." Coming up on tiptoes, she kissed Arman on the cheek, and Mia could almost see him melting on the spot, unable to withstand the potent force of the girl's charm.

With a big grin on his own face, Arman turned his attention back to Mia and Korum. "She's incorrigible," he said, and there was such happiness in his voice that Mia could only gape at him in open-mouthed amazement. "Please ignore her and follow me. The dinner is all ready."

They followed Arman into another room. In the middle of the room was another large floating plank, oval in shape, surrounded by four floating seats. Why all K furniture seemed to float, Mia had no idea. On the large plank—which Mia assumed functioned as a table—there were about twenty different dishes, ranging from familiar tropical fruits and vegetables to some exotic-looking salads, dips, and stew-like concoctions.

Sitting down on one of the chairs, Mia felt it adjusting to her body and smiled. All K inventions seemed to be designed with a focus on maximum comfort and convenience.

The dinner flew by, dominated by light conversation and amusing stories about the Costa Rican flora and fauna. Mia learned that Arman was an artist, and that he came to Earth to study human culture and the arts. He had met Maria shortly after his arrival. Her family used to own land in the area where the Ks had built their Center, and Arman had been one of the Krinar responsible for making sure that the displaced humans were appropriately compensated. Theirs seemed to be a love at first sight.

"From the moment I saw him, I knew I wanted him," Maria confided, her dark eyes sparkling. "I didn't care that he wasn't human, or that everybody was scared of them. I knew he couldn't be as bad as they said—he was far too nice for that." And reaching out, she squeezed his hand, beaming at Arman with a megawatt smile.

Observing the two lovers, Mia felt a strange pressure in her chest that was very much like jealousy. They seemed to be genuinely in love, despite the obstacles Mia had always viewed as insurmountable. And Maria was far too happy for someone who had so few rights in the

Krinar society. Clearly, her formal status as a charl had very little bearing on her relationship with Arman. If anything, it seemed that her K lover was quite content to let her take the lead in many things, his own laid-back personality complemented by her outgoing nature.

By the time the dinner ended, Mia found herself forgetting many of her concerns and simply enjoying the company of this likable couple. They were sweet and tender with each other, and Maria didn't seem intimidated by either of the two Ks. She even reprimanded Korum again for not giving Mia a proper tour of the Center, for which Korum laughingly apologized. It could've been a regular double-date, except that two of the participants were from a different galaxy.

Finally, Mia reluctantly said goodbye to them and headed home with Korum, mulling over the strangeness of what she'd just seen, her heart filling with hope for things she rationally knew had to be impossible.

* * *

The Krinar replayed the results of his latest experiment, watching the recording over and over again.

Everything seemed to be working as he'd hoped. Soon, he would be able to implement the next part of his plan. It was unfortunate that the Keiths had failed, but it was ultimately just a minor setback.

Now he wanted to look at his enemy again . . . and that little charl of his.

For some reason, he found those recordings to be particularly fascinating.

CHAPTER EIGHT

On the short ride back, Mia couldn't help thinking about the other couple. A human and a K, so happy together—it seemed to go against everything Mia had been told by the Resistance and everything she'd learned about the role of charl in Krinar society. How did they manage such a feat? And wasn't Maria worried that she would ultimately lose Arman when her beauty faded and he remained the same?

Of course, Arman was as different from Korum as anyone she'd ever met. It was difficult to believe that he was a member of the same predatory species. He seemed far too kind and gentle to be a K, and Mia couldn't imagine him holding Maria here against her will. Indeed, it seemed like Maria had been the one to initiate their relationship. Clearly, there were just as many varieties of personalities among Ks as there were among humans.

And Mia had managed to meet one who wouldn't have been out of place in the primeval Krinar forests of billions of years ago.

Korum would've been a very successful hunter, Mia decided, with his blend of ruthlessness and sheer smarts. His ambition had propelled him to the top of the modern Krinar society, and she had no doubt he would've been successful in any type of environment—it was just the way he was. He knew exactly what he wanted, and he didn't hesitate to go after it.

And for now, he wanted her.

Sighing, Mia looked at the floor as they landed in the clearing right next to Korum's house. The ship touched the ground softly, and one of its walls immediately disintegrated, creating an opening for them.

Getting up, she exited the aircraft and followed Korum to the house. "Are we far from the beach?" she asked, remembering Maria mentioning it earlier.

"No, it's actually walking distance," Korum said as they entered the house. "I'll show you the way tomorrow, if you'd like, so you don't have to be cooped up in the house when I'm not around. Just don't go into the ocean without me—the surf can be very strong here, and the currents are unpredictable."

"I'm a good swimmer," Mia told him. "You don't have to worry about me."

"It doesn't matter." Korum stopped and gave her a strict look. "You either promise me you won't go into the water alone, or you don't go to the beach without me at all."

Mia mentally rolled her eyes. The dictator was back. "Fine. I won't go into the water by myself." Having grown up in Florida, she knew exactly what to watch out for in terms of rip currents and rogue waves, and the ocean didn't scare her. Still, she didn't want Korum preventing her from going to the beach, so she decided against arguing with him further.

"Good." He sounded satisfied. "Then I'll take you there tomorrow morning."

"What about the trial?"

"It doesn't start until eleven in the morning. If you wake up before then, we can take a walk to the beach, and I'll show you some of the nearby sites. Later on, I'll give you a more thorough tour."

"That would be nice, thanks," Mia said. "Can I observe the trial again tomorrow? It was really fascinating . . ."

He smiled at her. "Of course. It will be Loris's turn to present—that should be particularly interesting to see."

"Why does he hate you so much?" Mia asked, curious to learn more about Krinar politics. "Did you have some kind of differences before his son was accused?"

Korum's lips twisted slightly. "Differences is one way of putting it. He had a company that competed with mine a few hundred years ago. His designs were far inferior, though, and he ultimately ended up having to close it down. His son—Rafor—worked with him at the time as one of his lead designers, and he lost a lot of his standing in society when the company went out of business. Loris had other ventures at the time, and he was deeply involved in politics, so his standing took a much smaller hit and recovered quickly. His son's, however, never did."

So Rafor was the Keith with the design background, the one who had provided the Resistance with K gadgets. It all made sense now. His designs had never been as good as Korum's; it was no wonder that the Resistance had failed.

"And Loris hates you for that? For Rafor losing his standing?" Mia wasn't sure she fully understood the standing concept, but it seemed to be quite important for the Krinar.

"He does," Korum said. "He hates it that his son wasn't good enough as a designer, and he blames me for Rafor never doing anything else productive with his life. And now that Rafor has also proven to be a pathetic traitor . . ."

"He blames you for that as well?" Mia guessed, staring up at Korum with a slight frown. "Is that why he intends to seek revenge?"

Korum nodded, his eyes glittering with something that looked like anticipation. "Indeed."

"It doesn't bother you?" Mia asked, trying to understand her lover better. He looked almost as if he were relishing the other K's hatred. "That someone hates you so much, I mean?"

"Why should it bother me?" He looked amused at the thought. "He's hardly the first, and he won't be the last."

Mia stared at him. "You don't care if people like you? If they are your friends or your enemies?"

Korum laughed. "No, my sweet, why would I? If someone wants to be my enemy, it's their choice—one that they will ultimately regret."

"I see," Mia said, another piece of the Korum puzzle clicking into place for her. She knew that there were people like that, individuals so confident in themselves—or arrogant, depending on how one looked at it—that they seemed to lack the usual drive to please others. And her lover appeared to be one of them. If anything, it looked like he thrived on conflict. She wondered if it was a K-specific trait or simply a part of Korum's personality.

Before Mia could finish fully analyzing that thought, Korum stepped closer and lifted his hand to brush her hair back from her face. "That's enough talk about politics," he said, cupping her cheek with one large warm hand, his eyes beginning to gleam with familiar golden undertones. "I can think of far more pleasant things we could be doing right now."

Mia's heartbeat immediately quickened, and the muscles deep within her belly tightened, reacting to his touch and the unmistakable sexual intent in his voice. Such a Pavlovian response, the psychology student in her noted wryly—her body was now fully conditioned to respond to him this way, to crave the pleasure that only he could provide. The lack of control over her own flesh bothered Mia on many levels, making her feel even less in charge of her own life, her own decisions.

Bending down, he wrapped one arm around her back and placed the other under her knees, effortlessly lifting her up into his arms. Mia closed her eyes, burying her face against his shoulder as he swiftly carried her toward the bedroom.

As he'd said earlier, the labels placed on their relationship didn't matter—at least not when it came to this.

* * *

When they got to the bedroom, he placed her down on the bed and straightened for a minute. Bemused, she watched as he placed a small white dot on his right temple.

"What is it?" she asked him warily when he leaned over her again.

"You'll see," he said mysteriously, with a wicked gleam in those amber eyes. And then he touched her temple as well. Startled, Mia raised her hand and felt a small protrusion. He had placed a dot on her also.

Feeling nervous, Mia opened her mouth to ask him again, but he kissed her in that moment and all rational thought left her head. His hand closed over her right breast, kneading the small globe, his thumb flicking lightly over her nipple, and Mia felt a surge of heat go through her. His other hand buried itself in her hair, holding her head still as his tongue invaded her mouth. She could taste the hunger in his kiss, and she wondered vaguely what had provoked him.

All of a sudden, she could no longer feel the softness of the bed beneath her and her ears were ringing from loud music, the pulsing beat reverberating through her bones. Gasping in shock, she pushed at Korum, and he let her go, watching with an unsettling mixture of amusement and burning lust as she sat up, gaping at the scene in panic and disbelief.

They were on the floor inside what looked like a large metal cage. All around them, Mia could see gyrating bodies, grinding and pushing against each other. Stunned, she realized they were dancing. The flickering lights above them cast everything in shades of blue and purple, adding to the surreal feel of the situation.

"Where are we?" she yelled, jumping to her feet and staring at Korum in frightened astonishment. Did he teleport them somewhere, or was this some strange and new virtual world?

He laughed, rising from the floor smoothly. "Come here," he said, pulling her toward him.

Angry and confused, Mia tried to resist, but it was useless, of course. Within seconds, he had her pressed against his body, and she could feel his erection pushing at her stomach.

"So I learned something interesting today," Korum said softly, his voice somehow carrying above the music. His eyes were nearly yellow in the strange flashing lights of the dance floor. "My sweet little charl seems to have a thing for touching me in public places—when she thinks no one is watching, of course. When she thinks I can't feel it."

Mia swallowed, remembering her actions earlier, before the trial began. She'd played with Korum, secure in the knowledge that no one would ever find out . . . yet somehow he knew. Was he mad at her? Did he intend to punish her somehow?

"Where are we?" she asked, staring up at him warily. "Why did you bring me here?"

"We're in the most exclusive nightclub in Beverly Hills," Korum told her. "And I'm going to give you exactly what you want."

Mia's stomach twisted with a strange mixture of fear and excitement. "Korum, please, I don't think—"

Before she could finish the sentence, he grasped her butt and lifted her up, pressing her back against the wall of the cage, her thighs spread wide and his pelvis flush against her own. Mia gasped again, feeling his cock prodding at her sex through the thin barrier of their clothing. Then his mouth was over hers again, his kiss so deep and penetrating that she could barely breathe.

He intended to fuck her in public, Mia realized with some semi-functioning part of her brain, horrified and yet unbearably aroused at the thought. Surely this couldn't be real, she thought desperately, surely he wouldn't do that to her . . . or would he?

She tried to twist away from his mouth, her nails digging into his shoulders, but he wouldn't let her, biting her lower lip in warning until she had no choice but to give in. The roar of her own heartbeat was almost louder than the blaring music around them as she fought to maintain some semblance of sanity in what seemed like an utterly insane situation.

Holding her up with one arm, Korum used his other hand to grasp the skirt of her dress and lift it higher, leaving the front portion of her lower body naked. Mia whimpered in panic, frantically raking her nails down his bare shoulders as he freed his cock too. She could feel the blunt force of it pressing against her delicate opening, and then he began to push inside, ignoring the way her muscles tightened in an attempt to deny him entry.

It was all happening so fast that Mia could barely process the situation, the flashing lights and the pounding music adding to her sense of disorientation. She felt unbearably hot, her body burning with a strange combination of searing shame and feverish desire as his cock continued to push deeper inside her, her narrow sheath reluctantly stretching around its thick girth. With her full weight supported only by his arm, she couldn't limit the depth of his penetration in any way, and he felt too large inside her, the head of his shaft almost bumping up against her cervix. For a few moments, pain threatened, but then her body adjusted, softening and melting around him, and the discomfort receded, leaving only a scorching need in its place. At the same time, his mouth continued to plunder her own, the invasion of his tongue mimicking the relentless push of his cock.

Her senses completely overwhelmed, Mia couldn't string together a single thought, could only feel as he began to move his hips, the force of his thrusts pressing her into the cage wall. The metal links dug into the soft skin of her exposed back, and the pulsing beat of the music seemed to echo inside her, the noise from the dancing crowd a dizzying buzz in her ears. Her vision darkened for a second, his kisses draining her of oxygen, but then his mouth lifted, letting her catch her breath, and the fainting sensation receded, bringing her back to semi-awareness of the situation.

Frantically sucking in air, Mia shut her eyes tightly and tried to pretend that this wasn't happening, that he wasn't truly fucking her in a cage in the middle of a nightclub. It couldn't be real, any of it; surely, she couldn't really feel the hard metal pressing into her back, couldn't hear the crowd screaming and whooping in tune to the blasting music. Yet the relentless thrust and drag of his cock inside her couldn't be mistaken for anything else, nor could the moist heat of his mouth as it traveled down the side of her neck.

A wave of hot shame rolled through her again, somehow adding to the powerful tension gathering inside her. His pace picked up, his hips hammering at her, and every muscle in her body seemed to tighten simultaneously, the pleasure so sharp it was almost intolerable . . . and then she could only scream as the climax crashed over her with the force of a tidal wave, her inner muscles squeezing and releasing his cock several times.

As the orgasmic sensation faded, Mia slumped in Korum's arms, burying her face in the crook of his neck. She could feel him shuddering as well, could hear his hoarse groan as his shaft throbbed and jerked inside her, releasing his seed in warm bursts.

Now that it was over, all she could feel was scalding embarrassment, and angry tears filled her eyes, leaking out through the corners. She didn't want to look around, didn't want to face the people who were sure to be avidly watching them.

More tears fell, moistening his neck. Mia wanted to disappear, to pretend this was all some horrible dream, but there was no escaping the stark sensations. His softening shaft was still buried inside her, and she could feel the cage digging into her back. And just when she thought she couldn't bear it any longer, he murmured in her ear, "We're not really here, darling. You know that, right?"

"What?" Mia jerked back, staring at him in shock and disbelief. She could hear the hypnotic beat of the latest dance-hop single, could feel him inside her, and he was telling her it was all happening inside her head?

His lips curled into a small smile. "Did you think it was real?"

"Let me down," she said quietly, hot fury rushing through her. "Let me down right now."

He actually listened to her this time and lowered her to the ground, slowly withdrawing from her. Her trembling legs refused to support her weight for a second, and he held her carefully, looking down at her with a slightly amused expression on his face. The dress fell back into place, covering her lower half again.

As soon as she could stand on her own, Mia pushed at Korum's chest, and he took a step back, giving her some breathing room. Just to confirm what he'd told her, Mia slowly turned in a circle, staring at the dancers outside their cage.

No one was looking at them. Not a single person. The music kept blaring, the dancers kept grinding against each other, and nobody was paying them any attention. *This wasn't real after all.* It was all happening virtually, just like at the trial. Or was it?

Turning back toward Korum, she asked evenly, "Did we just have sex, or did you simply mind-fuck me?"

Instead of replying to her question, Korum lifted his hand to his right temple and pressed on it lightly. The club dissolved around them, reality shifting and adjusting, and Mia found herself standing on the floor next to one of the bedroom walls. He was standing there too, less than a foot away from her, his shorts unfastened and his now-flaccid sex partially visible.

Blinking to clear the slight blurriness in her vision, Mia took stock of her current state. Her sex felt swollen and a little sore, like it usually did after intercourse, and she could feel the wetness of his sperm sliding down her leg.

So the sex part had definitely been real.

Mia couldn't decide if that made her feel better or worse about the situation. Now that the adrenaline rush was over, she found herself shaking slightly, feeling cold despite the warmth in the room.

"I need a shower," she told him, refusing to look at him.

"Mia," he said softly, his hand wrapping around her upper arm when she tried to walk past him, "you're not going to tell me you didn't like it, are you?"

"Of course I didn't!" Tears welled up in her eyes again as she relived the sharp feelings of burning humiliation and unwilling arousal, and she tried to yank her arm away from him. A useless effort, of course; he didn't even seem to feel her struggle.

"Liar," Korum said, and she could hear the amusement in his voice. "I could feel exactly how much you didn't like it when you came, your little pussy squeezing me for all its worth."

Mia felt her cheeks turning a bright red. "I'm going into the shower right now," she repeated, wanting nothing more than to get away.

"All right," he said. "I will go with you." And before she could object, he picked her up again and carried her into the bathroom, placing her on her feet next to the jacuzzi.

"I wanted to go alone," she told him mutinously as he pulled down her dress, leaving her standing there naked with the exception of the necklace around her neck and the soft booties on her feet. She touched the necklace lightly, finding the place where it apparently locked in place, and carefully took it off, placing it on the side of the jacuzzi. She had no intention of showering with a million-year-old piece of alien jewelry around her neck.

He smiled at her, taking off his own clothes. "Why would you want that?"

"Because I don't like you right now," she told him bluntly. Actually, that was a huge understatement. It was more that she felt like doing something violent to him—such as slapping that smile right off his beautiful face.

"Because I gave you what you wanted but would've been too scared to ask for?" he asked, cocking his head to the side.

"I didn't want that," Mia told him vehemently. "And the fact that I came has nothing to do with anything. I'm more than just the sum of my physical responses—"

"Of course you are," Korum said, coming up to her and crouching down to remove the boots from her feet. Mia stared down at him resentfully, fighting a ridiculous urge to stroke the dark, lustrous-looking hair on his head. Fluidly rising to his feet and looking down at her with a half-smile, he added, "If you had been truly uncomfortable or scared, I would've stopped immediately and brought us back here. I could feel your excitement, your pleasure at doing something forbidden. That's why you played with me in the virtual world today—because underneath that shy exterior, you secretly love the thought of being just a little bit bad . . ."

Mia didn't have a good answer to that, so she lowered her gaze and padded toward the shower. He came in with her as well, adjusting the settings so that the water cascaded over both of them. Pouring the pleasantly scented shampoo in his hand, he applied it to her hair, his strong fingers massaging away the tension in her scalp.

After her hair was clean and soft, he turned his attention to her body, tenderly washing each part until she forgot all about her anger in the sheer bliss of his skilled caresses. And just when she thought he was done, he knelt down and brought her to another peak with his mouth, his lips and tongue soft and gentle on her sensitive flesh.

Utterly relaxed and incredibly sleepy, Mia barely felt him toweling her off and carrying her to bed. As soon as her head touched the pillow, she passed out, not even cognizant of lying in his warm embrace.

CHAPTER NINE

The next morning, Mia woke up with the memory of their virtual sex session fresh in her mind.

She still couldn't believe that Korum had done that to her—that he had made her believe he was fucking her in public, of all things—and she couldn't believe she had responded like that, despite her feelings of embarrassment and humiliation. Even now, she could feel herself getting wet at the thought, and she cursed her own susceptibility to him. He seemed to know her sexual needs far better than she did, and had no hesitation about pushing her boundaries. She wanted to stay mad at him, she really did. But, if she were to be honest with herself, she had to admit that she had enjoyed the experience on some level. It had been terribly exciting, having sex in public like that—particularly since she now knew that there was no need for shame, as no one had actually seen them.

Stretching, she yawned and then remembered the promised beach outing. Jumping out of bed and putting on her robe, she went to brush her teeth and splash some water on her face before going to look for Korum.

To her surprise, he was nowhere to be found. Before she could wonder about his whereabouts, she heard something in the living room and left the kitchen to investigate. Sure enough, Korum was just walking in through the opening in one of the walls.

And Mia gasped in horrified shock at the sight.

Far from his usual immaculate self, her lover looked like he had just rolled in the mud, his clothes dirty and torn. And were those . . . *traces of blood* on his arms and face?

Seeing her standing there, Korum flashed her a quick grin, his teeth startlingly white in his dirt-streaked face. "You woke up early. I was hoping you'd still be asleep and I'd have a chance to shower before you saw me like this."

Mia finally found her tongue. "What happened? Are you all right?"

He laughed, his eyes glittering with excitement. "I'm fine. I was just out playing *defrebs*—it's a type of sport I enjoy."

"Oh . . ." Mia exhaled in relief. "So it's like a ball game or something?"

"More like a type of martial arts," he explained, walking toward the bathroom.

Curious, Mia followed him there, watching as he stripped off his dirty clothes, dropping them on the floor and revealing the magnificent body underneath. He smelled deliciously sweaty, and his golden skin gleamed with perspiration. He looked like a warrior fresh from battle, and she could now see that those were definitely scratches and bloody streaks on his arms and legs.

"Is that what you do for exercise? Martial arts?" she

asked, perching on the edge of the jacuzzi as he turned on the shower, adjusting the controls. The dirty clothes had already disappeared, having been absorbed into one of the walls, and the floor was again spotless. Another useful function of the house, Mia guessed.

"Pretty much," he admitted, stepping under the water. His voice sounded a little muffled by the water spray, so she came closer to hear him better. "We rarely exercise the way many modern humans do, in a gym environment or doing only one type of physical activity. Instead, we usually engage in some type of sports. Defrebs is particularly popular because it's the closest we get to fighting outside of the Arena—"

"Arena?"

"Ah, you haven't gotten to that part of your reading yet . . ." He paused for a few seconds, lathering his hair and rinsing out the shampoo before continuing. "The Arena is a place where our citizens get to resolve certain irreconcilable differences. If, let's say, I believe that someone has done me irreparable harm, I can challenge him to the Arena—and he would have to accept my challenge or lose much of his standing."

Mia looked at the foggy shower glass with surprise. "So what would you do in the Arena? Fight?"

"Exactly. No weapons are allowed, but everything else goes. The goal is to win, to subdue your enemy completely while everyone watches . . ."

Mia laughed incredulously. "What, like gladiators in ancient Rome?"

"Where do you think the Romans got the idea?"

"What? Seriously?"

Korum shut off the water and opened the door, grabbing a towel from a nearby rack. "Absolutely. The same group of scientists I told you about earlier—the ones who had been the source of many of your Greek and Roman myths—they're responsible for that as well. A couple of them missed that aspect of life on Krina, so they gradually introduced the tradition into Roman culture and then it took on a life of its own. We were quite surprised, actually, how long the games persisted and how popular they became."

Mia could hardly believe her ears. "And you still have these games? In the modern era?"

"Sure," he said, his eyes bright with golden undertones. "It's a way for us to satisfy certain . . . urges . . . that would otherwise get in the way of a peaceful and prosperous society."

Urges? She blinked, watching him warily as he finished drying himself off. So the Krinar did still have the violent tendencies she'd just finished reading about. No wonder there had been so many rumors about their brutality during the days of the Great Panic—

Before she could analyze that thought any further, he came up to her and lifted her up by the waist. Startled, Mia grabbed his shoulders as he slanted his mouth over hers, kissing her with tightly leashed aggression. Playing the sport had clearly excited him, and she could feel his cock hardening against her leg even through the thick fabric of her robe. Her own response was instantaneous, her sex clenching with desire and her nipples pinching into tight buds.

Sensing her arousal, he growled low in his throat and backed her up against the wall, his hands tearing at the tie holding her robe together. Bending his right knee, he set her astride it, causing her naked sex to grind against his leg, and Mia moaned into his mouth, the pressure on her clitoris turning her on even more. His hands migrated lower, grabbing her thighs and opening them wide, and then he was inside her, impaling her with no further preliminaries.

Mia cried out at the hard force of his entry; as aroused as she was, he was still too large for her to accommodate easily, and her delicate inner channel felt stretched to the point of pain. He paused for a second, letting her adjust, and then he slowly began thrusting, still holding her legs open, preventing her from controlling the sexual act in any way. The thick head of his cock nudged her G-spot with each stroke, and the wide-open position allowed his pelvis to press against her clitoris each time he bottomed inside her, causing the pressure to build further and further.

Finally, she climaxed with a scream, her entire body spasming in his arms. Unable to resist the rhythmic pulsations of her inner muscles, he came too, groaning harshly against her ear.

Panting, Mia hung in his grasp until he carefully lowered her to the ground, slowly withdrawing from her and handing her a tissue.

Her knees wobbled a little, and he held her up, staring down at her with a slightly perplexed look on his beautiful face. "Believe it or not, I didn't really mean for this to happen," Korum said, a self-deprecating smile curving his lips. "I honestly don't know why I don't seem to have any control around you. It's like I have to get inside you every chance I get . . ."

Her pussy still throbbing with the remnants of her orgasm, Mia moistened her lips and shrugged slightly, absurdly flattered by his admission. "It's okay . . . It's not like I don't enjoy it . . ."

"Oh really?" he teased, a big grin breaking out on his face. "You enjoy it? I would've never guessed—"

Mia frowned at him, cleaning herself up with the

tissue. "You did promise me a trip to the beach, though," she reminded him, wanting to change the topic. The strength of her own sexual response to him—of her feelings for him in general—still made her uncomfortable. Why couldn't she have fallen for someone less complicated? Why did it have to be this hard, uncompromising man with his domineering nature? Even Arman would've been an easier person to have a relationship with; at least with someone like him, she would've felt a little more in control, instead of constantly feeling off-balance.

"We should still be able to make it," Korum said, creating an outfit for himself with the aid of the nanomachines and putting it on. "I'll make you breakfast and we'll go."

"Okay," Mia said. "I'll grab a quick shower and be right there."

* * *

Seven minutes later, Mia entered the kitchen and saw that Korum was making something green in a regular human blender.

"What is that?" she asked him, curiously observing the strange concoction.

Korum smiled, his features lighting up at the sight of her. "Ah, I was hoping you'd be quick." Taking two steps toward her, he dropped a light kiss on her forehead and then returned to his task. "This is a blend of mango, banana, spinach, and bowit—that's a type of sweet nut from Krina. Are you hungry?"

"Always," Mia admitted with a sheepish smile. The smoothie sounded very promising. "Do we have enough time to swim before the trial begins?"

"Absolutely," he said, and then started up the blender. Mia put her hands over her ears at the noise, which thankfully lasted only about ten seconds. Once the room was quiet again, he added, "We have about two hours, so I should be able to show you some interesting places around here and then we could go for a quick swim."

"That would be great," Mia said, eager to get out and explore the area. "I was feeling pretty cooped up yesterday—"

"Of course," he said, pouring the green shake into a tall, clear cup and handing it to her. "I don't want you to feel that way. Try this—it should be quite good."

Mia took a sip of the thick concoction, and her tastebuds nearly exploded with the sweet, rich taste. It was unlike anything she'd ever tasted before, with hints of chocolate, cream, and a completely indescribable something underneath the more familiar fruity flavors. "Wow." She swallowed and licked her lips. "Whatever that bo-thing is, it's absolutely amazing."

Pleased at her reaction, Korum smiled. "Yes, it's my favorite as well. It takes the bowit plant five years to reach full maturity, so this is the first time we've been able to harvest these nuts here, on Earth. They're quite tasty and go with a lot of different dishes."

"Can I take this with me?" Mia asked, wanting to get a head start on the day. "That way, I can just dress quickly and we could go . . ."

"Sure, why not?" Korum poured a cup for himself as well. "Let me show you our swimwear."

Leaving the kitchen, he walked toward the bedroom, sipping his shake. Mia followed him, curious to see what a K version of a bathing suit was like.

Entering the room, he placed his cup on the commode and headed toward the closet. Pulling out what looked like a tiny scrap of white fabric, he laid it on the bed and said, "This is what our women typically wear."

Mia stared. "Uh . . . I don't see how that would fit me." Her parents' Chihuahua, maybe, but definitely no one bigger than that.

He laughed. "The material is stretchy. Try it on."

Still dubious, Mia put down her own shake and approached the bed. Picking up the material, she carefully examined it.

"It goes on over your head," Korum said. "Here, take off your robe, and I'll show you how to put it on."

"Okay," Mia said, untying the robe and dropping it on the bed. She was completely naked underneath, and she could feel the heat of his gaze as it traveled down her body. When his eyes came back up to her face, they were almost purely gold in color. Mia's breathing quickened, and she could feel her nipples tightening, her body responding to his need.

She heard him take a deep breath, as though inhaling her scent, and then he said huskily, "Here, this goes on like this." Stretching the bandana-like piece in his hands, he lowered it over her head, letting go when it was securely sitting around her hips. His fingers brushed against her stomach in the process, causing her to feel all warm inside again.

Her lips slightly parted, Mia stared at him, unable to believe she could want him again so soon.

"Don't look at me like that," he said, his voice sounding rough. "I promised you an outing this morning, and that's what we're going to do."

Mia flushed. "Of course." This was ridiculous; he was turning her into a nymphomaniac. Surely, it couldn't be normal, to want someone like that all the time.

Trying to distract herself, she looked down at the

bandanna-like piece of cloth. To her surprise, it had stretched to cover her torso, turning into an unusual one-piece swimsuit. The fabric looped between her legs, concealing her pubic region and the center of her butt, then ran up the sides of her ribcage and lightly cupped her breasts, hiding the nipples from view. Like all K clothing, the material adhered to her shape perfectly and seemed to be sitting on her quite securely despite the fact that there were no ties of any kind to hold it up.

The overall effect was incredibly sexy, Mia realized, and her cheeks turned pink at the thought of leaving the house like that. "Is that all I'm going to wear?" she asked, looking up at Korum.

He shook his head. "No, you would also wear this on top," he said, handing her what looked like a basic white sheath. "You can take it off when we get to the beach."

Mia wriggled into the sheath and walked over to the mirror to take a look. It seemed like a simple tube-top dress, just made of some thin and clingy fabric. Not all that different from a coverup one might wear on a Florida beach.

"You can put on these boots," Korum said, handing her a pair of grey knee-highs. "Since we're going on foot and you don't like insects, these might be the best option for you."

Willing to wear anything to minimize exposure to Costa Rican creepy-crawlies, Mia pulled on the boots. Casting one last look at her reflection in the mirror, she picked up her smoothie from the commode. "I'm ready."

"Let's go then." Grabbing his own cup, Korum led her out of the house and into the green jungle outside.

The first place Korum showed her was a beautiful grotto

with two mid-sized waterfalls. The water fell from a distance of about twenty feet into a small, shallow pool and then drained into a small river. On the side of the river, there were a number of large rocks, and the grass looked soft and green. A very inviting place to just relax and read, Mia decided, noting the grotto's location.

After the waterfalls, they walked over to another, larger river—an estuary draining into the ocean. According to Korum, it was an excellent place to view the local wildlife, including various species of birds and howler monkeys. "That sounds fun," Mia told him, and he promised to take her on a boat tour one of these mornings.

Following the estuary west, they finally arrived at the beach. As Korum had warned her, the surf was quite healthy, with reasonably sized breakers pounding against the shore. In the distance, Mia could see some people—likely Krinar—enjoying the ocean as well, but the area around them was completely deserted.

"We only have about thirty minutes at this point," Korum told her. "After that, I have to get to the trial."

"Of course," Mia said, grinning. "How about a quick swim then?" And without waiting for his response, she pulled off her boots, wriggled out of her sheath, and ran toward the ocean.

He caught up with her immediately, swinging her up into his arms before she could get so much as a toe into the water. "Gotcha," he said, his eyes filled with warm amusement.

Mia laughed, the feeling in her chest lighter than anything she'd experienced in recent weeks. Looping her arms around his neck, she told him, "Okay, but now you have to go in with me. And if the water is too cold for you, I don't want to hear any complaints."

"Oh, a challenge?" he said, raising one eyebrow at her. "We'll see who complains first . . ." And holding her in his arms, he strode decisively into the waves.

Shrieking with laughter at the sudden immersion into cool water, Mia held her breath as a big wave covered their heads. She could feel the strong pull of the current and realized that Korum was likely right about the potential dangers of swimming by herself. With him, however, she felt completely safe; he could obviously resist the drag of the water with ease, his Krinar strength more than a match for the surf.

The wave receded, and Mia rubbed her eyes with one hand, trying to get the salt water out. When she finally opened them, Korum was looking down at her with a strange smile.

"What?" she asked, feeling a bit self-conscious.

"Nothing," he murmured, still smiling. "You just look very cute like this, with your eyelashes and hair all wet. Reminds me of that day when you were caught in the rain."

"You mean the second time I saw you, when I sneezed all over you?" Mia asked wryly, still somewhat embarrassed at the memory.

He nodded. "You were the cutest thing I'd seen in a long time, all dripping curls and big blue eyes . . . and I could barely stop myself from kissing you right then and there."

Mia gave him a disbelieving look. "Really? I thought I looked terrible, like a drowned rat."

He laughed. "More like a drowned kitten, if you want to use animal analogies. Or a wet fregu—that's a cute, fluffy mammal we have on Krina."

"Do you have any of them here?" Mia asked, suddenly excited at the prospect of seeing some alien fauna. "In

Lenkarda, I mean—"

Korum shook his head. "No, the fregu are not domesticated in any way, and we don't take wild animals out of their habitats. We don't domesticate animals in general."

"So no pets of any kind?" Mia asked, surprised.

Another wave approached at that moment, and Korum lifted her higher, enabling her to keep her head above water this time. "No pets," he confirmed once the wave passed. "That's a uniquely human institution."

"Really? I would've never thought that. My parents have a dog," Mia confided. "A little Chihuahua. She's very cute."

"I know," Korum said. "I've seen recordings."

Somehow Mia wasn't shocked. "Of course you have," she said, sighing. She knew she should be upset at this invasion of her family's privacy, but she felt oddly resigned instead. Her lover clearly had no sense of proper boundaries, and Mia was too content right now to spoil it with another argument. Still, she couldn't resist asking, "Is there anything you don't know about me or my family?"

"Probably not much at this point," he admitted casually. "Your family is fascinating to me."

Her family? "Why?" Mia asked, puzzled. "We're just a regular American family—"

"Because *you* are fascinating to me," Korum said, looking at her with an inscrutable amber gaze. "And I want to better understand who you are and where you're coming from."

Mia stared at him. "I see," she murmured, but she didn't see, not really. Why someone like him—a brilliant K with such a high standing in their society—would be interested in a regular human girl was beyond her comprehension.

Suddenly, he grinned at her, and the strange tension dissolved. "So how about you show me just how good of a swimmer you are?" he suggested playfully, letting go of her.

Mia grinned back, feeling almost unbearably happy. "Watch and learn," she told him cockily, and headed for the ocean depths with a strong, even stroke, secure in the knowledge that she was far safer with Korum in deep water than she would be in a kiddie pool with a lifeguard.

* * *

The Krinar watched his enemy frolicking in the water with his charl.

Initially, he hadn't really understood the girl's appeal; she'd seemed like a typical human to him. A pretty little human, but nothing truly special. However, as he kept observing her, he'd slowly begun to notice the fine delicacy of her facial features, the creaminess of her pale skin. Her body was small and fragile, but it was perfectly curved in just the right places, and there was an innocent sensuality in the way she moved, in the angle at which she held her head when she spoke.

To his shock, the K realized that he wanted to bury his fingers in her thick, curly hair and inhale her scent, to lick her neck and feel the warm rush of blood in her veins through that soft skin. That was the best part about sex with human women—the knowledge that just a tiny bite away, paradise awaited.

The craving caught him by surprise. It wasn't part of his plan. He'd thought himself above such nonsense, such primitive urges. He rarely indulged these days; he couldn't afford the distraction. There was too much at stake to throw everything away for the sake of fleeting physical pleasure.

With a heroic effort, he pushed away the fantasy and focused on the task at hand.

CHAPTER TEN

After their swim, Korum brought her back home, jumped into the shower, and left within two minutes, moving like a whirlwind. Bemused, Mia could only watch as he paused to brush a quick kiss on her forehead and then practically flew out the door.

Following his departure, Mia also took a shower and fortified herself with a snack of mango and walnuts, preparing for another potentially lengthy presentation. Then, putting on the bracelet Korum had given her yesterday, she settled comfortably on the couch and immersed herself in the show.

The second day of the trial started with the now-familiar chime.

As before, Mia found her way through the crowd toward Korum's podium and perched on top of it. This time, she refused to touch his virtual self in any way, her cheeks heating up at the memory of what he'd done to her last night as a result of her actions yesterday.

Today there were fewer greetings and preliminaries. After the accused and the Protector appeared in the arena, the audience went completely silent, watching with tremendous interest as the proceedings unfolded.

Like the last time, Loris was dressed in all black. The expression on his face was pinched and strained, and the look he threw in Korum's direction was filled with so much rage and bitterness that Mia involuntarily shivered. After a few seconds, he seemed to get himself under control, and his features smoothed out, his face becoming expressionless.

Stepping forward, he addressed the spectators in a loud, ringing voice. "Dear Earth inhabitants and fellow citizens of Krina! You have been shown evidence of a terrible crime—a crime so horrifying that it is almost beyond belief. And if you were to believe the recordings shown to you yesterday, you would obviously judge these people—and my son among them—to be guilty.

"But you have to ask yourself, is this plausible? How can seven young people with no history of social deviancy all of a sudden conspire to forcibly deport fifty thousand Krinar from Earth, endangering all of our lives in the process? Endangering *my* life in the process? How can they hatch this elaborate plot, arming humans with Krinar weapons and technology? And for what? A chance to help the humans? Does that make sense to any of you?"

The crowd was deathly silent. Mia held her breath, unable to tear her eyes away from the black-clad figure standing so imposingly in the arena.

"Well, it didn't make sense to me. I know my son, and he has his faults—but would-be mass murderer is not among them. And that's why I had to step forward and take on the role of the Protector—because this trial is a farce. It's a very real attack on these young people, and I have no choice but to defend them—"

Turning around for a quick second, Mia peeked at Korum, trying to see his reaction to all of this. There was a look of calm amusement on his face, and he seemed to be watching the proceedings with polite attentiveness.

"I have spoken with Rafor and each of his friends extensively, and none of their stories match," Loris continued. "In fact, they are downright confused. So confused that they don't recall doing anything along the lines of what they have been accused of—so confused that they can barely remember many of the key events of the past year . . .

"Now I know what many of you are thinking. Obviously, if they were guilty, pretending not to remember would be a good way to stall the proceedings, to cast some doubt on the validity of these accusations. And that was my initial thought as well . . . which is why I commissioned a memory scan to be done by the leading mind experts based here on Earth. Four different mind laboratories have performed their examinations—laboratories based in Arizona, Thailand, Fiji, and Hawaii—and the results are indisputable.

"All seven of the accused have had their memories tampered with."

A shocked murmur ran through the crowd, and Mia could see the surprised looks on the Councilors' faces. Sneaking another look behind her, she could see that there was now a very slight, almost imperceptible frown on Korum's face. He seemed puzzled.

"Now many of you know that there aren't many people capable of doing something like that. In fact, I believe that there are fewer than thirty individuals on this planet who have anything to do with mind manipulation. However, one esteemed member of the Council does comes to mind—"

Another murmur ran through the crowd at the last sentence, and Saret slowly rose from behind the podium. "Are you accusing *me* of something?" he asked in a tone of utter disbelief.

"Yes, Saret," Loris said, and Mia could hear the barely suppressed rage in his voice again. "I am accusing you and your friend Korum of tampering with the memories of my son and the others. I am accusing you of violating their minds with the goal of advancing your own political agenda. I am accusing Korum of staging the whole sequence of events, right down to the attack on the colonies, with the sole purpose of destroying me and upsetting the balance of power on this Council to satisfy his own insatiable ambition. And I am accusing you of helping him cover his tracks by mind-raping my son and the other young people standing in front of you here today!"

The crowd broke out into a cacophony of arguments and shocked exclamations, and Mia turned around again to look at Korum. She had no idea how to react to Loris's words. Could there be any truth to them?

Korum was sitting there outwardly calm, his expression completely unreadable. Only the faint yellow striations around his pupils gave away any hint of the emotion inside. Getting up slowly, he approached the center of the arena where the Protector was standing.

"Very nicely done, Loris," Korum said, his tone light and mocking. "That was quite creative. I have to say, I wouldn't have expected you to go in this direction at all—though I can see why you would. Kill two birds with one stone and all that . . . Of course, there are still all the recordings, not to mention all the witnesses, that clearly show your son and his cohorts acting quite rationally, with no trace of mental confusion whatsoever—"

"Those recordings are worthless," interrupted Loris, his face taut with barely controlled anger. "As we all know, someone of your technological prowess can fake anything along those lines—"

"I will gladly submit the recordings for examination by the experts," Korum said, shrugging nonchalantly. "You can even choose some of these experts—as long as they stake their reputation on the veracity of the results. And of course, other Councilors have already interrogated the witnesses. Councilors, was there anything in anyone's story to contradict the recordings?"

Arus rose in response. Swallowing nervously, Mia watched as yet another one of Korum's opponents walked toward the center of the arena. What if he sided with Loris? Would Korum be in trouble then? She couldn't bear the thought of anything happening to him as a result of these accusations.

"I will speak on behalf of the Council," Arus said in a deep, calm voice. Once again, there was something about the open, straightforward look on his face that made Mia want to trust him, to like him. A very useful trait for a politician to have, she realized—especially for an ambassador.

"As much as I'd like to support Loris's quest to protect his son," he said, "there is no doubt that all the witnesses interviewed thus far—from human Resistance members to the guardians involved in the operation—told a very similar story. And unfortunately, Loris, the story substantiates the recordings." There seemed to be genuine regret in Arus's voice as he was saying this.

"Witnesses can be bribed—"

Arus shook his head. "Not so many. We have gathered over fifty testimonies from completely different individuals, both human and Krinar. I'm sorry, Loris, but there are simply too many of them."

"Then how do you explain the memory loss?" Loris asked bitterly, staring at Arus with resentment.

"I can't explain that," Arus admitted. "The Council will have to investigate the matter—"

"I can perhaps venture a guess," Korum said, and Mia could practically feel the buzz of anticipation in the crowd. "There is a human trial defense strategy that's frequently utilized in developed countries. It involves trying to prove that the accused is insane, mentally incapable of standing trial. Because, you see, if they are judged to be mentally ill, then they can't be held responsible for their actions—and instead of getting punished, they are sent for treatment.

"Now the Protector is fully aware that the evidence points to the guilt of the accused. Of course, he can't claim that his son is insane and therefore didn't know what he was doing. No, he can't claim that at all—but he *can* say that his son's mind has been tampered with, that he's had his memories forcibly erased. Of course, the fact of the matter is there is only one person who would benefit from Rafor and the other traitors losing their memories—and that's neither me nor Saret."

"Are you accusing me of violating my own son's mind?" Loris asked incredulously, and Mia could see his hands clenching into fists.

"Unlike you, I don't accuse without evidence," Korum said, giving him a cold smile. "I am merely venturing a guess."

The noise from the crowd grew in volume. Curious to see how Saret was reacting to all of this, Mia turned her attention to his podium. He was watching the proceedings with a slightly bemused look on his face, as if he couldn't quite believe he'd gotten dragged into this. Mia felt bad for him. Not that she knew much about Krinar politics, but Korum's friend seemed like someone who didn't enjoy getting caught in the crossfire.

Her lover, on the other hand, was clearly in his element. Korum was enjoying his enemy's helpless rage.

"All the guesses and accusations are useless at this point," said Arus, and the crowd fell silent again. "The Council will have to examine the results from the laboratories before we can proceed in that direction. In the meantime, we'll show the testimonies from all available witnesses to shed further light on this case." And with a small gesture, he called up a three-dimensional image, just as Korum had done yesterday.

More recordings, Mia realized, sighing at the thought that today's proceedings were likely to last even longer. If they were showing testimonies from fifty witnesses, then the trial could last well into the night.

Settling even more comfortably on Korum's podium, Mia prepared for a lengthy and potentially boring viewing session.

* * *

The Krinar watched the recordings with satisfaction.

It had all worked out so perfectly, just as he'd hoped. No one would know the truth, not until it was too late for them to do anything.

He was glad he'd had the foresight to erase the Keiths' memories. Now they would never be able to explain, to point to him as the leader behind their little rebellion.

He was safe, and he should be able to implement his plan in peace.

Particularly if he could manage to keep his mind off a

certain human girl.

CHAPTER ELEVEN

After about five hours of watching the recordings, Mia had finally had enough. Exiting the virtual trial, she got up from the couch and went into the kitchen to get something to eat. It was truly exhausting, paying attention for so long, and she had no idea how Korum and the other Ks sat there so attentively this whole time.

As before, the house gladly provided her with a delicious meal. Feeling daring, Mia asked for the most popular traditional Krinar dish—provided that it was suitable for human consumption. When the dish arrived a few minutes later, she nearly moaned with hunger, her mouth salivating at the appetizing scent. It appeared to be a stew again, with a rich, salty flavor that was vaguely reminiscent of lamb or veal. Of course, she hadn't had those delicacies in over five years, so that could be simply her imagination. Like all K food she'd tried so far, this stew was also entirely plant-based.

It was still light out when Mia got done with her meal,

so she decided to venture outside for a bit. Putting on a pair of boots and a simple ivory dress, she told the house to let her out and smiled with satisfaction when the wall dissolved for her, just as it usually did for Korum. Grabbing the tablet-like device Korum had given her yesterday and a towel from the bathroom, Mia headed to the waterfalls, looking forward to spending a couple of hours reading and learning more about the early history of the Krinar.

Arriving at her destination, Mia located a nice patch of grass that didn't seem to be near any ant hills. Spreading out her towel there, she lay down on her stomach and immersed herself in the drama of the end of the first Krinar Golden Age.

"Hello? Mia?" The sound of an unfamiliar voice calling her name jolted Mia out of her absorption with the story.

Startled, Mia looked up and saw a young human woman standing a few feet away. Dressed in Krinar clothing, she had a vaguely Middle Eastern look to her, with large brown eyes, wavy black hair, and a smooth olive-toned complexion.

"Yes, hi," Mia said, getting up and staring at the newcomer. At first glance, the woman—more of a girl, really—seemed to be in her late teens or early twenties, but there was something regal in the way she held herself that made Mia think she might be older. Although she lacked Maria's vivid looks, there was a quiet, almost luminous beauty in her heart-shaped face and tall, slender figure. Another charl, Mia realized.

"I'm Delia," the girl said, giving her a gentle smile. She spoke in Krinar. "Maria told me she'd met you yesterday, and I wanted to stop by and welcome you to Lenkarda."

"It's nice to meet you, Delia," Mia said, giving her an answering smile. "How did you know where to find me?"

"I stopped by Korum's place, but no one seemed to be home," Delia explained. "So I was actually taking the scenic route home and saw you reading here. I hope you don't mind—I didn't mean to interrupt . . ."

"Oh, no, not at all!" Mia reassured her. "I'm very glad you came by! Please have a seat." Gesturing toward the other end of the towel, Mia sat down on one end of it. Delia smiled and joined her, gracefully lowering herself onto the fabric.

"Have you been living in Lenkarda long?" Mia inquired, studying the other girl with curiosity.

"I've been here since the Center was built," Delia said. "You could say I'm one of the original residents, in fact."

Mia's eyes widened. This girl had been a charl for almost five years? She had to have met her Krinar right after K-Day. "That's amazing," she told Delia earnestly. "How do you like living here?"

Delia shrugged. "It's a little different from what I'm used to. I prefer our old home, to be honest, but Arus needed to be here—"

"Arus?" Could this be the same Arus she'd just seen virtually?

"Yes," Delia confirmed. "Have you already heard the name?"

"I have," Mia told her carefully, not sure how much she should say to someone who was apparently with Korum's opponent. "He's on the Council, right?"

Delia nodded. "Yes, and he's also in charge of relations with the human governments."

"Oh, yeah, that's right," Mia said, trying to figure out how much the girl knew about the apparent tension between their lovers.

As though reading her mind, Delia gave her a reassuring look. "You don't have to worry, Mia," she told her. "Even though our *cheren* have had their share of political differences, I'm not here as Arus's representative or anything like that. I just thought you might be feeling a little overwhelmed with everything and could use someone to talk to—"

Mia gave her a sheepish smile. "I'm sorry, I didn't mean to imply—"

Delia smiled back. "You didn't. Don't worry about it. I just wanted to clear up any misunderstanding and set your mind at ease."

"So how long have you and Arus been together?" Mia asked, eager to change the subject. "And is that what you would call Arus, your cheren?"

"Yes," Delia said. "Cheren is what a charl would call his or her lover."

"I see." Now she had a Krinar term for what Korum was to her. "So when did you meet Arus? Was it when they first arrived?"

"I met him a long time ago." Delia gave her a calm smile. "What about you? Have you been with Korum long?"

Mia shook her head. "Not at all. I only met him about a month ago in New York, in Central Park."

"When you were part of the Resistance?" Delia asked, staring at her with those large, liquid brown eyes.

Mia flushed slightly. Everyone in Lenkarda seemed to know her involvement with the attempted attack on the colonies. "No," she said. "I only met the Resistance fighters later."

"So you became Korum's charl first and *then* joined the Resistance?" Delia seemed perplexed by that sequence of events.

Mia sighed. "They approached me soon after I met him, and I agreed to help. I thought I was doing the right thing at the time."

"I see," Delia said, studying her carefully. "I guess Korum is not the easiest cheren, is he?"

The color in Mia's cheeks intensified. "I'm not sure what you mean," she said, staring at Delia with a slight frown on her face.

"I'm sorry." Delia looked apologetic. "I didn't mean to pry into your relationship. It's just that you seem so young and vulnerable . . ."

"I can't be that much younger than you," Mia said, somewhat offended by the girl's assumption.

Delia laughed, shaking her head ruefully. "I'm sorry, Mia. I put my foot in it again, didn't I? Look, I didn't mean to insult you in any way . . . All I wanted to say is that I know how difficult it can be in the beginning, being involved with one of them. Your cheren also has a certain reputation for ruthlessness, and I guess I just wanted to make sure that you're okay—"

"I'm fine," Mia said, frowning at Delia again. She didn't need to hear about Korum's reputation from this girl; she knew better than anyone just how ruthless her lover could be.

"Of course," Delia said gently. "I can see that you are."

"How did you meet Arus anyway?" Mia asked, wanting to shift the conversation in a different direction.

Delia smiled. "It's a long story. If you'd like, I can tell you sometime." Getting to her feet, she said, "Arus just told me that the trial is over and he's on his way home. I should be getting back. It was really nice to meet you, Mia. I hope we get to see each other again soon."

Mia nodded and got up also. "Thanks, it was really nice to meet you, too. I should probably head back as well."

"That's not a bad idea," Delia said, still smiling. "I'm sure Korum will be wondering where you are."

Mia waved her hand dismissively. "Oh, he knows, with the shining and all."

"Of course," Delia said, and for a second, there was something resembling pity on her beautifully serene face. Before Mia could analyze it further, the girl added, "Listen, Maria is organizing a little get-together on the beach in about three weeks—a picnic of sorts, if you will. It's her birthday, and she mentioned that she wanted me to invite you if I saw you today. Most of the charl from Lenkarda will be there, and it might be a good way for you to meet some more of us and make some friends . . ."

A charl beach party? Mia grinned, excited at the idea. "Oh, I'll definitely be there," she promised.

"That's great," Delia said, the smile returning to her face. "We'll see you there then." And raising her hand, she lightly brushed her knuckles down Mia's cheek in a gesture that almost seemed like a caress. Surprised, Mia lifted her hand to her cheek, but Delia was already walking away, her graceful figure disappearing into the trees.

* * *

Entering the house, Mia heard rhythmic thumping sounds coming from the kitchen. Curious, she went to investigate and saw that Korum was already there, chopping up some vegetables for dinner. Mia's stomach grumbled, and she realized that she was quite hungry.

Seeing her walking in, Korum looked up from his task and gave her a slow smile that made her feel warm inside. "Well, hello there. I was just beginning to wonder if I'll have to go searching through the woods for you. You didn't get lost, did you?"

"No," Mia told him, grinning. "I just met another charl, actually. A girl named Delia . . . and she invited me to a beach party!"

"Delia? Arus's charl?"

Mia nodded enthusiastically. "Do you know her?"

"Not well," Korum said. "I've met her a few times throughout the years." He didn't seem particularly happy at this turn of events, his expression cooling significantly.

"You don't like her?" Mia asked, some of her earlier excitement fading. "Or is it just because she's with Arus?"

Korum shrugged. "I don't have anything against her," he said. "What did you talk to her about? And what beach party is this?"

"It's Maria's birthday, and she's organizing a get-together for the charl living here in Lenkarda," Mia told him. "And we really didn't have a chance to talk much. Delia said she's been with Arus for a long time—I think she must've met him shortly after you guys arrived. Mostly she was just being friendly, though. Oh, and she told me a new term I've never heard before: cheren."

Korum smiled, and Mia thought he almost looked relieved. "Yes, that's what you would call me."

"What does it mean, exactly? Is there a comparable human word for it?"

"No, there isn't," Korum said. "Just as there isn't one for charl. It's unique to the Krinar language."

"I see," Mia said, walking over to the table and sitting down. "Well, the beach party will be in three weeks. It's all right if I go, right?"

"Of course," he said, looking up to give her a warm smile. "You should definitely go if you want, make some friends. I think Maria is very nice, and she seemed to like you quite a bit yesterday."

"I liked her, too," Mia admitted, smiling at the thought of seeing Arman's charl again. "She's exactly how Latino women are often portrayed in the American media—really pretty and outgoing. By the way, I forgot to ask Delia today . . . Do you know where she's from? Delia, I mean . . ."

"Greece, I think," Korum replied, placing cut vegetables into a big bowl and sprinkling them with some brownish powder. Swiftly mixing everything, he brought the salad to the table and ladled it onto each of their plates.

Mia quickly consumed her portion and leaned back against the chair, feeling replete. Like everything Korum made, the meal had been delicious, with the familiar flavors of tomatoes and cucumbers mixing well with the more exotic plants from Krina. It was also surprisingly filling, considering that it was only vegetables. "Thank you," Mia told him. "That was great."

"Of course. I'm glad you enjoyed it."

"So I read some more of your history today," Mia told him, watching as he fluidly rose from the table and carried the dishes to the wall, where they promptly disappeared.

"And what did you think?" He came back to the table carrying a plate of strawberries.

"I was pretty shocked," Mia told him honestly. "I can't believe your society survived the plague that almost wiped out those primates. I'm not sure if humans could've gone on if eighty percent of our food died out in a span of a few months."

"We almost didn't survive it," Korum said, biting into a strawberry, and licking the red juice off his lower lip. Mia suppressed a sudden urge to lick the juice off him herself. "More than half of our population was killed in fights and battles during that time, and many others died from the lack of the necessary hemoglobin. If the synthetic blood substitute hadn't come through in time, we would've all perished. As it was, it took millions of years for us to recover, to get back to where we were before the plague almost wiped out the lonar."

Mia nodded. She'd read about that. The aftermath of the plague had been horrible. At the core, the Krinar were a violent species, and that violence had been unleashed when their survival was threatened. Regions fought other regions, centers attacked other centers within their region, and everyone tried to hoard the few remaining lonar for themselves and their families. Even after the synthetic substitute became available, bloody conflicts had continued, as tremendous losses suffered during the post-plague days had left deep scars on K psyche. Almost every family had lost someone—a child, a parent, a cousin, or a friend—and the quest for vengeance became a feature of everyday life.

"How were you able to move past that? All the wars and the vendettas? To get to where you are today?" The brief glimpse she'd had of Krinar life in Lenkarda seemed greatly at odds with the history she'd just learned.

"It wasn't easy," Korum said. "It took a long time for the memories of that time to fade. Eventually, we implemented laws curbing violent behavior and outlawed vendettas. Now, Arena challenges are the only socially and legally acceptable way to seek revenge and settle disputes that cannot otherwise be resolved."

Mia studied him curiously. "Have you ever fought in the Arena?"

"A few times." He didn't seem inclined to elaborate further. Instead, he rose from the table and asked, "How do you feel about a post-dinner walk on the beach?"

Mia blinked, surprised. "Um, sure. You don't think it'll get too dark soon?"

"I can see pretty well in the dark, plus there is some moonlight. You have nothing to be afraid of."

"Okay, then sure." If she didn't get eaten by mosquitoes, then this could be really nice.

Taking her hand, Korum led her outside. The sun had just set, and there was still an orange glow behind the trees, which appeared like dark silhouettes against the bright sky. The temperature was getting a little cooler, the day's heat starting to dissipate, and Mia could hear the chirping of some insects and the rustling of leaves in the warm, tropical-scented breeze. A few feet away, a large iguana scooted off a rock and into the shrubs, apparently seeking to avoid them.

"How did the rest of the trial go?" Mia asked. "I stopped watching all the witness testimonies after about five hours."

"It was fairly uneventful," Korum said, smiling down at her. "You didn't miss much."

"Do you think anyone believed Loris when he made those accusations against you?"

"I'm sure some did." He didn't sound overly concerned about that. "But he has no evidence to substantiate his claims."

"Arus seemed to be on your side," Mia said, carefully stepping around a fallen log. It was getting darker by the minute, and they were still a good distance away from the beach.

"He has no other choice," Korum explained. "He has to side with the evidence."

"Why don't you like him?" Mia asked, looking up to him. "He doesn't seem like a bad person . . ."

"He's not," Korum admitted. "Just misguided in some ways. He doesn't always see the big picture."

"And you do?"

Korum's smile widened. "For the most part."

For the next couple of minutes, they walked in companionable silence, with Mia concentrating on where she was stepping and Korum seemingly absorbed in thought. There was something very peaceful about this moment, from the soft glow of the twilight to the quiet roar of the ocean in the distance.

For the first time, Mia fully realized just how tumultuous her relationship with Korum had been thus far. In many ways, it was like a roller coaster ride, with plenty of passion, drama, and excitement, but very few moments like this, where she got to spend time with him without her pulse racing a mile a minute from either sexual arousal or some strong emotion. When she'd imagined herself having a boyfriend, this was always how she'd pictured it—long, pleasant walks together, quiet time spent simply enjoying the other person's presence. And in this moment, she could pretend that's exactly what Korum was to her—a boyfriend, a regular human lover whom she could take to meet her parents without worry, someone with whom she could have a future . . .

Suddenly, her foot hit a rock, and Mia stumbled. Before she could do more than gasp, Korum caught her and lifted her up into his arms.

"Are you all right?" he asked, looking down at her with concern.

In response, Mia wrapped her arms around his neck and lay her head on his shoulder, feeling unusually needy. "I'm fine. Just being a klutz."

"You're not a klutz," Korum denied. "You just don't see well when it gets dark."

"True," Mia said, inhaling the warm scent of his skin near the throat area. She felt strangely content like this, being held so gently in his powerful arms. It occurred to her that she no longer feared him, at least on a physical level. It was hard to believe that just a few days ago, she thought he might kill her for helping the Resistance.

He walked for a few more minutes, carrying Mia, until they reached the beach. Setting her down carefully, he kept his hands on her waist. "Do you feel up for a swim?" he asked, and Mia could make out the sensuous curve of his lips in the faint light of the almost-full moon.

"I'm not wearing a bathing suit," Mia said, looking up at him. The night air was also getting a little cooler—perfect for a walk, but likely less pleasant on wet skin.

"There's no one around," he told her. "Except me. And I've seen you naked."

For some reason, that simple statement jolted Mia out of her calm contentment. Her lower belly tightened with arousal, and her nipples hardened. She felt much warmer all of a sudden, as though the hot sun was still beaming down on them. Staring up at him, she asked, "What if someone comes by?"

"They won't," Korum promised. "I reserved this portion of the beach just for us tonight."

He had reserved the beach just for them? She hadn't realized someone could do that. But it made sense, of course, that if anyone could, it would be Korum; as a Council member, he likely enjoyed special privileges in Lenkarda.

Apparently getting impatient with her lack of response, Korum decided to take matters into his own hands. Taking a couple of steps back, he stripped off his own clothes and removed his sandals, dropping everything carelessly on the sand. Mia's breathing quickened. His tall, powerfully muscled body was now completely naked, and the moonlight revealed the hard erection between his legs.

"Take off your clothes," he ordered softly. "I want you naked right now."

Staring at him, Mia licked her suddenly dry lips. She could feel the soft material of her dress rubbing against her hard nipples and the moisture starting to gather between her thighs. Her whole body felt sensitized, her heart beating harder and blood rushing faster through her veins. Memories of last night's disturbing—yet incredibly erotic—experience were suddenly at the front of her mind, and she swallowed nervously, wondering if he intended to teach her another lesson or fulfill some other fantasy she didn't know she had.

He didn't say anything else, just stood there waiting, watching her expectantly. Mia wondered just how good his night vision was. She couldn't see the expression on his face in the dim light and had no idea what he was thinking right now.

Her hands trembling a little, she slowly pulled off her boots. The sand felt cool under her bare feet, no longer retaining the warmth of the sun.

"Now the dress," Korum prompted, and there was a roughness in his voice that made her think his patience was near the end.

Mia obeyed, pulling the dress over her head and dropping it on the sand. She was now completely naked, and she could feel herself shivering slightly in the evening ocean breeze.

He stepped toward her then and reached out to cup her shoulders, pulling her closer to him. "You're so beautiful," he whispered, leaning down to kiss her. His hands left her shoulders and curved around her butt cheeks instead, lifting her up against him until the hardness of his cock pressed into her belly.

His mouth slanted over hers, and she could feel the smooth warmth of his lips and the insistent push of his tongue penetrating her mouth. Everything inside her softened, melted, and she moaned quietly, wrapping her arms around his neck. His hands tightened on her butt, squeezing the small round globes, and then he was lowering her to the ground, putting her down on top of their clothes. His right hand found its way down her body, forced apart her legs, his fingers exploring her tender folds with a maddeningly gentle touch. Mia squirmed, her hips lifting toward him, wanting more, and he obliged, one long finger penetrating her opening and finding the sensitive spot inside. The familiar tension began to gather in her belly, and she twisted her hips, needing just a tiny bit more . . . and then she was hurtling over the brink with a small cry, her inner muscles pulsing in orgasmic relief.

Lying there bonelessly in the aftermath, she felt his hands pulling her legs wider apart. His arousal brushed against her thighs, the tip of his cock impossibly smooth and hot. He was pressed against her opening, and Mia's breath caught in anticipation of his entry, her body instantly craving more of the pleasure she had just experienced.

"Tell me you want me," he whispered, and there was something strange in his voice, some dark note she'd never heard before.

"You know I do," she told him softly, feeling like she would die if she didn't have him right now. Her skin felt too tight, too sensitive, as though it couldn't contain the need that was burning her from the inside.

"How much?" he demanded roughly. "How much do you want me?"

"A lot," Mia admitted, staring up at him, her pelvic muscles clenching with desire and her clitoris throbbing. What did he want from her? Couldn't he tell how much her body yearned for his?

He lowered his head then, kissing her again, even as his cock pressed forward and entered her in one powerful thrust. Mia cried out against his lips, suddenly filled to the brim. Before she could fully adjust to the sensation, he began to move, his hips thrusting and recoiling, the hard rhythm reverberating through her insides in a way that made her forget all about his strange behavior. She heard her own cries, though she wasn't conscious of making them, his roughness somehow adding to the coiling tension inside her—

And then he stopped, just as she was seconds away from finding release. Frustrated, Mia moaned, writhing underneath him, unable to control the convulsive movements of her body. "Korum, please . . ."

"Please what?" he murmured, withdrawing from her. His hand found its way between their bodies, and he pressed his fingers lightly against her clitoris, keeping her balanced on the exquisite edge of pleasure-pain. "Please what?"

"Please fuck me," she whispered, nearly incoherent with need. He pressed harder against her folds, and Mia cried out, the knot of tension inside her growing even tighter.

"Tell me you love me," he ordered, and Mia froze, the unfamiliar words reaching through her daze, startling her for a second out of her sensual fog.

"Tell me, Mia," he said sharply, and his finger slipped

inside her, finding the spot that always drove her insane and pressing on it rhythmically until she was almost crying with frustration, her body writhing and twisting in his arms.

Nearly incoherent, she screamed, "I do! Please, Korum . . . I do!"

"You do what?" He was relentless, completely unyielding in his demand.

"I love you," she sobbed, knowing that she would regret it later but unable to help herself. "Korum, please . . . I love you!"

His fingers left her then, and she could feel his cock again, pushing into her, and she shuddered with relief as he resumed his thrusting, reaching deeply inside her, filling the pulsing emptiness within. At the same time, his hand buried itself in her hair, arching her throat toward him, and Mia felt the heat of his mouth on her neck and the familiar slicing pain signifying his bite. Almost instantly, her world dissolved into a blur of sensations, the long-awaited climax rushing through her with so much force that she blanked out for a few seconds, barely cognizant of his harsh cry as he found his own release a minute later.

The rest of the night passed in a haze, with him taking her again and again in blood-induced frenzy until she could come no longer, her throat hoarse from screaming and her body wrung dry from unending orgasms. It didn't seem real, any of it, with her senses unbearably heightened from the chemical in his saliva and her mind empty of all thought, her entire being caught up in the extreme ecstasy of his touch.

Finally, at some point before dawn, Mia passed out in his arms, with the ocean waves pounding against the shore a few feet away and the moon shining down on their entwined bodies.

CHAPTER TWELVE

Opening her eyes the next morning, Mia stared at the ceiling as the memories of last night flooded her brain.

She'd told him she loved him, she remembered with a twisting sensation in her stomach. Like an idiot, she'd let him rip away her one remaining shred of protection, baring her heart and soul. Now he could toy with her feelings, just as he played with her body. And why? Why had he done this to her? Wasn't it enough for him that he fully controlled her life? Did he have to possess her on an emotional level as well, stripping away her last bit of privacy?

She could deny it today. She could say that he had tortured the words out of her—and that much would be true. But he would know that she was lying if she tried to go back on her reluctant confession.

Groaning, Mia buried her face in the pillow, wishing she could sleep longer. The last thing she wanted was to face him today.

After about a minute, she talked herself into getting up and going into the shower. To her surprise, there was no trace of sand anywhere on her body. Korum must've brought her home and washed her last night—or at some point this morning. She didn't remember that part at all. She was also surprised that she didn't have any soreness after last night's sexual marathon; in New York, Korum would often have to use his healing device on her after a night like this. He had probably done it when she was sleeping, Mia decided.

Stepping under the hot spray of the shower, she closed her eyes and tried to think about something else besides seeing Korum today.

It turned out to be an impossible task. Her mind kept dwelling on what she would say to him when she saw him next, how he might act, whether he would be his usual mocking self... She desperately wished she could get away for a couple of days, just go home to her own apartment—but that was obviously not a possibility.

Exiting the shower, Mia toweled off and put on the robe. Steeling herself for a potential encounter, she ventured into the living room. To her relief, Korum wasn't there. He must be at the trial, Mia realized. Checking the time, she was shocked to see that it was already three in the afternoon.

Padding into the kitchen, she requested a plate of fruit for breakfast and brought it with her into the living room. It was probably too late to go into the virtual world of the trial; if it started at the same time as yesterday, the presentations would be wrapping up in another couple of hours. So instead, Mia curled up on the couch and tried to distract herself by reading the latest Dan Brown thriller.

Looking up from the book, Mia checked the time. It was almost five o'clock. Her stomach rumbled, reminding her that she had barely eaten today. She was also still wearing her bathrobe and house slippers.

Getting up, Mia went into the bedroom and put on a pretty white-and-pink dress and a pair of flat, strappy sandals. She had no idea when Korum would be done with the trial, but yesterday he was home by early evening and already making dinner when she got back from her conversation with Delia. For some reason, she didn't want to look like a slob when he got home tonight, although she had no idea why she cared about that. For a brief second, she thought about leaving to take a walk in the hopes of avoiding him for a while longer, but then she decided not to be a coward. It's not like she could go far, or even someplace where he wouldn't immediately find her. The tracking devices embedded in her palms broadcast her whereabouts to him at all times. It was best to just face him and get it over with.

He came home an hour later.

Hearing Korum enter, Mia looked up from her book, and her heart skipped a beat at the sight. Dressed in the more formal trial clothes, he looked simply gorgeous, his bronze skin contrasting beautifully with the white color of his shirt and his powerful physique emphasized by the tight fit of his outfit. The look in his amber eyes was surprisingly warm, as if he hadn't spent last night torturing her with the goal of exposing her silly feelings.

As Mia watched warily, he approached and picked her up from the couch, lifting her up for a brief kiss.

"I have a surprise for you," he said, carefully placing her back on her feet and keeping his hands still on her waist.

"A surprise?" Mia asked, startled.

Korum nodded, smiling down at her. "We're going out for dinner with Saret and one of his assistants."

"Okay . . ." Mia said, frowning at him slightly. "That sounds good, but what's the surprise?"

His smile widened. "The reason why we're meeting with them is because they want to find out more about your psychology knowledge and experience, to better figure out how and where you could be of most use in Saret's lab."

"What do you mean?" Mia could hardly believe her ears. "What does Saret's lab have to do with anything?"

"Well, since school and career are so important to you," said Korum, "I wanted to make sure I'm not depriving you of anything by bringing you here. You seemed interested in Saret's specialty earlier, and, from what I understand, your field of study is similar to his. One of his assistants recently left, creating an opening at his lab. Of course, there are already about ten applicants for the position, but I convinced him to take you on for a couple of months, just to try things out. Obviously, this will be a great learning opportunity for you, but you might also provide him with some unique insights, given your background—"

"And he agreed to take me on? A human?" Mia asked incredulously, her heart jumping in her chest.

"He did," Korum answered. "He owes me a couple of favors, plus he said he likes you."

"You're telling me that I can work in a K laboratory alongside your top mind expert?" Mia said slowly, needing to hear him confirm it just in case. She was nearly hyperventilating with excitement. This was an unbelievable, impossible opportunity. How many humans had a chance like this, to study Krinar minds from their own perspective? Scientists would sell their soul to the devil to be in her shoes right now. Mia wanted to jump up and down and laugh out loud, and she knew there was a huge grin on her face.

"If you're interested," he said casually, but there was a gleam in his eyes that told her he knew exactly how much this meant to her.

"*If* I'm interested? Oh, Korum, I don't even know how to thank you," Mia told him earnestly. "Obviously, this is a phenomenal opportunity for me! Thank you so, so much!"

He smiled, looking pleased with himself. "Of course. I'm happy you like the idea. As to how you can thank me . . ." His eyes took on a familiar golden tint, and he sat down on the couch, pulling her down next to him. "A kiss would be nice," he told her softly.

Mia's grin faded and she tensed, remembering last night. For a moment, she'd forgotten what he'd done, what he'd forced her to say, too distracted by the amazing opportunity he was presenting her with. But now it was at the forefront of her mind again. Was he going to act like it hadn't happened? If so, she would be more than happy to play along.

Staring him in the face, Mia buried her fingers in his hair and brought his head toward her. His hair felt thick and soft in her hands, and his lips were smooth and warm underneath hers. He tasted delicious, like some exotic fruit and himself, and she kissed him with all the passion and excitement she was feeling. When she finally stopped, his breathing was a little faster, and Mia could feel her own nipples pinching into tight buds underneath her dress.

"Mmm, that was quite a thank-you," he murmured, looking at her with a soft smile. "Maybe I should find internships for you every day."

"I might expire from excitement if you do," Mia told him honestly. "Seriously, this is more than I could've ever expected or imagined. Thank you again."

"You're welcome," he said, obviously enjoying her reaction. "Now, are you ready to go? The dinner is in fifteen minutes, and we shouldn't be late."

Mia got up and twirled in front of him. "Can I wear this, or should I change?"

"This is perfect. Just add some jewelry, and you're good to go."

* * *

They left the house a few minutes later, after Mia put on her million-year-old shimmer-stone necklace. Korum had already created the small aircraft that would take them to dinner, and Mia climbed in through the dissolving wall, sitting down on one of the floating planks and making herself comfortable. She was already starting to get used to this mode of transportation.

"Are we meeting them at a restaurant?" she asked, curious if such a thing existed in Lenkarda. Thus far, the only meal she'd had outside of Korum's home was at Arman's.

Korum nodded. "Something like that. It's called the Food Hall, and we get a private booth there. The idea is similar to a human restaurant, but there are no waiters of any kind. The food tends to be much fancier than what you'd get at home, with more exotic ingredients than something my house or I would typically go for."

"So do Ks meet at this Food Hall, just as we would go to a restaurant to socialize?"

"Exactly," Korum confirmed. "It's a popular place for business meetings and other such occasions. Dates, also, but most prefer a bit more privacy for that."

"Why?" Mia asked as the little aircraft took off soundlessly.

"Sex in public is considered rude," Korum explained, looking at her with a wicked smile. "And dates frequently result in sex."

Mia felt her face getting warm. "I see. More frequently than in human society?"

"Probably—though I haven't seen any hard data to substantiate that assumption. Our society tends to be much more liberal about such matters. With the exception of mated couples, everyone's on birth control, so we don't have to worry about unwanted pregnancies. Also, there is no such thing as a sexually transmitted disease among the Krinar. There's really no reason for us not to enjoy ourselves."

Mia suddenly felt extremely and irrationally jealous, imagining Korum "enjoying himself" with some unknown Krinar female. He'd told her she was the only woman in his life and had been ever since they met, and she believed him—there had been no reason for him to lie. Still, she couldn't get the images of Korum entwined with some beautiful K woman out of her mind.

Before she could ask him any more questions, the aircraft landed softly in front of a large white building. Shaped similarly to Korum's house, it was also an elongated cube with rounded corners, only much bigger in size.

Korum exited first and then held his hand out to her. Mia accepted it, gripping his palm tightly. This was her first public outing in Lenkarda, and she felt both excited and nervous about encountering other Krinar. Mostly, though, she hoped she wouldn't seem like an idiot to Saret and his assistant. She wished she'd had a chance to review notes from some of her classes, just in case they decided to quiz her on what she'd learned thus far in her psychology studies.

Holding her hand, Korum led her toward the building. As they approached, the wall dissolved to let them in, and they entered a large hallway with opaque walls and a transparent ceiling. Nobody came out to greet them, but there were a number of Ks milling about, both males and females, dressed in a mix of formal and casual clothing.

At their entrance, several dozen heads turned their way, and Mia gripped Korum's hand tighter, startled to be the center of attention. Korum, however, didn't acknowledge the stares in any way, walking at a leisurely pace down the hallway. Mia did her best to imitate his composure, looking straight ahead and concentrating on not gawking at the gorgeous creatures who were openly—and rudely, in her opinion—studying her and her lover.

Just before it seemed like they would reach the end of the hallway, the walls to their right parted, and Korum led her into the opening. It turned out to be a small, private room where Saret and another male Krinar were already waiting for them.

As they entered, Saret rose from his floating seat and stepped toward Korum, greeting him with the palm on his shoulder. Her lover reciprocated the gesture with a small smile.

"I'm glad you could come out tonight," Saret said, looking at them both. "Mia, is this your first time visiting the Food Hall?"

Mia nodded, feeling a little nervous. If all went according to plan, this K would soon be her boss. "Yes, I haven't been out too much yet."

"Of course," Saret said. "Your cheren has been occupied with the trial, like many of us. Now, Korum, have you met Adam?"

"I haven't had the pleasure," Korum said, turning to the other Krinar. "But I've heard quite a bit about this young man."

Adam got up and, to Mia's surprise, held his hand out in a very human gesture. "I've heard quite a bit about you as well," he said. His voice was deep and smooth, and the way he pronounced certain words in Krinar made him seem almost like a foreigner.

Smiling slightly, Korum reached out and shook Adam's hand. "I see you haven't quite gotten the hang of our greetings."

The other K shrugged. "I'm familiar with the customs by now, but they still don't come naturally to me. Since you've lived in New York for quite some time, I figured you wouldn't mind." Then, turning to Mia, he smiled at her warmly and said, "I'm Adam Moore. And you must be Mia Stalis, the girl I've heard so much about."

Mia blinked, not sure if she'd just imagined hearing a K introduce himself with what seemed like a human first and last name. "Yes, hi," she said, giving him a smile in return. Korum had called him a young man, and she wondered how old he really was. Physically, he seemed to be about the same age as Korum and Saret.

"Adam has a very unusual background," Saret said, apparently sensing her confusion. "Come, have a seat, and we can chat more over dinner."

"That sounds like a good idea," Korum said, pulling a pair of floating seats toward them. Mia perched on one of them, letting it adjust to her body shape, and Korum did the same. The seats floated closer toward the other two Krinar, who had also sat down by that time. Now the four of them were arranged in a circle around what looked to be a tiny floating table. Upon closer inspection, Mia could see that the table was actually more like a tablet of some kind, filled with Krinar writing and images of various appetizing platters. A menu, she realized.

"We've already requested our meal," Saret told them. "You can go ahead and choose."

"Do you want me to order for you?" Korum asked Mia, his lips curving into a dimpled smile.

"Sure," Mia told him, happy to delegate that task. Even though her embedded translator made it possible to read Krinar writing, she had no idea what most of the dishes were.

Korum waved his palm over the table. "Okay, I just ordered for both of us. The food should get here in a few minutes."

Mia thanked him and turned her attention back to the other Ks, giving them a smile.

Saret smiled back at her, his brown eyes twinkling. "How are you enjoying your first few days in Lenkarda?"

"It's a beautiful place," she told him honestly. "The beach is very nice. I grew up in Florida, so I really miss it in New York. I mean, we have the ocean and everything there, but it's just not the same."

"Too dirty and polluted, right?" Saret said.

"It's pretty dirty," Mia admitted. "And crowded. Even in the summer, the beaches right around the city are not the greatest. And, of course, the weather is not optimal for beach-going most times of the year—"

"Do you ever go out to Jersey Shore or the Hamptons?" asked Adam. "Those beaches are much nicer."

"No, I haven't had a chance," Mia answered. "I don't have a car, and I'm not usually in New York during the summer, anyway. During the school year, the weather is nice enough for a beach outing only in September, and

I'm typically too busy to take the bus somewhere for an entire weekend. Why, have you been there?"

"I actually grew up in Manhattan," Adam said. "So I've gone out to both Jersey Shore and the Hamptons quite a bit with my family."

Mia's eyes widened in shock. "Your family?"

Adam nodded. "I was adopted by a human family when I was a baby. They had no idea what I was, of course, and neither did I, at least until K-Day."

"Really?" Mia stared at him in fascination. To her, he looked very much like a K, with his dark brown hair, golden skin, and hazel eyes. He also had their way of moving, an almost cat-like grace common to many predators. Of course, prior to K-Day, nobody knew that the Krinar existed, so it was feasible that he could've been mistaken for a human. "So you only recently discovered that you're a K?"

"I knew that I was different, of course," Adam said with a shrug. "But I had no idea I was actually from another planet."

"But how did no one find out? I mean, you must've been much stronger and faster than the other kids... And what about blood tests and immunizations?"

"It wasn't easy," Adam admitted readily. "My parents are amazing people. They realized early on that I was not a regular kid from Romania and did everything in their power to protect me."

"But how did this even happen?" Mia was still trying to wrap her brain around such an improbable situation. "How did you end up on Earth as a baby—and before K-Day, no less?"

"It's a long story," Adam replied, suddenly looking colder and much more dangerous. Watching him now, Mia could easily imagine him filling Korum's shoes in another couple of hundred years. "And probably not a good fit for dinner conversation."

"Of course," Mia apologized swiftly. Clearly, she'd hit a sensitive spot. "I didn't mean to pry—"

"No worries," Adam said, smiling at her again. "I know the whole thing is very strange, and I don't blame you for being curious."

The food appeared in that moment, with dishes emerging from the wall to Mia's left and floating to land on the table—which immediately expanded into a fairly sizable surface. Mia's plate seemed to be a mixture of some strange purplish grain and a bunch of green and orange bits of unfamiliar-looking plants. Everything was arranged in elaborate flower-like shapes and swirls, resembling a work of art more than actual food.

Korum appeared to have ordered the same thing for himself. Taking a bite of the concoction, Mia almost moaned in pleasure, her tastebuds in heaven from the incredible fusion of sweet, salty, and tangy flavors. For a couple of minutes, there was only silence as all four of them concentrated on their meal.

Saret finished his food first and pushed away the plate, which immediately floated away. Coming back to the earlier topic of conversation, he told Mia, "As you can imagine, Adam is still trying to figure out our way of life. In some ways, you two actually have a lot in common, which is why I brought Adam with me today. Despite his youth, he's one of my most promising assistants—and that's partially because of the unique perspective he brings as a result of his background. I would not normally take on someone in their twenties—an adolescent in our society—but Adam is much more mature than a typical Krinar of that age."

Mia nodded, her palms beginning to sweat. Now they

were getting to the reason behind this dinner. She pushed away the rest of her food to better concentrate on Saret.

"Korum tells me that you have a strong interest in all matters of the mind—that, in fact, it's your chosen field of study. Is that right?" he asked, looking at her expectantly.

"I'm a psychology major at NYU," Mia confirmed. "From what I understand, psychology is much narrower in scope than your specialty . . . but I would love to learn about anything having to do with the mind."

"And how much do you know already? What did they teach you at NYU so far?"

Mia felt herself shifting into her "interview mode," her nervousness somehow translating into a greater clarity of thought and speech. Drawing on everything she remembered, she told Saret about her basic psychology classes, as well as the more advanced, specialized courses she'd begun to take recently. She spoke about the paper she'd just finished writing for Child Psychology and about the internship she had last year at a Daytona Beach hospital counseling victims of domestic abuse. She also explained her plan to get a Master's degree and work as a guidance counselor, so she could positively influence young people at an important time in their lives.

Saret and Adam both listened attentively, with Saret occasionally nodding as she mentioned some of the key concepts she'd learned in her classes. Korum observed everything quietly, seemingly content to just watch her as she spoke animatedly about her education.

Finally, Saret stopped her after about a half hour. "Thank you, Mia. This is exactly what I wanted to know. You do seem quite passionate about your chosen . . . major . . . and I think you could be a useful addition to my team. Would you be able to start tomorrow?"

Mia almost jumped from excitement, but controlled herself in the last moment and simply gave Saret a huge grin. "Absolutely! What time do you want me there?" Then, remembering that she should probably consult the K who ran her life, she quickly looked at Korum. He nodded, smiling, and Mia's grin got impossibly wider.

"Can you be there by nine in the morning?" Saret asked. "I know you need more sleep than us, but I believe that's a standard business start time among humans . . ."

"Of course," Mia said eagerly. "I can also come earlier, whatever the regular time is for you—"

Out of the corner of her eye, she saw Korum shaking his head at Saret.

"No, there's no need," Saret said. "There's absolutely no urgency, and you'll be of greater use to us if you're not sleep-deprived. Just come at nine, okay?"

Mia nodded, feeling like she was floating on air. "Sure, I can't wait!"

Adam smiled at her enthusiasm. "It's a very steep learning curve," he warned. "I've been working in this lab for the last two years, and I can tell you that I'm still learning fifty new things a day."

Mia grinned again, too hyper to feel properly intimidated. "That's fine—I love to learn." Turning to Saret, she told him earnestly, "Thank you for this opportunity. I will do my best to make myself useful."

"Of course," Saret said with a smile. "I look forward to seeing you tomorrow." And getting up, he repeated the earlier greeting, touching Korum's shoulder before walking out.

Adam followed his boss's example, rising to his feet and shaking Korum's hand again before departing. Mia noticed that he didn't offer his hand to her for some reason, even though he had to know that it was somewhat rude to ignore her like that. She guessed there was a taboo of some kind about touching women—or maybe just other Ks' charl—likely having to do with the Ks' territorial nature. Since even Adam was following this particular custom, there had to be a fairly compelling reason.

Finally, Korum and Mia were left alone.

Getting up, her lover smiled at her warmly. "You did great—I could tell that Saret was impressed. I'm very proud of you."

Mia gave him a big smile and got up also, his words filling her with a happy glow. "Thank you. And thanks again for making this possible."

"Of course," Korum said, pulling her closer to him and burying his hand in her hair. Holding her pressed against his body and her face tilted up toward him, he said softly, "Now tell me again that you love me."

Staring up at him, Mia froze, her euphoria fading and a terrible sense of vulnerability taking its place. He *wasn't* planning to ignore what happened last night.

She moistened her lips. "Korum, I . . ." She tried to lower her gaze, to look away, but it was impossible with the way he was holding her.

"Tell me, Mia." His eyes were turning a deeper shade of gold. "I want to hear you say it again."

She desperately wanted to deny him, to tell him that she'd been out of her mind last night, but the words simply wouldn't form on her tongue.

Because she did love him, so much that it hurt, so much that she could barely think past the powerful emotions filling her chest. At some point in the last few weeks, he'd gone from being an aloof and dangerous stranger to someone she couldn't imagine her life without. And as much as she hated her loss of freedom, she also loved the numerous little kindnesses he showed her on a daily basis, the way he made her feel so alive . . .

He was right: she had been merely content with her life before she met him. She'd had a comfortable, mostly happy existence. But she hadn't truly lived.

"Tell me, my darling," he urged softly, his hand slipping out of her hair to gently cup her cheek. "Tell me . . ."

"I do. I love you," she whispered, staring up at him, wondering what he would say now, whether he would somehow use her admission against her.

But he just smiled and leaned down to kiss her, his beautiful lips touching hers so tenderly that she felt her heart squeezing in her chest. "Does it make you happy, being able to have an internship here?" he murmured, lifting his head and regarding her with a warm glow in his golden eyes.

Mia nodded. "Of course," she said quietly. "You know it does."

"Good. I want you to be happy here," he said softly, stepping back and releasing her from his embrace. And then, taking her hand, he led her out of their private room and into the hallway.

* * *

They arrived at the house a couple of minutes later.

During the short ride, Mia kept her gaze trained on the transparent floor, though she could hardly see the scenery below with her mind occupied by the evening's events. In some strange way, it was almost liberating to open herself up to Korum like this, to tell him how she really felt. Now she didn't have to constantly be on her guard, worried that he would guess that she'd fallen in love with him. She didn't have to fear that he would mock her for being a silly young girl and confusing sex with emotions.

No, he hadn't mocked her at all. Contrary to her expectations, he seemed to welcome the emotional aspect; in fact, he'd practically forced her to admit she loved him. He hadn't reciprocated with his own words of love, but then she hadn't really expected him to. He'd said in the past that he cared for her, and she believed him. But love? Could someone like Korum truly fall in love with a human? Arman seemed to love Maria, but their relationship was so different from what Mia had with her cheren.

No, she didn't know if Korum could ever love her, and she didn't want to drive herself insane wondering—not right now, not when she felt so happy and was so eagerly looking forward to starting her internship tomorrow.

They exited the aircraft, and Korum swiftly disassembled it, activating the nanomachines with a small gesture. Mia watched him, her heart feeling like it would burst from her chest, unable to contain the feelings within. Every movement of his tall, muscular body was imbued with barely leashed strength, his Krinar hunter heritage evident in the predatory grace with which he held himself. He was so far from someone she could've ever imagined herself with—and so wrong for her in many ways—yet he was the only man who had ever made her feel this way.

After the ship was gone, turned back into its individual atoms, Korum lifted her into his arms and carried her into the house, heading straight for the bedroom. Mia clung to him, desperately craving physical contact, wanting the incredible pleasure only he could give her.

They entered the bedroom, and he gently placed her on the bed. Lying there, Mia watched as he removed his shirt, revealing his powerfully built chest and muscular stomach. His shorts were next, and then he was fully naked, his large cock already hard and his balls swinging heavily between his legs. His body was the epitome of masculine beauty, Mia thought hazily, her own body reacting to the sight with almost instant arousal.

Before she had a chance to fully admire him, he climbed on top of her and pulled up her dress, exposing her nether regions to his burning gaze. Without any preliminaries, he spread her legs and paused for a few seconds, seemingly fascinated by her sex.

Her entire body flushing, Mia tried to close her legs, feeling far too exposed like that, but he wouldn't let her, not until he'd had a chance to look his fill. Finally, raising his head, Korum murmured, "You have the prettiest little pussy I've ever seen. Did I ever tell you that?"

Mia shook her head, flushing even hotter.

"You do," he said softly. "All delicate pink folds and tiny clit—like the prettiest little flower." And before Mia could say anything, he bent his head toward the object of his admiration, carefully separating the said folds with his fingers, his tongue unerringly finding the sensitive area around her clitoris.

Startled by the sudden lash of pleasure, Mia cried out and arched against his mouth, her entire body tensing from a sensation so intense that it was almost intolerable. Her hands somehow found their way into his hair, tightening there, trying to force him into a harder rhythm that would give her immediate release. But Korum refused to be rushed, and his tongue continued its maddeningly light strokes around her nub, keeping her hovering right on the edge. And just when Mia thought she would go out of her mind, he finally pressed the flat side of his tongue against her clit, moving it back and forth with just enough force for her to reach her peak with a loud scream, her whole body quaking from the strength of her climax.

Panting and weak, she lay there as he watched her sex pulsating from the orgasm, his interest apparently still not fully satisfied. Once she had recovered a bit, he started to climb on top of her again, but Mia whispered, "Wait."

To her surprise, he listened, pausing for a second.

Still trembling slightly in the aftermath of what she'd just experienced, she sat up and gave Korum a challenging smile, her left hand reaching out to stroke his balls. "Turnabout is fair play," she said softly. "Why don't you lie down now?"

His eyes turned a deeper shade of gold, and Mia could feel his balls tightening within her hand. It excited him, she realized, when she took the initiative like that.

"How about I stand?" he suggested instead, and Mia nodded, liking the idea even more. Getting on her knees on the tall bed, she reached out and ran her hands down his chest, reveling in the feel of hard muscle covered by soft skin. His flesh was hot and firm to the touch, and she could almost believe he was a statue of some Greek or Roman god come to life.

Her right hand traveled lower, down the taut muscles of his stomach and followed the faint trail of hair down to his sex. Wrapping her fingers around his shaft, Mia felt it growing even harder in her grasp. She stroked it gently, enjoying the velvety texture of his skin there, and he groaned, closing his eyes, the expression on his face almost bordering on pain.

Encouraged, Mia pressed her lips against his chest and kissed her way down his body, slowly kneeling until her mouth was hovering just above his cock. His breath caught in anticipation, and Mia smiled and licked him, her tongue flicking lightly over the sensitive tip. He hissed, his hips thrusting at her. His hands buried themselves on her hair, bringing her face closer to his sex, until Mia had no choice but to open her mouth and let him in.

At the feel of her lips closing around his cock, he shuddered, and she could taste the faint saltiness of pre-cum. Her inner muscles tightened as a tremor of arousal ran through her.

His pleasure turned her on, Mia realized, reveling in the effect she had on him. She rarely got a chance to do this, to take him in her mouth and make him come, because he was always so focused on driving *her* crazy, making *her* scream with ecstasy in his arms.

Cupping his balls with her left hand, she wrapped the right one lower around the base of his shaft and began a slow rhythmic movement, taking him deeper into her mouth every time. She couldn't accept his full length, of course, but he didn't seem to care, his fingers tightening in her hair almost to the point of pain.

Then she could feel him swelling up even further, getting impossibly long and thick, and a warm, salty liquid spurted into her mouth as he came with a harsh cry, his head thrown back in ecstasy.

After a minute, Korum's fingers slowly unclenched in her hair as he withdrew his softening shaft from her mouth. Looking down at her, he smiled. "That was amazing," he told her and Mia stared up at him, slowly licking her lips and tasting the remnants of his seed there. She didn't know why she found it so exciting, giving him pleasure, but she did. She was fully aroused again, as though the powerful orgasm she'd just had was days in the past, instead of just minutes.

Climbing onto the bed, he brought her toward him and pulled her dress off over her head. At the sight of her naked body, his sex stirred again, and Mia's stomach clenched with anticipation as he drew her toward him, covering her mouth with his in an all-consuming kiss.

And then he took her, possessing her with his body even as he now owned her heart and soul..

CHAPTER THIRTEEN

Over the next ten days, Mia fell into a routine. Her days were almost entirely consumed with her apprenticeship at Saret's lab, while Korum occupied her evenings and—quite frequently—nights.

Interning at the lab proved to be a grueling and mentally exhausting job, yet Mia learned more in a few days there than she had during her entire three years of college. Saret made no allowances for her ignorance or for the fact that, as a human, she was slower at certain tasks than his other assistants. On the very first day, he paired her up with Adam and assigned them three projects, the most interesting of which was to figure out how to improve the process of knowledge transfer for Krinar children. Knowledge transfer, Mia had learned, was the way in which Ks educated their young—essentially imprinting the necessary information on their maturing brains, thus eliminating the need for rote learning of such basics as reading, writing, math, and history.

After giving her a whirlwind tour of the highly

advanced technology used in the lab, Saret told Adam to explain to Mia the research they'd done thus far and to show her the necessary recordings and readings. By the time Mia left the lab on her first day, it had already been ten in the evening, and she had been completely exhausted. Korum had been furious with Saret, but her new boss proved surprisingly inflexible: Mia was either working as hard as the other apprentices, or he had no room for her in his lab. After a major argument between the two Ks, which included several thinly veiled threats from Korum, Saret had reluctantly agreed that Mia would go home at seven on most nights—except when they were running critical simulations. On those days, she would have to stay until midnight, same as the rest of the lab crew. Mia had protested that she didn't mind, that she loved to learn and would stay as late as necessary, but Korum refused to hear it. "You're human, and you're my charl. I'm not letting you wear yourself out like this," he told her flatly.

And her routine was thus set.

In an effort to keep up with the tremendous amount of information coming her way on a daily basis, Mia placed a number of work-related recordings on the paper-thin tablet Korum had given her earlier. The tablet turned out to be waterproof, and Mia multitasked by watching some videos during her showers. Korum had been less than pleased when he'd found out, muttering that she was even more obsessed with this internship than she'd been with her schoolwork, but he didn't stand in her way. In fact, he even set up a comfortable place for her in his office, where she could study next to him in the evenings while he worked on his designs.

Adam proved to be indispensable as a lab partner, and Mia quickly realized that Saret had done her a huge favor by putting them together on the projects. The young K—he was only twenty-eight, she'd learned—was razor-sharp and extremely comfortable working with a human. As a teenager, he had apparently already made a fortune in the stock market and set up his adopted human family with a sizable trust fund, ensuring that they would always have a comfortable life. He also held a number of microchip patents that Intel and Apple were bidding for and was hoping to do an apprenticeship with Korum's company in a few years. To her surprise, she learned that he actually had a human girlfriend (he refused to call her his charl). When Mia tried to pry further, sensing a fascinating story, he refused to divulge any other details. He did promise to have Mia meet her one day, and she had to be content with that.

In the first few days, Mia felt so overwhelmed that she wanted to cry, her brain hurting from the sheer amount of learning that she was trying to accomplish each day. To help her, Adam suggested that they try imprinting her with some of the necessary information, just like they would a Krinar child. Mia initially resisted the idea, but after struggling with basic data collection using some of the more complex lab equipment, she grudgingly agreed. Saret had been delighted to have a live subject to experiment on, even if she didn't qualify as either a child or a Krinar, and requested Korum's permission to try the new imprinting procedure on Mia. After grilling both Saret and Adam about the process's safety and potential side effects, her cheren gave his consent, telling Mia that he hoped it would help her with the difficulty of the initial adjustment period. As a result, Mia spent the majority of the weekend inside the imprinting chamber, her brain rapidly absorbing all the information that Saret had deemed to be useful to his assistant.

By the time Mia left the chamber on Sunday evening, she felt dizzy and nauseated, but she knew enough neurobiology to qualify for an honorary doctorate in the subject. She could also potentially perform brain surgery, particularly on a Krinar subject—although she didn't think she'd enjoy the physical aspects of that specific task. At the same time, she had—at least theoretically—mastered all the equipment in Saret's lab and now felt infinitely more comfortable with Krinar technology overall.

After the imprinting, a whole new world opened up to Mia, and her second week in Saret's lab was significantly less stressful than the first. Instead of feeling like a bumbling idiot all the time, she actually knew how to do all of the simple—and many of the more advanced—tasks that Saret required from his assistants. The three other apprentices in the lab—who had initially looked amused at her presence there—began to treat her as more of an equal, letting her share some of their tools and equipment. They were still reserved around her, as if uncertain about a human in their midst, but Mia didn't let it bother her. There had been plenty of Krinar applicants for her position, and she was only there because of Korum. It was understandable that the other apprentices thought she didn't really deserve this opportunity. Mia was determined to prove them wrong.

Now that she had a solid foundation with the imprinting, she became much faster at learning and was even able to offer some suggestions to Adam about potential improvements in the imprinting process. He had already thought of most of them, of course, but he nonetheless told Saret about Mia's progress, and her boss said that she appeared to have a natural aptitude for his field—words of praise she would've never expected to hear from a Krinar.

She loved working at the lab so much that she wondered why the previous assistant had left.

"I'm not sure," Adam told her. "Saur just up and left one day. He told Saret he was quitting, and the next day he was gone. He was always a little strange, kind of a loner—none of us knew him that well. But he was really smart. He did a lot of work with mind manipulation, which is the most complex part of what we do. Nobody has seen him since he left. I don't think he's in Lenkarda anymore."

On the home front, her relationship with Korum had undergone a significant change. After her first, rather unwilling confession of love, she felt like she had nothing left to hide, and the words now came quickly and easily to her tongue. Korum seemed to revel in the new situation, frequently demanding that she tell him how much she loved him, and there was a constant warm glow in his eyes when he looked at her. At times, she thought that he had to love her back, at least a little bit, but she didn't want to ask for fear of spoiling the fragile truce that now seemed to reign between them. Instead, for the first time in her life, she chose to live in the moment and not dwell on the past or worry about the future.

Korum's own days were occupied with the trial and all the associated politics, and he would often tell her about it over dinner. The Council had commissioned an investigation into the supposed memory loss of the Keiths, and various mind experts—including Saret—had to testify as to the validity of these findings. It was beginning to seem that the memory loss was indeed real, and the final verdict was put off until the Council could find out what exactly had happened and who was behind these strange events. Korum still suspected that Loris was the culprit, but he didn't have enough evidence to sway the rest of the Council. As a result, the Keiths enjoyed a temporary reprieve while the investigation was ongoing.

Every night, Korum made dinner for them, constantly introducing her to new and exotic foods from Krina. Afterwards, they would either go for a walk on the beach or sit in his office, quietly working side by side. Whenever Mia allowed herself to think about her life in Lenkarda, she was struck by just how different—and amazing—it was compared to her initial expectations. Far from feeling like Korum's human pet, she woke up every morning with a sense of purpose, excited to face the day ahead and learn everything her new job could teach her. Her evenings were spent enjoying the company of her lover, while her nights were consumed with passionate sex.

In bed, Korum was insatiable, and Mia realized that he had been holding back in New York. His hunger for her seemed to know no bounds, and he would often fuck her until she was completely worn out and literally passing out in his arms. Surprisingly, her body appeared to have acclimated to his lovemaking, and Mia no longer had to worry about internal soreness or achy muscles in the morning. Even on those occasions when he took her blood, she recovered with unusual ease.

He also began to introduce virtual reality into their sex life. Now, at least a couple of times a week, they had sex in a variety of public and private settings, ranging from the stage at a Beyonce concert to the top of Mount Everest (which had been far too cold for Mia's taste). After that first time in the virtual club environment, he didn't push her too far beyond her comfort zone, although she had no doubt that he'd just begun to scratch the surface of everything he ultimately planned to do with her in bed.

On some days, she marveled at her own seemingly

inexhaustible energy. While she definitely tired more easily than her Krinar counterparts in Saret's lab, she managed to work ten-plus hours a day and then spend several hours more with Korum, of which at least a couple were in bed—or wherever they happened to be when the mood struck him. She should've been exhausted and dragging all the time, but she felt great instead. She chalked it up to the fresh Costa Rican air and the general excitement of her new job.

She called Jessie after a week and told her how happy she was.

"Really, Mia? You're happy there?" Jessie asked disbelievingly. "After everything he's done to you?"

"It's different now," Mia explained to her roommate. "I was wrong to be so frightened of him in the beginning. I think he truly does care for me—"

"A blood-drinking alien who pretty much kidnapped you? Are you suffering from some weird version of Stockholm's Syndrome?"

Mia laughed. "Hey, I'm the psych major here. And no, I don't think so . . ." She didn't go into all the details about her improved relationship with Korum—it still felt too fragile and precious—but she did tell Jessie about her internship and described some of the cool new things she was learning.

"Oh my God, Mia, you're going to be an expert on the Ks when you come back," Jessie said jealously. "Okay, I can see that he's not exactly mistreating you—"

"No, far from it," Mia told her earnestly. "I actually think I'm happier than I've ever been in my life."

"But you *are* coming back to New York, right?" Jessie asked worriedly. "You're not just going to decide to stay there, are you?"

"No, of course not," Mia reassured her. "I have to

finish college and everything . . ." Even if the thought of returning was not nearly as compelling as it had been just a few days ago.

She called her parents a couple of times as well, telling them that all was well and that she would be arriving home on Friday, almost exactly two weeks after she was initially scheduled to be there. Korum had cleared her vacation with Saret, telling him that Mia needed to see her family. Her boss had been less than pleased that Mia would be gone for an entire week, but he accepted it, particularly after she promised to stay in touch with Adam and keep up with the latest developments on her projects.

"What flight will you be on?" her mom asked eagerly. "We need to know so we can pick you up."

Mia winced, glad that her mom couldn't see her. She had no idea how she was going to get to Florida, and she'd been so busy at work that she'd forgotten to ask Korum about the specifics of their trip.

"I'm currently on a waitlist for an early morning flight," Mia lied, cringing internally at yet another falsehood she had to tell her parents. "But it might end up being in the afternoon, so I really don't know at this point. But don't worry—the professor arranged a rental car for me, so I don't need to be picked up at the airport."

"Okay, honey," her mom said, sounding surprised. "If you're sure . . . We truly don't mind. Are you flying into Orlando or Jacksonville?"

"Orlando," Mia told her. It sounded plausible enough.

* * *

On Thursday evening, right before their departure for Florida, they were scheduled to attend a celebration.

Korum's cousin Leeta had apparently been with her mate for forty-seven years—a major milestone in Krinar culture. In Earth time, it was actually closer to fifty years, as Krina traveled around its sun at a slightly slower pace than Earth.

It was Mia's first public event in Lenkarda.

"We don't have marriage and weddings in the human sense," Korum explained, watching her get dressed in a beautiful dress that he had created for her. "Instead, when a couple wants to make a permanent commitment, they come to a verbal agreement and then document that with a recording. At that point, it's really no one's business. They don't have a party or anything like that, and their union is not considered permanent until they are together for at least forty-seven years—"

"Why forty-seven?" Mia asked curiously, sliding her feet into a pair of sparkly sandals that went with the white shimmery material of her dress. The dress itself was form-fitting, showing off every curve of her body. It was also incredibly sexy, with her back entirely exposed. Around her neck, she was wearing Korum's beautiful necklace, and her hair was decorated with a fine silvery mesh that had somehow worked its way into her hair, carefully defining and separating each curl. She looked as good as she could possibly look, and she was grateful that Leeta had taken the time to send her recorded instructions on what to wear. Korum had apparently insisted on it, wanting to make sure that Mia didn't feel uncomfortable at her first big party in Lenkarda.

"Because it's a number that we consider special. It's a fairly large prime number, and several important historical events on Krina happened in years that ended with forty-seven. Plus, it's considered to be a sufficient length of time for a couple to know if they are compatible for the long term or not. Before the Celebration of Forty-Seven, it's very easy to walk away from the union; however, the event we're about to attend tonight makes the union binding. After that point, a couple whose union falls apart loses some of their standing in society. Of course, if one person cheated or did something else to cause the union to end, his or her standing suffers the most, while the innocent party is less impacted."

"So divorces are rare among the Krinar?"

Korum nodded, smoothly rising off the bed where he had been lounging. He himself was wearing a pair of fitted white pants tucked into knee-length grey boots and a sleeveless white shirt that was made of some kind of stiff, structured material. It was apparently the traditional Krinar attire for such celebrations, and he looked simply stunning in it.

"Yes, divorces—or union dissolutions—are uncommon. However, permanent unions are also unusual. Many Krinar don't find the person they want to be with for centuries or even thousands of years, and some never enter into a traditional union for a variety of reasons. So, you see, the Celebration of Forty-Seven is a major event for us, and it will be widely attended. We can't be late."

"Of course," Mia said, following him toward the bedroom door.

Leaving the house through the usual dissolving wall, they climbed into the aircraft that Korum had sitting next to the house in preparation for their journey. The celebration was here in Lenkarda, but not within walking distance. Over the past two weeks, Mia had learned that the Krinar traveled in two ways—on foot or via small flying pods. There were no cars or ground transportation of any kind.

Sitting down on the intelligent seat, Mia enjoyed the sensation of being completely comfortable. Although it was already 10 p.m. and she'd had a long day at the lab, she was feeling quite hyper at the thought of attending this celebration. Tapping her foot on the floor, she watched as the ship took off, swiftly carrying them toward the center of the colony.

A minute later, they landed in front of a large building Mia had never seen before. Instead of being planted on the ground, it floated in the air a few feet above the tree tops. A long pathway connected one wall to the ground, serving as a bridge of sorts.

"It's the Celebration Hall," Korum explained as they exited the aircraft and walked up the pathway toward the imposing structure. The building looked to be about twenty stories high and the size of a city block. Mia was surprised she hadn't seen it on the virtual map of Lenkarda earlier.

"Is this building always here?" she asked, seeing other ships landing all around them and hundreds of Krinar stepping out.

"No," Korum answered, leading her toward the building and ignoring all the stares in their direction. "It was constructed specifically for this purpose, and it will be unmade after today. There is a much larger Celebration Hall on Krina, and that one is permanent, but there are too few of us here on Earth to justify having such a large building around all the time. The Celebration of Forty-Seven is one of the very few events that brings together the entire Krinar population of Earth. Many from Krina will also be watching virtually."

The entire Krinar population of Earth? All fifty thousand? Mia hadn't realized the full scope of this event. Nervous and excited, she clutched at Korum's arm as they entered the building.

The noise inside was nearly deafening. It appeared that thousands had already gathered, and Mia couldn't help gawking at the gorgeous creatures all around her. The females were dressed in shimmering, light-colored dresses similar to Mia's, while the male outfits resembled Korum's. Even the shortest Krinar women were several inches taller than Mia, making her wish she were wearing high heels. The building itself was beautifully decorated, with flowers and glittering surfaces everywhere. The walls were not transparent, as was usual for Krinar structures; instead, they seemed to be reflective, making the already enormous hall seem even larger.

Like at the Food Hall, the Krinar around them stared at Mia and Korum. Mia wondered if that was because they hadn't seen a lot of humans—unlikely, given the fact that they all lived on Earth—or because they were surprised to see Korum with a charl. She decided that it was the latter. Probably it was just the novelty factor of seeing a Council member accompanied by a human girl.

As they made their way through the crowd, Korum put a possessive hand around her back, pressing her closer to him. Mia had learned over the past two weeks that it was considered a serious offense for a Krinar male to touch another man's female, whether she was his mate or his charl. It was a strange throwback to their territorial beginnings. The Krinar were very liberal when it came to sex, and Krinar women had all the same rights and freedoms as Krinar men. However, once they entered into a committed relationship, no other men were allowed to touch the women without explicit consent from their cheren or their mate. In some cases, violating that rule could even lead to an Arena challenge.

Korum was particularly bad in this regard. When he

picked her up at the lab on her second day there and saw Adam leaning over her to help her with one particular testing device, he had nearly flipped out. Mia had been impressed with Adam's composure in that situation; instead of cowering at Korum's rage, the young Krinar had calmly explained that he was helping Mia do her job and hadn't laid a finger on her. Thankfully, Korum hadn't done more than glower at him—Mia would've hated to see those two come to blows. Still, after that incident, Adam was particularly careful around her, always maintaining at least two feet of space between them. The last thing he needed was a jealous cheren after him, he'd explained with a laugh.

So now Korum kept her close as they walked toward the center of the giant hall. God forbid another male brush against her, Mia thought with exasperation.

As they approached the center, Mia saw a floating platform with a couple standing on it. She recognized the dark red hair of Korum's cousin, whose union celebration they were attending. It was an unusual hue for a Krinar, and Mia wondered if it was natural or dyed. Leeta's mate was as gorgeous as she was—tall, muscular, and with the typical dark Krinar coloring. They were each dressed in unusual robe-like outfits, pale mint-green in color, and stood completely still, just facing each other.

Hundreds of floating planks were arranged in circular rows all around the platform, and Korum led her to the front row. As a relative and a Council member, he apparently got the best seats in the house.

Looking around, Mia spotted a familiar figure a couple of rows behind them. Raising her arm, she waved to Delia and smiled when Arus's charl waved back at her. Turning his head to see what Mia was looking at, Korum saw Arus and gave him a cool nod of acknowledgement. The other

Councilor responded in kind. Clearly, the political tensions between the two had not improved since Mia had observed their interactions at the trial.

"So what's going to happen?" Mia asked, watching as more and more Krinar piled into the building. Maybe it wasn't quite fifty thousand yet, but it certainly looked like a huge number.

"In another few minutes, they will join together and then everyone will celebrate by dancing all night," Korum said, and there was a wicked gleam in his eyes.

That gleam usually meant he was up to something. "What do you mean, join together?" Mia asked warily. Her mind was beginning to wander in a strange and inappropriate direction.

His lips parted in a smile, exposing the dimple in his left cheek. "Exactly what you think it means, my sweet. They will mate publicly, thus binding their union in the way of our ancestors."

"They will have sex in front of everyone?"

She must've turned red because Korum burst out laughing. "Yes, my darling. But don't worry, the robes they're wearing are specifically designed to give them privacy. Your delicate sensibilities won't be too offended."

"My sensibilities aren't delicate," Mia hissed at him, knowing that all the Krinar around them could probably hear their conversation. Like the vampires of legend, Ks had sharper senses than most humans, with better hearing, eyesight, and sense of smell—all courtesy of their hunter heritage.

"No?" he teased, raising his hand to stroke her cheek. "You're used to public orgies?"

Mia swatted his hand away and determinedly turned her attention to the couple on the platform. Sometimes

Korum liked to play with her, telling her all kinds of naughty things just to watch her blush. Mia was not a prude, but she couldn't help her skin's involuntary reaction—and he seemed to enjoy that fact quite a bit.

In that moment, the hall darkened and the noise of the crowd abruptly subsided. A soft light came on, spotlighting the platform only. It was like a stage, Mia realized, her cheeks heating up again at the thought of what was to come. In general, she found the Krinar culture to be quite paradoxical; while their science and technology were incredibly advanced, some of their customs—like the Arena fights and now this bonding ritual—were almost barbaric.

A strange music, unlike anything Mia had heard before, began to play. The melody was haunting and powerful, and the underlying beat was both rhythmic and irregular at the same time, making Mia want to squirm in her seat. It was not dancing music, but there was something oddly sensual in it, with a few tones almost caressing her skin. She had no idea what musical instruments were used, but she had to admit that the overall result was beautiful. Korum had let her listen to some Krinar music before, and she'd found it to be quite unusual—but nothing like what she was hearing right now.

"This is the traditional bonding song," Korum whispered to her. "It's one of our oldest melodies—it dates back more than a billion years."

"It's incredible," Mia whispered back, feeling the fine hairs on the back of her neck rising as the tempo picked up.

The couple—who had been standing on the stage this whole time without movement—took a step toward each other. Their arms came up, their palms joining together, and the robes that they were wearing seemed to expand and curve around their bodies, creating a tent of sorts. Only their heads were visible now, and the expressions on their faces were calm, as though they were not about to do something very intimate in front of fifty thousand spectators.

As the music continued to play, Leeta's mate started speaking, his voice echoing throughout the hall. "For the past forty-seven years, you have been my companion, my love, my life. Without you, my future has no meaning. You are the air that I breathe, the water that I drink, the food that I consume. You are a part of me, and you will always be a part of me."

He stopped, and Mia blinked to get rid of the sudden moisture in her eyes. While simple, the words seemed truly heartfelt, and she couldn't help envying Leeta for having someone who loved her so deeply.

Leeta spoke next. "You are my mate, my love, my life," she said solemnly. "Without you, my future has no meaning. You are the air that I breathe, the water that I drink, the food that I consume. You are a part of me, and you will always be a part of me. I will be with you for forty-seven more years to come, and forty-seven years after that, and every forty-seven years into infinity."

She fell silent, and then they spoke together. "We are united," they said, and their vow reverberated throughout the building.

The music quieted for a second, and then it picked up again, only this time the beat was deeper, more sexual. To her surprise, Mia felt herself beginning to get turned on, her pulse speeding up and her belly muscles tightening at the unusual, but melodious tones. She'd never imagined that music could do something like that to her.

And apparently, she wasn't the only one. The mood of

the audience seemed to shift, and Mia could sense the sudden tension in the atmosphere. A warm male hand landed on her thigh, caressing it lightly, and Mia turned her head to see Korum looking at her with a familiar glow in his amber eyes. "Now the fun part begins," he mouthed to her, and Mia's cheeks got warm again.

Surreptitiously glancing around, she saw that the other spectators were staring at the stage with a rapt expression on their faces.

In the meanwhile, the couple on the stage came even closer to each other. Even though Mia couldn't see their bodies, she could tell that they had to be touching at this point. Leeta's eyes were now closed, and she looked flushed underneath her light golden skin, while her mate seemed to be breathing harder as he gazed at her beautiful face. They didn't kiss, and there was no visible physical contact of any kind, but Mia's heart still pounded at the knowledge of what they were doing. The scene playing out on the platform was unbelievably erotic, made even more so by the fact that so much was left to the viewers' imagination.

Enthralled, Mia stared at the stage, unable to tear her eyes away.

* * *

A couple of rows away, the Krinar watched Korum's charl observing the bonding ceremony.

Her little face was pink with color, and her lips were slightly parted. He could see her small chest rising and falling with every breath, and his fingers itched to pull down her dress and expose those perfectly round, pink-tipped breasts to his gaze.

In the past two weeks, his craving had turned into an

almost unbearable obsession. When he tried to analyze it logically, he knew it had something to do with the fact that she belonged to his enemy. He'd hated Korum for a long time, and the thought of taking away something he loved was exceedingly appealing.

But it went deeper than that. He found himself thinking about her constantly, fantasizing about touching her, tasting her . . . Fucking her, as he'd seen Korum do on the beach. To this day, he hadn't been able to watch that incident fully, rage and bitter jealousy coursing through his veins at the sight of his nemesis enjoying something he so desperately wanted himself.

It was incredibly dangerous, this obsession of his. He was starting to have trouble controlling himself, and he couldn't afford to let his true feelings show. There was too much at stake to throw everything away for the sake of one human girl, no matter how much he hungered for her delicate little body.

Besides, if he succeeded in his plan, she would be his.

Everything would be his.

CHAPTER FOURTEEN

After the bonding ritual was over, an opaque wall rose up around the edges of the platform, hiding the couple from view, and the music quieted down.

Her cheeks flaming, Mia rose from her seat, following Korum's example. What she had just witnessed had been far from pornographic, yet she couldn't get the rapturous expressions on the couple's faces out of her mind. Their sexual act had been hidden from view, but their feelings and emotions during the ritual had been on display for everyone to see. At the end, the music had reached a crescendo, and Mia realized that it was both imitating and facilitating their lovemaking.

Now everyone was standing. Glancing up at Korum, she saw that he was looking straight ahead. All of a sudden, he stomped his foot, once and then again and again. His actions appeared to serve as a signal of some kind because the hall was suddenly filled with loud stomping noises, as every person in the audience followed Korum's lead. Uncertain at first, Mia did it too, deciding that it was probably the K version of clapping. Korum turned his head and gave her an approving smile.

The spotlight on the stage faded, and the hall gradually became lighter. All the seats rose into the air and floated away, leaving a large empty area where the spectators had been sitting.

A different song began to play, this one more along the lines of what Mia had listened to before in Korum's house. It sounded like a mix of some kind of synthesizer, with weeping undertones and a pulsing beat. Krinar party music, Mia guessed, watching as everyone started milling about and gathering into small groups.

"What did you think?" Korum asked, putting his hand on her shoulder and looking down at her with a smile.

"I thought it was beautiful," Mia told him sincerely, and his smile widened.

"Do you want to stay for the dancing or are you too tired?" he asked.

"Oh, no, I'd love to stay!" What kind of an idiot would she be to miss out on her first Krinar dancing party?

"Well, then, let's go dance."

He led her away from the platform toward one of the corner areas that apparently functioned as dance floors. As they walked through the crowd, other Krinar stepped to the side, letting them pass. Korum nodded to a few people in acknowledgment, pausing to briefly say hello and introduce Mia to a few Ks here and there. Everyone they met seemed to treat Korum with some mixture of deference and respect, and Mia realized yet again just how powerful her lover was in the K society.

When they reached one of the corner dance floors, Mia stopped and simply stared. There was no way she would be able to dance like that. Simply no way.

The athletic grace displayed by the dancers was

unbelievable—and inhuman. They didn't move—they simply *flowed* from one dance step into another. It was a spectacle unlike any other Mia had ever seen, and she tried to imagine what K athletes or professional dancers would be like—if such a thing existed.

Looking up at Korum, she said wryly, "I think I'll watch from the sidelines. This might be just a tad too advanced for me."

"Don't worry about it," Korum said, grinning down at her. "You can just follow my lead."

And before she could protest, he swept her onto the dance floor, his hands firmly holding her waist. Startled, Mia grabbed his shoulders, clinging to him as he launched into an unfamiliar series of moves.

Dancing with Korum was an experience unlike any other. She wasn't sure one could even call it dancing—it was more like being picked up and carried by a tornado. For the next hour, her feet barely touched the floor as he whirled her around in a complex routine. Laughing and gasping at some of the more extreme moves, Mia could only hold on as the room spun around her. Finally, thirsty and out-of-breath, Mia had to beg him to stop.

"That was amazing!" She couldn't help the huge grin on her face as they stopped by one of the floating tables that held a variety of interesting-looking liquids.

Korum grinned back at her. "See? You can dance." Filling a rounded cup with a pink liquid, he handed it to her.

"More like I can hang on to you as you spin me around," Mia said, laughing at the image they must've presented. She'd felt like she was flying, and it had been an incredible sensation. Taking the cup from him, she took a sip and immediately downed the whole glass.

"That was yummy," she said. "What is it?" It tasted

like juice, but had a cool, refreshing aftertaste.

"It's a type of fruit cocktail. Very common at parties and other events."

"You don't drink alcohol?"

"We do." Korum pointed at the other drinks on the table. "But it's nothing that you can have. Those are designed to give *us* a buzz, so they'll probably knock you on your sweet little rear end. So stick to this cocktail, okay?"

Mia pretended to pout. After the club incident in New York, Korum seemed to go out of his way to limit her alcohol intake. She didn't actually want anything strong enough to get a K drunk, but she found it funny that Korum felt the need to warn her away.

"Don't give me that look," he said softly, his eyes glued to her mouth. "It makes me want to bite that delicious lower lip of yours."

Surprised by the sudden shift in Korum's mood, Mia reflexively moistened her lips—and realized her mistake when she heard him inhale sharply.

"That's it," he said quietly, and his voice sounded a little hoarse. "We're going home."

And before she could say anything, he ushered her quickly through the crowd, heading decisively for the exit.

When they arrived home, he stripped off her clothes as soon as they entered the house. Bemused, Mia stood there naked, watching as he disrobed as well. He was already fully aroused, and a familiar heat burned in her belly at the hungry look in his eyes.

"You're driving me crazy, you know that?" he said roughly, stepping toward her and lifting her up to stand on the couch. From this vantage point, she was a little taller than him, and she enjoyed the novelty of looking down at him.

"I'm not doing anything," Mia protested, then moaned as he pressed his hot mouth to her neck, nibbling on the sensitive spot in the area. Tremors of pleasure ran down her body, and her eyes closed as he pulled her closer to him, his large hands stroking her naked back. His lips traveled down her neck to her collarbone, then lower, until his tongue was slowly swirling around her right nipple. Her insides clenched at the sensation.

He lifted his head, looking up at her with a burning amber gaze. "You exist. You make me want you just by breathing. Everything about you appeals to me—your taste, your scent, the look on your face when I am deep inside you. I can't go a single fucking day without touching you, without feeling you in my arms. I can't even go a few hours. And it's not enough, Mia . . . I want more. I want everything."

Mia's breath caught in her throat as she stared at him. His intensity was almost frightening.

"You have everything," she whispered, clutching his powerful shoulders. "I love you. You know that—"

"Do I?" His hands slid down her back, cupped her butt cheeks. He pulled her closer to him until her lower body was pressed against his, the tip of his hard cock prodding between her thighs.

"Of course . . ." Mia gasped as she felt him beginning to push inside.

"Tell me you're mine," he ordered, and she wondered at the dark need she saw on his face. His face was flushed and his eyes glittered with some strange emotion.

Mia licked her lips. Only the head of his cock was inside her for now, and she was desperate for more. "I'm yours," she told him softly, and then immediately cried out, her head falling back, as he entered her fully with one thrust.

"That's right," he whispered savagely, "you're mine. You will always be mine."

And for the next several hours, Mia didn't doubt him for even a second.

* * *

"How are we getting to Florida? And can you please make some more human clothes for me? I don't think I have enough here . . . And shoes . . . Maybe we should get some of my new clothes from New York?"

Feeling like a bundle of nerves the next morning, Mia paced up and down the kitchen, too wired to sleep past 7 a.m. despite getting less than four hours of sleep last night.

"I don't think I've seen you this nervous even when you were spying on me," Korum observed with amusement, slicing up a papaya for her breakfast smoothie. He was back to his normal self, having apparently gotten over whatever weird mood he was in last night.

Mia took a deep breath and plopped down on one of the chairs. "No, but seriously, I have nothing to wear. All I have are those jeans and the T-shirt that I was wearing earlier—"

"Do I ever not take care of that for you?"

It was true, he did. He always handled all the logistics, and everything came out perfectly fine.

"Okay, I am nervous," Mia confessed, bringing her thumb toward her mouth to bite at the nail before she remembered that she'd gotten rid of that nasty habit in high school.

"Why? You should be happy. You're going to see your family. Isn't that what you wanted?"

"They're going to find out I lied to them," Mia impatiently explained, giving Korum a don't-you-get-it look. "And then they're going to flip out when they meet you—"

He sighed with exasperation. "They're not going to flip out. We've discussed it already. You're going to first tell them about me, and then I'll do my best to reassure them of your safety and wellbeing."

Mia jumped up, unable to sit still. "I know, but I don't see how they would *not* flip out. I've never brought home a boyfriend before, and here I show up with a K. They've never even seen one of you except on TV."

"Well then, they'll have a new experience."

Korum was completely inflexible on this topic. As far as he was concerned, her parents would just have to get used to the fact that their daughter was now his charl. Whenever Mia tried to bring up the idea of her going to Florida by herself, he would immediately shoot it down. Far too dangerous, he'd told her, and, besides, he had no intention of not seeing her for a week. When Mia had argued that they could still see each other at night—since his super-fast aircraft could get anywhere within the globe in a matter of minutes—he reminded her of the first part of his statement. Not all the Resistance fighters had been caught yet, he explained, and thus it was not safe for her to go anywhere outside of Lenkarda by herself.

Mia blew out a frustrated breath. "Okay, fine. So are we going there by the same ship that brought us here to Costa Rica?" At Korum's nod, she continued, "And where are you planning to land? In my parents' backyard?"

He laughed. "No, my sweet. That might frighten them

too much, not to mention bring a lot of unwanted attention to your family. We're going to land at a special section of the Daytona Beach International Airport, and I will make us a car there. Then we'll drive to your parents' house. Your arrival is going to be very human and straightforward."

"And you'll what? Sit in the car while I explain the whole thing to them?"

"I'll drop you off and go for a drive to explore the area. You'll call me when you're ready for me to come by. Here, drink your smoothie and stop stressing. It's going to be fine," Korum said soothingly, handing her the shake.

"Thank you," Mia told him after a few sips of the flavorful concoction. She was starting to feel marginally better. Maybe she *was* over-thinking it. "So when are we flying out?"

He shrugged. "Whenever you're ready. We can go now if you want."

"What? Like right this second?" Her nerves were back in full force.

Korum looked exasperated. "I said whenever you're ready. Finish your shake, do whatever you need to do, and then we'll go."

"Shouldn't I also get dressed?" Mia asked, giving him an anxious look. She was currently wearing her bathrobe and house slippers.

"Yes, you should. And if you'll look in the closet, you'll find an outfit I prepared specifically for today," Korum told her patiently. "Now stop panicking and get ready. Your family is waiting."

Almost vibrating with tension, Mia ran into the bedroom

and opened the closet. Sure enough, Korum had prepared a pretty blue sundress for her and a pair of silvery flip-flops. There were no labels on either the dress or the shoes; her lover had obviously created them himself. He'd gotten the style right, however; the dress had the wide scooped neckline that had been featured in all the fashion magazines, and the flip-flops had just the right amount of sparkle to make them "casual daytime glam"—or whatever the magazines had labeled that look most recently. There was also a set of underwear for her: a sexy pair of lacy boy-cut panties and a matching strapless bra. Korum had clearly thought of everything.

Putting on her new human-style clothing, Mia studied herself critically in the mirror, trying to figure out how her parents would perceive her. In her own not-overly-modest opinion, she looked unusually well. Her skin was clear of all imperfections—even the freckles had somehow faded despite the hot sun—and her dark brown curls were smooth and glossy. The color of the dress complemented her eyes, turning them a deeper blue. Overall, she looked exactly as she felt—happy and healthy. Hopefully, that would help mitigate her parents' concern about the situation.

Exiting the bedroom, Mia found Korum sitting in his office, apparently tweaking a design. He had changed as well, into a pair of jeans and a white polo shirt that hugged his powerfully muscled body to perfection. On his feet, he wore a pair of brown loafers that managed to look both casual and elegant.

"I'm ready," Mia told him bravely, feeling like she was going to face the guillotine instead of her loving parents.

At the sight of her, Korum slowly smiled and golden flecks appeared in his expressive eyes. "Come here," he said softly, pulling her onto his lap before she had a chance to protest.

Leaning down, he kissed her deeply, his tongue delving into her mouth even as his hand found its way under her skirt, pressing against her lace-covered pussy. Her body reacted with swift arousal, her nipples pinching into tight buds and her sheath moistening in preparation for him.

Coming up for air, Mia moaned, "What are you doing?" His wicked fingers were now inside her panties, and she could feel them starting to stroke the area directly around her clitoris. Unable to sit still, she squirmed on his lap, feeling the tension starting to build. She couldn't believe he was doing this to her right now, so soon after last night's sexual marathon.

"I'm making sure you're less stressed when you see your parents," he murmured, and she heard the sound of a zipper being lowered. Before she could say anything else, he pulled down her underwear, leaving it hanging around her ankles, and raised her skirt. Now her naked bottom was on his lap, and his hard cock was pressing against her butt cheeks.

"Korum, please . . . I'm not sure that's a good idea . . . Oh!" she gasped as he entered her suddenly, pushing into her without any preliminaries. With her feet bound by her panties, she couldn't spread her legs wider for a more comfortable fit and he felt huge inside her, his shaft like a heated baton burning her from within.

"Shh," he whispered, his fingers finding her clitoris again. "Just relax. There's a good girl . . ."

Mia whimpered, feeling both uncomfortably full and unbearably turned on as he began to move inside her, his cock nudging at her G-spot. At the same time, he started rubbing her clit, keeping the pressure firm and steady.

Without any warning, a powerful orgasm ripped

through her body, and Mia cried out, her sheath spasming around the large intruder. Korum groaned as well, his cock jerking inside her, releasing his seed in warm spurts as the rhythmic squeezing of her inner muscles sent him over the edge.

Feeling like a rag doll, Mia slumped against him. Her entire body was still trembling with small aftershocks, and she could hear his breathing slowly beginning to return to normal.

After about a minute, he rose and gently set her on her feet, handing her a soft tissue to wipe away the remnants of their lovemaking. "Feeling better now?" he asked, smiling at her.

Mia certainly felt less tense, but she was now worried about showing up at her parents' house looking and smelling like a nymphomaniac. She gave him a reproachful look as she cleaned the traces of his sperm on her inner thigh. "Now I need a shower before going anywhere . . ."

"All right." Korum grinned. "Let's take a quick rinse and then we go. Five minutes should do it." And picking her up, he quickly carried her into the bathroom, moving with inhuman speed.

True to his word, they were done and heading out within a few minutes. The pod that had brought Mia to Costa Rica was already assembled and sitting next to the house. Korum had apparently widened the clearing around his home to accommodate the ship instead of having them walk a few minutes to the spot where they had landed two weeks ago.

Entering through a dissolving wall, Mia studied the now-familiar-seeming transparent ivory walls and floating seats. The ship still didn't look like the complex piece of technology that it was, with no visible electronics or controls. Nonetheless, she knew it was capable of carrying them thousands of miles in a matter of minutes, with no ill effects from traveling so fast.

Perching on one of the seats, Mia sighed as she felt it adjusting around her, conforming to the shape of her body. It was one of the things she would miss the most in Florida—all the intelligent technology that seemed designed solely for the purpose of making their lives easier and more comfortable. She resolved to ask Korum to remake his home back into what it was before he "humanized" it for her sake; now that she had mostly acclimated to Krinar technology, she was very curious to see what his house normally looked like.

And then they were on the way, the ship rising silently and carrying them toward Florida, where Mia's parents were still blissfully ignorant of the surprise their youngest daughter had in store for them.

* * *

The Krinar watched as the ship took off.

They were gone. *She* was gone.

Watching her dance with his enemy last night had been almost intolerable. *He* wanted to be the one to have her light body pressed against him, to take her home for the night. He'd spent the next several hours imagining her in Korum's bed, and quiet rage had burned in the pit of his stomach. Maybe it was for the best that she was leaving. It would minimize the distractions in the next week.

She had looked happy, laughing as Korum twirled her around. Foolish girl. If only she knew the truth.

She would be sympathetic to his cause once he explained everything to her. She would understand—the K was certain of that.

She would want Earth to be saved.

CHAPTER FIFTEEN

"Can you please drop me off here?" Mia asked Korum as they turned onto her parents' street. "They might see the car if you pull into their driveway."

"Sure," he said, and the unimaginably expensive Ferrari Spider convertible came to a smooth stop a few houses away from Mia's childhood home.

Why Korum had chosen to make this particular car, Mia had no idea. She vaguely remembered Jessie's brother raving about it a few months ago; supposedly, it cost more than three average houses put together. When Mia had protested that a Toyota would get them around just as well, her lover had simply raised his eyebrows. "It's one of the nicer cars," he told her, "and I would like to enjoy the experience of operating one of these human vehicles. Not to mention that this is the only car design I bothered to adjust to make it reproducible by our nanotechnology."

And that was that. The little sportscar had zoomed

down I-95 at over a hundred miles per hour, getting them to their destination in Ormond Beach in record time. It seemed that one of the perks of traveling with a K was not having to worry about speeding tickets; any state trooper unfortunate enough to stop them would have immediately backed off when he saw the driver.

"All right, just call me when you want me to come by. And stop worrying," Korum told her, leaning over to open the door for her and giving her a quick kiss on the lips.

"Okay, sure."

Mia climbed out of the car and shut the door, watching as he drove away. Then, taking a deep breath, she headed toward her parents' house.

The street on which Mia grew up was in a slightly older part of the city. The majority of houses there were built in the eighties and nineties, before the big real estate boom of the mid-2000s. As a result, some of their neighbors' roofs looked a little dated, with few of them covered by the solar panels that were all the rage these days. In general, the houses didn't have that glossy, brand-new look and feel that characterized some of the wealthier and more expensive parts of the area. However, the landscaping here was much nicer, with large trees providing solid shade and cutting down on energy bills.

Walking down the street, Mia absorbed the familiar atmosphere, with each house, each shrub triggering some childhood memory. There was her friend Lauren's house, where she had spent many hot summers swimming in their pool. And there were the tall oaks that they used to climb, as careless with their safety as only children could be. Lauren had ultimately gone to college in Michigan, and Mia rarely saw her these days, though they would usually catch up on the phone or Skype every couple of months.

Like many others, Mia's parents had moved to Florida from Brooklyn, lured by warm weather and affordable housing. It was a decision they'd never regretted, quickly adjusting to the slower pace of life there. Marisa had been three years old at the time, and New York had been too expensive for the young couple to purchase anything bigger than a studio there. So instead, they scraped and saved for two years—no eating out in restaurants for that entire time, her mom had proudly told her—and made a downpayment on a nice four-bedroom home in a pretty middle-class neighborhood of Ormond Beach.

Approaching the house, Mia hesitated for a second, trying to control her nervousness. Not wanting to tell any more lies, she had decided against calling her parents to let them know what time she would be arriving. Simply showing up and then explaining the whole story seemed easier. Checking her phone, she saw that it was only nine in the morning, so her parents were most likely home.

Raising her hand, she rang the doorbell. Immediately, a loud barking noise pierced the silence as Mocha, her parents' Chihuahua, did her duty by announcing the visitors. Her parents had gotten the dog when Mia left for college—as a replacement for her, her dad had always said jokingly.

Twenty seconds later, her mom opened the door. "Oh my God, Mia!"

Before Mia had a chance to say anything, she was pulled into a warm, familiar embrace. As usual, Ella Stalis smelled like lemons and some Chanel perfume.

Grinning, Mia hugged her back before pulling away. "Hi, mom. Surprise!"

"Oh sweetie, we had no idea you were arriving so early! Why didn't you call us? And where is your car?" Her mom was looking over Mia's shoulder and seeing an empty driveway. "And all your luggage?"

"It's a long story, mom. Is dad home? There's something I have to tell you."

A look of immediate concern appeared on her mom's softly rounded face. "Mia, honey, are you okay? What happened? Here, come inside—"

"Nothing happened, mom," Mia reassured her, walking into the hallway leading to the spacious living room. Mocha immediately ran away. Her parent's dog was shy with strangers and persisted in thinking of Mia as such, despite the fact that she'd seen her dozens of times. "Everything is fine. I just have an interesting story to tell you, that's all. Is dad home?"

"He's in his office," her mom said, then yelled, "Dan! Come and see who's home!"

Daniel Stalis came into the living room, still wearing his pajama pants and a robe. At the sight of Mia, his face brightened. "Mia, hon! What are you doing home so early? When did you fly in?"

Smiling, Mia stepped toward him and gave him a big hug, inhaling the familiar scent of aftershave and minty toothpaste. "Hi, dad. Oh, I missed you guys so much!"

Her dad grinned, hugging her back. "Oh, I always forget how tiny you are after not seeing you for a while. Seriously, honey, you should eat more."

"I eat like a horse and you know it," Mia told him, grinning.

"Mia has something she wants to tell us," her mom said, and Mia could hear the worried note in her voice.

Her dad frowned. "Is everything okay? Does it have something to do with that professor?"

"Yes and no." Mia was not even sure where to start. "Why don't we all sit down and get some tea? It's kind of a long story."

Her mom slowly nodded. "Of course. Let me make some tea right now. Are you hungry? Have you had breakfast? I can make some potato pancakes . . ."

"I already ate, mom, thanks. But definitely another time." Sitting down at the table, Mia twisted her hands nervously, watching as her mom put water to boil. Her dad sat down too, studying his daughter silently while the tea was getting prepared. When the water had boiled, Mia got up to help her mom carry the cups over to the table. Finally, the three of them were sitting around the table, with hot green tea steaming in front of them.

"All right, honey. Now tell us," her mom said, visibly bracing herself for the worst.

"Okay," Mia said slowly. "So I haven't been entirely honest with you guys about what's been going on in my life for the past few weeks. There was no professor, and I didn't stay in New York for this volunteer project . . ."

Seeing the surprised looks on her parents' faces, Mia plunged ahead. "You see, I actually met someone . . ."

"See, Ella, didn't I tell you Mia was acting strangely?" Her dad looked smug for a second, but her mom continued to stare at her worriedly.

Taking a deep breath, Mia continued. "The reason why I didn't tell you this is because he's not someone you would normally be comfortable with, and I didn't want you to worry—"

"Who is he, Mia?" her mom asked sharply. "A drug dealer? Someone with a criminal record?"

"No, nothing like that!" Although it might've been easier for her parents to accept if he had been. "Korum is a K."

For a moment, there was dead silence around the table. Her parents looked shellshocked, stunned speechless.

Her dad cleared his throat. “A K? As in, the aliens?”

Mia nodded, taking a sip of her tea. “I met him in a park in Manhattan a few weeks ago. We’ve been involved ever since.”

Her mom’s chin quivered. “What do you mean, involved? Involved how?”

“Ella, don’t be silly,” her dad said, his tone surprisingly calm. “Clearly, Mia is trying to tell us that she has a boyfriend who’s a K. Isn’t that right?”

Her dad was very good under stressful circumstances. “Exactly,” Mia told them, her stomach twisting into knots as her mom’s face crumpled and fat tears rolled down her cheeks. Feeling like the worst daughter in the world, Mia tried to reassure her. “Look, you can see that I’m perfectly fine. I know how they are portrayed in the media, and the reality is not the same at all. He’s actually very caring, and he makes me happy—”

“Caring? How can those monsters be caring? Mia, they say that they drink blood!” Her mom was beside herself, her normally pale face turning red and splotchy.

“Do they drink blood?” her dad inquired, looking mildly curious.

“Only recreationally and in small quantities,” Mia admitted honestly. “It’s just a pleasant thing for them—they don’t actually need it anymore.”

Her mom buried her face in her hands. “Oh my God, I feel sick!”

“Ella, stop it,” her dad said, his voice unusually firm. “Your reaction is exactly what Mia was afraid of and why she didn’t tell us earlier.”

Mia smiled, the knot in her stomach unraveling a bit.

"Thanks, dad. Look, I know how it sounds, but believe me when I tell you that he treats me really well and makes me very happy—"

"Is he the reason you couldn't come home on time?" her dad asked, while her mom raised her head to stare at Mia with eyes that were still swimming with tears.

"Yes. We actually went to Costa Rica after my finals were over," Mia said. "I have an internship there, at a neuroscience lab, and I'm working on some really interesting projects—"

"In Costa Rica?" Her dad looked puzzled for a second, and then his eyes widened. "The K Center in Costa Rica?"

Mia gave him a big grin. "Yep. Korum got me an internship there. I'm working alongside one of their top mind experts, and you can't even imagine how much I'm learning—"

"You're working in a K Center in Costa Rica?" Her mom looked absolutely floored. "With Ks?"

"I know, I can hardly believe it myself," Mia told them, grinning hugely. "And I can now speak so many languages . . ."

"What? What do you mean?" Her dad rubbed his temples. "What languages?"

"All languages," Mia told him in Polish, knowing that he would understand her. "All human languages, plus Krinar. It's a really cool translator that Korum got me." She decided against telling them about the brain implant part of things.

Her dad's jaw dropped. "You speak Polish without an accent! Mia, how did you . . . ?"

"Krinar technology," she explained with a smile. "You can't even imagine some of the things they can do—"

"But, Mia, he's not *human* . . ." Her mom seemed to be in shock. "How can you even . . ."

"Mom, they're very similar to humans in many ways. You do know that they made us in their image, right?"

Her mom shook her head, apparently unable to believe her ears. "And that makes it okay? How did you even manage to get involved with him? You met him in the park and then what, you went on a date?"

Mia hesitated for a second. "Yes, pretty much. He actually sent me flowers, and we went to a really nice restaurant. And we've been seeing each other ever since . . ."

"Just like that?" Her mom was incredulous. "You meet one of these creatures in a park, and you go on a date with him? What were you thinking?"

She was thinking that she didn't want to die or get kidnapped. But her parents didn't need to know that. "He's very good-looking," she told them honestly. "And it was the first time I was attracted to someone so strongly."

"So you completely ignored the fact that he wasn't human? Mia, that doesn't sound like you at all . . ." Her mom was looking at her like she'd grown two heads.

"How did you get here from Costa Rica?" her dad asked quietly, watching her with an unreadable expression on his face. As usual, he was the only one who could think clearly under difficult circumstances.

Mia looked at him. "Korum brought me. We flew to Daytona on one of their ships, and then he dropped me off in a car, so I could talk to you."

"And how long are you staying?"

"What do you mean, Dan, how long is she staying? For the rest of the summer, right?" her mom asked, sounding panicked.

Mia shook her head. "I'm here for a week, mom. Unfortunately, I can't be away from the lab that long—"

Her mom burst into tears. "Oh my God, we are seeing you for the last time . . ."

"What? No! Of course not! I just have to finish out my internship, that's all. I'll come back here soon, and you can come see me in New York during the school year—"

"Where is he now?" her dad asked coolly. "If he brought you here, then where is he?"

Mia took a deep breath. "I have to call him. I wanted to have a chance to talk to you first, to explain a little bit before you meet him. But he would like to meet you himself, to reassure you that everything is fine and I'm safe with him."

"We're going to meet a K?" Her mom seemed stupefied by this turn of events.

"Yes," Mia told her. "And you'll see that there's really nothing to be afraid of." She crossed her fingers that Korum would be on his best behavior.

"All right, Mia," her dad said. "Why don't you call him? We'd like to meet this K of yours."

* * *

Half an hour later, the doorbell rang.

Mia had managed to explain a little more to her parents about Korum and their relationship, emphasizing solely the good parts. She told them how he took care of her and about his cooking hobby (her mom's face brightened a little at this), how he was genius-level smart and ran his own company, and about the incredible opportunity he'd given her by getting her this internship. As a result, by the time Korum showed up, Mia was reasonably certain that her parents were calm enough to be somewhat civil. Still, she couldn't help her anxiety as she opened the door and saw her lover standing there, looking far too gorgeous to be human.

"Hello," he said softly, leaning down to give Mia a kiss on the forehead.

"Hi. Come on in." Mia grabbed his hand and led him into the house. Pausing in the hallway for a second, she gave him an imploring look and squeezed his hand, hoping that he understood her wordless plea.

Korum smiled and whispered, "Trust me."

Mia had no other choice. Bracing herself for the worst, she led Korum into the living room.

At their entrance, her parents stood up from the couch and simply stared. Mia couldn't blame them: Korum was a striking sight. Dressed in a white polo shirt and blue jeans, her lover was the epitome of casual elegance. With his glossy black hair and golden skin, he could have been a model or a movie star, except that no human had eyes of that unusual amber hue—or moved with such animal grace. And even standing still, he projected an unmistakable aura of power, his presence dominating the room.

Taking a step toward her parents, he smiled widely, revealing the dimple on his left cheek. "You must be Ella and Dan. I'm very pleased to meet you. Mia has told me so much about her family."

Mia noticed that he didn't offer to shake their hand or make any other move to touch them. It was probably the right thing to do. Her parents were already tense enough at having a K in their house.

Her dad nodded curtly. "That's funny, because we just heard about you today."

"Dan!" her mom whispered fiercely, clearly afraid of their extraterrestrial guest's reaction. She seemed unable to take her eyes off Korum, staring at him with a dazed look on her face. Mia knew exactly how she felt.

Korum didn't seem offended at all, giving her dad a warm smile instead. "Of course," he said softly. "I understand that this is all a huge shock for you. I know how much you love your daughter and worry about her, and I would like to set your mind at ease about our relationship."

Mia's mom finally remembered her manners as a hostess. "Can I offer you anything to eat or drink?" she asked uncertainly, still staring at Korum like she wasn't sure whether she wanted to run away screaming or reach out and touch him.

"Sure," he said easily. "Some tea and fruit would be great, especially if you join me."

Mia blinked in surprise. She hadn't known that Korum drank tea. And then she realized just how extensive his file on her family had to be: he had unerringly picked the one thing guaranteed to make her mom more comfortable—her parents' daily ritual of making and drinking tea.

"Of course." Her mom looked relieved to have something to do. "Please have a seat in the dining room, and I'll bring some tea. We have some really nice local oranges . . . You do eat oranges, right?"

Korum grinned at her. "Definitely. I love oranges, especially the ones from Florida."

Ella Stalis smiled at him tentatively. "That's great. We have really good ones this week—juicy and sweet. I'll bring them right out." And blushing a little, she hurried away, looking unusually flustered.

Mia mentally rolled her eyes. Apparently, even older women were not immune to his charm.

"The dining room is this way," her dad said, looking slightly uncomfortable at being left alone with Mia and her K.

Mia walked over to Korum and took his hand, determined to show her dad that there was nothing to worry about. Smiling, she led him toward the table.

The three of them sat down.

At that moment, Mocha appeared, her little tail wagging. To Mia's huge surprise, she came directly to Korum and sniffed at his legs. He smiled and bent down to pet the dog, who seemed to revel in his attention. Mia watched the scene with disbelief; the Chihuahua was normally very reserved around strangers.

After a minute, Korum straightened and turned his attention back to the human inhabitants of the house.

"So Mia tells us she has an internship in your colony," Dan Stalis said, looking at Korum as though studying a new and exotic species—which, actually, he was. "How exactly does that work? I assume she can't really understand a lot of your science and doesn't know your technology . . ."

"On the contrary," Korum told him, "Mia is a very fast learner. She's made tremendous progress in the last couple of weeks. Saret—her boss at the lab—tells me that she's already making herself quite useful."

Mia smiled, tickled pink by his praise. "Like I told you, dad, Saret is one of their top mind experts. He's at the cutting edge of Krinar neuroscience and psychology. And I get to work with him. Can you imagine?"

Her dad rubbed his temples again, and Mia saw him wince slightly. "I can't, to be honest. The whole thing has been rather overwhelming. You'll excuse us if we're not exactly jumping for joy right now—"

"Of course," Korum said gently. "I wouldn't be either if it were my daughter."

"Do you have children?" Dan asked bluntly.

"No, I don't."

"Why not?"

"Dad!" Mia was mortified by this line of questions.

Korum shrugged, apparently not minding the prying. "Because I don't have a mate, and I wouldn't want to raise a child without one."

Her dad's eyes narrowed. "How old are you?"

"In your Earth years, I'm about two thousand years of age."

The look on her dad's face was priceless. "T-two thousand?"

In that moment, her mom walked in, carrying a bowl of oranges and a tray with tea cups.

Mia got up and rushed toward her. "Here, let me help you with that," she said, grabbing the bowl from her.

"Thanks, sweetie," her mom told her, and Mia breathed a sigh of relief that at least one parent seemed to have recovered her composure.

Setting the cups filled with hot tea around the table, Ella asked Korum, "Would you like some cream or sugar? We have coconut cream, almond cream, soy cream . . ."

"No, thank you," Korum replied politely, giving her a dazzling smile. "I prefer my tea plain."

"So do we," her mom admitted, blushing again. Mia barely stopped herself from snickering—her parent appeared to have developed a little crush on her lover.

"Ella," Mia's dad said slowly, "Korum here is apparently much older than we thought . . ."

"Oh?" her mom inquired, sitting down and reaching for an orange. Methodically peeling the fruit, she gave her husband a questioning look.

"He's two thousand years old . . ." Her dad seemed awed by that fact.

"What?" The orange dropped on the table, landing with a soft plop.

"Mom, you knew the Ks are long-lived," Mia said, getting exasperated with their reactions. "You and I watched that program together a couple of years ago, remember? It was one of those Nova documentaries about the invasion."

"I remember," her mom said, still looking like she'd been hit with a hammer. "But I didn't realize that meant thousands of years . . ."

"How exactly does something like that work if you're in a relationship with a human?" Her dad was back to being his blunt self. "Because Mia can't possibly live that long—"

"That's between me and your daughter, Dan," Korum said gently, but there was a steely note in his voice that warned against pushing in this direction. "We'll figure everything out in due time." And picking up an orange, he calmly peeled it, his fingers moving faster and more efficiently than her mom's had been.

"By the way," he added, biting into the orange, "Mia mentioned that you tend to get frequent headaches, and I couldn't help but notice that you've been rubbing your temples. Are you suffering from one now?"

Caught off-guard, her dad nodded.

At the affirmative gesture, Korum reached into his jeans pocket and pulled out a tiny capsule. Handing it to Mia's dad, he said, "This is something that should take care of the issue. One of our top human biology experts developed it specifically for cases such as yours."

"What is it? A painkiller?" Her dad studied the little capsule with no small measure of distrust.

"Yes, it works immediately as such. But it should also prevent any future occurrences."

"A migraine cure?" her mom asked, and there was a desperate look of hope in her eyes.

"Exactly," Korum confirmed, and Ella Stalis's eyes lit up.

Her dad frowned. "Are there side effects? How do I know it's safe?"

"Dad, their medicine is wonderful," Mia told him sincerely. "Truly, you have nothing to be afraid of."

"Mia is right. There are no side effects when it comes to our medications. And, Dan, the last thing I would want is to hurt the people Mia loves the most. I know you have very little reason to trust me yet, and I hope that changes in the future. If you don't want to take the medicine, it's entirely up to you. I just wanted you to have it in case you are in pain."

"Just take it, Dan. Right now," Ella ordered, giving her husband a determined look. "I don't think Mia's boyfriend would give you something bad for you. If there's even a small chance that it can really cure you, then you owe it to yourself and to your family to try it—particularly if Korum says there are no side effects."

Her dad hesitated, studying Korum's face for a few seconds. Whatever he saw there seemed to reassure him. "Do I just swallow it?"

"Squeeze it into a cup of water, and then drink it," Korum said. "It works quicker that way."

Mia's mom was already on her feet and pouring her dad a cup of water from a pitcher sitting on the table. "Here," she said, thrusting it at him.

Dan Stalis took the cup slowly and pinched the capsule between his fingers, squeezing out two drops of liquid into the water. "Is this it?" he asked, looking up at Korum.

Her lover gave him an encouraging smile. "Yes."

Cautiously sniffing it, Mia's dad took a sip. "This actually tastes good." He sounded surprised.

"Most of our medicines do."

Bringing the cup to his mouth, her dad drank the rest of the water. Almost immediately, Mia could see the tense muscles around his jawline relaxing. Smiling at him, she said, "It's working, right? You can feel it right away."

Her dad looked pleasantly surprised, and her mom's face was shining with happiness. "Yes. It seems to be instant." Turning to Korum, he said, "Thank you. That was very nice of you."

"Of course," Korum said softly. "I would do anything for Mia and the people she loves."

CHAPTER SIXTEEN

"I have to talk to my sister too," Mia said as she got into the car and waved goodbye to her parents. Her mom was holding Mocha, who very nearly followed them out, having developed an inexplicable doggy crush on Korum. "I know mom is calling her right now, but I'd like her to hear it from me as well. I told her something earlier, and I would really like a chance to explain, so she doesn't get the wrong idea about our relationship."

"What did you tell her?" Korum asked, smoothly pulling out of the driveway. He drove like he did everything else—with skill and efficiency.

"I told her I had a lover who was from Dubai," Mia admitted, blushing a little. "And I said that things wouldn't work out between us because he had to leave soon."

"I see," Korum said, and there was a noticeable chill in his voice. "And when did you tell her this?"

Crap. She really shouldn't have brought this up—but

it was too late now. "When I thought you might be leaving for Krina," she confessed. "Before, you know . . ."

"Before your betrayal?"

Mia sucked in her breath. "Are you still mad at me? You said you'd let it go . . ."

"I let it go as far as I'm not going to punish you for it. But I can't quite forget it, my sweet. Not yet."

Mia bit her lip, feeling upset. "I don't understand you sometimes," she said quietly. "One minute you're so nice to me and my family, and the next you're talking about punishing me for a situation that wasn't exactly my fault—a situation that you manipulated to your advantage. What did you expect me to do? Just calmly accept the fact that I might end up as a sex slave?"

"You could've talked to me at any point and asked me whether it's true." He kept his eyes on the road, but Mia could see a tiny twitch in his tightly clenched jaw muscle.

"And if it were? What would I have done then? I would've endangered John and everyone in the Resistance and lost my only chance to help them and myself."

"At what point did I ever treat you as a sex slave?" Korum asked, and his even tone made her shiver a little. He was still not looking at her. "I gave you everything, Mia, and you kept acting like I was a villain."

Mia swallowed. "You knew I was afraid in the beginning, and you didn't give me any choice," she said, feeling old resentment rising up. "And besides, what is a charl, really? What rights do I have in your society? I know you don't treat me poorly, but you could, right? If you wanted to keep me locked up in your house, would anyone stop you?"

He didn't answer, and she could see his jaw tighten further.

They turned off Granada Boulevard onto A1A, and he drove for another few minutes before pulling into the winding driveway of a large beachfront mansion. At their approach, the wrought-iron gates swung open, letting them through.

"Where are we?" asked Mia, breaking the tense silence. She felt sick in her stomach. She hated arguing with Korum, and the last few days had been so nice, so peaceful. Why had she stupidly reminded him of what happened before?

The car came to a stop, and he put the clutch in "park" mode before turning to look at her. "Come here," he said roughly, burying his hand in her hair and leaning over to give her a deep, penetrating kiss. By the time he let her come up for air, Mia was melting bonelessly into him, almost trembling with need.

Letting her go, he climbed out of the car and came around to open the passenger door. Mia climbed out on somewhat unsteady legs as he watched her with hungry gold-tinted eyes.

She looked up at him.

"We're in a house I rented for the week," he told her. "Let's go inside." And taking her hand, he led her up the steps and into the stately white building.

The interior of their "rental house" could've easily been featured in *Architectural Digest* magazine, with its sharply designed white furniture and open layout with gleaming hardwood floors. One wall—the one facing the ocean—was made entirely of glass and provided a breathtaking view.

Turning Mia toward him, Korum bent down and kissed her again, lightly. "Why don't you go call your sister now?" he suggested, and his voice sounded a little hoarse. "When you come back, I have some plans for you."

* * *

Trying to calm her elevated heartbeat, Mia walked upstairs and into a room where she spotted an old-fashioned landline phone. When she was sure she had herself sufficiently under control and could think of something besides Korum's plans, she called her sister, dialing her cell phone number from memory.

Marisa picked up on the fifth ring. "Hello?"

"Hey, Marisa, it's me . . ."

"Mia? I was just on the phone with mom! Holy shit! You're dating a K?!?"

Mia sighed. "Yep. Listen, remember that thing I told you?"

"About your supposed wealthy executive lover?" Her sister's tone sounded caustic. "Yes, I remember perfectly."

Mia winced. "Well, I was not fully honest with you—"

"No shit!"

"I'm sorry," Mia said sincerely. "I really thought he might leave for Krina at that point and I would never see him again. I needed to talk to someone, but I just didn't feel like I could tell the whole story . . ."

For a second, there was silence. "Mia," Marisa said, sounding upset, "you can always tell me the whole story, even if it's worthy of being on the cover of *National Geographic*. I'm your sister, and if anyone can understand, it would be me."

Mia squeezed her eyes shut, feeling ashamed. "I know. I'm sorry. There was just a lot going on and I wasn't thinking clearly at the time—"

"What *was* going on? And what changed? How did it

go from 'this can never work out' to meeting the parents and spending the summer in Costa Rica?"

"We worked out our differences," Mia said, not wanting to go into the particulars. "And he's staying here, on Earth."

There was again silence for a second. Then her sister said, "Seriously, Mia? A K? You couldn't choose someone of the same species?"

Mia smiled, relieved. The worst seemed to be over. "I know, it's insane—"

"Insane is putting it mildly," Marisa said seriously. "Freaking awesome is how I would phrase it."

Mia laughed, startled. "What?"

"My baby sis is dating a super-hot, wealthy alien genius who just cured dad's migraines? Hell yeah, it's fucking amazing!"

Mia couldn't believe her ears. "You're not going to read me a lecture and tell me how foolish I am to get involved with someone so dangerous and not human, and blah, blah, blah?"

"Oh please, I'm sure the parents already did that. What can I say that'll be in any way additive? No, baby sis, I'm happy for you. You've walked the straight and narrow for way too long. A little danger and spice in your life is exactly what you need. And besides, from what mom tells me, he's unbelievably gorgeous and has been around since the dawn of time. It really doesn't get any cooler than that . . . I can't wait to meet him!"

Mia grinned hugely. Her sister always managed to surprise her. "You're the best sister ever," she told Marisa. "So when am I seeing you and Connor?"

"Tonight at six. Apparently, your extraterrestrial lover invited the whole family for dinner."

"He did? When?" Mia couldn't remember him doing

anything of the sort.

"I don't know. I wasn't there. Shouldn't *you* be the one to know? I thought he did it at your request . . ."

"Um . . . he takes initiative a lot when it comes to these things." Too much, considering that Mia didn't even know about the invitation. He must've talked to her parents when she visited the restroom. "So are we meeting at a restaurant somewhere?"

"It's kind of crazy that I'm the one telling you this, Mia." Marisa sounded like she was laughing. "We're coming over to your rental house. He's cooking. Still doesn't ring a bell?"

"That does sound like something Korum would do." Mia smiled, even though Marisa couldn't see her. "You're in for a treat—he's an amazing cook."

"And does the laundry, right? Unless you made up that part too?"

"Nope," Mia said, grinning. "He definitely did the laundry when we were in New York. He has this weird thing for human appliances. I think it mostly has to do with his cooking hobby, which is strange in and of itself. They have these intelligent houses that *cook* for them, Marisa. He doesn't need to lift a finger to have gourmet meals, and yet he does—"

"Oh my God, where can I find a K for myself? I'm already in love and I haven't even met the guy yet!"

Mia burst out laughing. "Hey, this one's taken! And besides, wouldn't Connor have something to say about his pregnant wife hooking up with an alien?"

"Connor would gladly give his pregnant wife to an alien right about now," Marisa said, and Mia could hear the serious undertone in her voice. "I'm so moody these days that he's slinking around the house like I might bite him. Which I might, at any moment. My emotions are beyond wacky. Don't get pregnant, sis—it's so not fun . . ."

Mia immediately sobered up. "Oh, Marisa, I'm so selfish. I haven't even asked you how you're feeling!"

"Well, I didn't exactly give you a chance, did I? But yeah, I'm still feeling crappy. The nausea is just not going away. I lost another pound in the last week. The doctor doesn't know what to do. I've been resting a lot, I tried yoga and meditation—none of it seems to work."

"Oh Marisa . . ."

"Think your boyfriend could help with that?" her sister joked.

"I don't know," Mia said seriously. "Maybe. I'll ask him. He's not a doctor, but he might have access to one of their wonder drugs."

"Oh, no, you don't have to do that . . . I was just kidding—"

"Well, I'm not. I'll ask him right now."

"Mia, please, that'll be embarrassing. I'm sure I'll get over it in another few weeks . . ."

"Uh-huh," Mia said. "By then you'll be skin and bones, if you aren't already. You don't exactly have a ton of fat to spare."

She could hear Marisa sighing with what sounded like exasperation. "Fine, you can ask, I guess. I just don't want him to feel like we're taking advantage of him—"

"Oh please, Korum *offered* the migraine cure to dad. I didn't even know there was such a thing, much less that he brought it with him. Stop worrying, please—it's not good for you right now."

"Fine, fine . . ." Her sister sounded distracted all of a sudden. "Hold on, babe, I'm talking to Mia!"

"You have to go?" Mia guessed.

"Oh, it's just Connor . . . We were supposed to go

grocery shopping when mom called and then you . . ."

"Oh, well, go then. We'll see each other tonight. I can't wait!"

"Me too. Love you, baby sis! See you soon!"

"Love you too!" And hanging up the phone, Mia went to look for Korum.

She found him outside, swimming in the Olympic-sized infinity pool that apparently came with the property. He was gliding through the water like a shark, moving with unbelievable speed.

"Hi," Mia called out, and then remembered the mysterious plans he had for her. Was it something sexual? Her breathing quickened at the thought. Telling herself to focus on Marisa, she decided to ask Korum about the medication right away, before he had a chance to implement whatever those plans were.

Swimming up to the edge of the pool, Korum lifted himself out effortlessly, using only his arms. His black hair was wet and slicked back against his skull, and water droplets glittered like tiny diamonds on his golden skin. He looked mouthwateringly sexy, and Mia swallowed, realizing yet again just how gorgeous her lover truly was. Walking toward the edge of the pool, she sat down on one of the lounge chairs conveniently placed there.

"Hi yourself," he said, smiling at her warmly and sitting down on the chair next to her. He seemed to have forgotten about their earlier disagreement, and Mia smiled back at him, relieved.

It seemed like as good of a time as any to ask about Marisa. "Do you know anything about pregnant women?" she blurted out, and then flushed for some reason.

Korum's eyebrows rose, and he looked amused. "I assume you're talking about your sister?"

Mia nodded. "She's having a difficult pregnancy. Really bad nausea and all. I was wondering if maybe you might have some anti-nausea medication or something that might settle her stomach . . ."

Korum considered it, looking thoughtful for a second. "I don't have it with me, but I can probably get someone to bring it here. However, it would only be a temporary fix . . . If there's something wrong that's causing your sister to feel this way, the medicine wouldn't do anything except mask the symptoms."

"Oh, I see . . ."

"The best thing for your sister would probably be Ellet. I'll ask her to swing by this week and examine Marisa—"

"Ellet?" The name sounded oddly familiar, even though she couldn't remember where she'd heard it.

Korum smiled. "She's our human biology expert in Lenkarda. Her lab designs many of the drugs I've given you in the past, as well as the one I just gave your dad. She's excellent at what she does and knows more about human health than all of your doctors put together."

Something nagged at Mia, some elusive memory that she couldn't place. After trying to remember for a second, she gave up and returned to the issue at hand. "Oh, I see . . . Yeah, if she could take a look at Marisa, that would be phenomenal. Would she seriously do that? Come all the way out here for this?"

He shrugged. "She owes me a few favors."

"Is there anyone in Lenkarda who doesn't owe you a few favors?" Mia asked wryly, staring at him. Her lover always seemed to have something up his sleeve.

"Not many," Korum admitted, smiling at her. "I believe in having leverage—comes in handy in situations like this. Of course, Ellet would probably come out here regardless. She has a soft spot for pregnant humans."

Mia grinned, wanting to hug and kiss him in gratitude. She didn't want to fight with him; she loved him too much. Giving in to the urge, she got up and sat down on his lounge chair, ignoring his wet shorts pressing against her dress. Taking his head between her hands, she pulled his face closer and gave him a tender kiss on the lips. "Thank you, Korum," she said softly, looking him in the eyes. "I really appreciate everything you've done for me and my family."

He smiled, and his eyes held a warm amber glow. "Of course, my darling . . ."

"I love you," Mia told him sincerely. "I love you so much, and I'm sorry about everything that happened before. You're right—I should've trusted you more. Do you think you'll be able to forgive me some day?"

It was the first time she had apologized for spying on him, and she could see that she'd pleasantly surprised him. Raising his hand, he lightly stroked her cheek. "Of course," he said softly. "Rationally, I know why you did what you did, but I have a difficult time being rational when it comes to you. When you first agreed to work with the Resistance, I let anger at your betrayal cloud my thinking instead of giving you more time to adjust to our relationship. I'm sorry for that, and for the stress and worry I caused you as a result. But I'm happy you're here now, with me . . ."

"I'm happy too," Mia said, and she knew he could see the full depth of her feelings on her face. "I really am . . ."

His eyes flaring brighter, Korum leaned toward her and kissed her hungrily, as though he wanted to consume her. His hands curled around her shoulders, and he pulled her closer, dragging her onto his lap, his erection pressing into her through the wet material of his swimming trunks.

Feeling buffeted by his passion, Mia could only cling to him as he greedily devoured her mouth, his hands roaming over her body, ripping off the clothing that prevented him from touching her naked skin. His hot mouth moved to her neck, nipped the skin lightly, and she cried out, her head falling back as if it were too heavy for her neck to support. She felt unbelievably hot, like she was burning inside from a liquid flame, every inch of her sensitized and craving his touch. He seemed to feel the same, his erection throbbing against her leg and his hands moving over her almost roughly.

Her fingers curved into claws, dug into the back of his shoulders. "Please, Korum . . ." She wanted him inside her with a desperation that didn't fully make sense. "Please . . ."

He rose, still holding her in his arms, and flipped her over, putting her down on the lounge chair on all fours. And then he was bent over her, driving into her with one powerful thrust, his hard cock penetrating her without restraint.

Mia gasped, shocked at the sudden entry, her inner muscles straining with the effort to adjust to his thickness, but he didn't give her any time. Grasping her hips, he fucked her relentlessly, his hips hammering at her with such force that she couldn't catch her breath, utterly overwhelmed by the sensations. She could hear his harsh breathing and her own screams, and then her whole world consisted of nothing more than the physical, the pleasure and the pain intermingling until there was no way to tell them apart and one could not exist without the other . . . until she was nothing more than an animal, besieged by the most basic need.

It seemed to go on forever, and then he came with a guttural groan, grinding into her as though trying to merge them together. The pulsations of his cock inside her sent her over the edge, and the orgasm tore through her body, leaving her weak and shaking in its wake. Only his hands on her hips kept her from collapsing onto the lounge chair, her arms and legs trembling too much to support her weight.

After about a minute, his breathing had calmed and he withdrew from her, separating their bodies. Mia felt too worn out to move, so she was glad when he picked her up and carried her into the house.

Wrapping her arms around his neck, she mumbled into his shoulder, "Was this what you had in mind when you said you had plans?"

"Pretty much," Korum admitted, walking up to the second floor. "I did envision something more civilized, but I don't seem to have any control over myself when it comes to you. I didn't hurt you, did I?"

He had, a little, but it had only enhanced the pleasure. And besides, she felt perfectly fine now, with all traces of soreness seemingly gone. "No," Mia reassured him. "I loved it."

He walked into a large, luxuriously appointed bathroom and placed her on her feet next to a large, claw-footed tub. "That's good," he said, turning on the water and smiling at her. "Still, I think you could use a nice bath, and so could I."

And, as Mia watched, his cock began to harden again.

CHAPTER SEVENTEEN

Marisa and Connor arrived first, their 2012 Toyota pulling into the driveway five minutes before six o'clock. Korum was finishing setting the table, so Mia came out to greet them by herself.

"Oh my God, Mia! Baby sis, it's so good to see you! You look phenomenal! What has he been feeding you?" Marisa burst out as soon as she exited the car. "And holy cow, look at this place! He must be a gazillionnaire!"

Laughing, Mia gave her sister a big hug, sobering a bit when she felt the unusual fragility of her frame. "Marisa! Oh, it's so good to see you too! And Connor!"

Smiling, her brother-in-law bent down to hug her too. "There's my favorite sister-in-law. How are you?"

"Oh, I'm doing great! Here, let's go inside! Korum is just putting the finishing touches on the dinner—which should be amazing, by the way."

"Any meat?" Connor asked with a hopeful look on his face as they followed Mia toward the house. A former college quarterback, Marisa's husband was still having trouble adjusting to the post-K-Day diet.

"No, sorry, they're mostly plant-eaters. But it's really yummy stuff, anyway."

"I still find it hard to believe that vampires are vegetarians . . ." Connor muttered, and Mia laughed again.

"They're not really vampires—they're past that now," Mia explained. "And some of the plants on Krina are very rich-tasting and dense in calories. I think if we had them here, we might not have been eating meat either."

"Ooh, you've tried plants from Krina?" Marisa sounded envious. Her sister was normally an adventurous eater, and the two of them would frequently try unusual restaurants when Marisa came to visit Mia in New York.

"Yep," Mia confirmed, grinning. "And they're really tasty. But that's only in Lenkarda. Tonight, we're eating much more local."

"Ugh, I hope I can eat something. I was sick again on the way here," Marisa confided. She did look pale and rather ill. "We had to stop by a rest area. I'm surprised we got here before the parents—"

"Oh, I was just about to tell you," Mia said, pausing for a second before entering the house. "I spoke to Korum, and he's going to have one of their doctors look at you to determine what's causing the problem."

"A K doctor?" Connor looked surprised.

"Actually, she's more of a human doctor—a Krinar specializing in human biology. Korum said she's really good."

"Wow, Mia, I don't even know what to say . . ." Marisa's eyes were suddenly swimming with tears.

"Oh no, don't worry about it! It's really not a big deal—"

"Hormones," Connor explained, pulling his wife closer to him for a hug.

"Ah, I see." Mia gave Marisa a few seconds to get her emotions under control. Then, smiling at them, she asked, "Ready to go in?"

Marisa nodded, looking much sunnier, and Mia led them into the house.

Korum must've just finished what he was doing because he came into the living room at the same time. As always, he looked stunning, with the golden hue of his skin contrasting with the white color of the simple button-up shirt he was wearing. And even though they had spent most of the afternoon in bed, Mia couldn't help the twinge of arousal she felt at the sight.

Spotting her sister, he gave her a big smile and walked up to them. "You must be Marisa," he said warmly. "I can definitely see the resemblance . . ."

Marisa nodded, looking uncharacteristically shy and flustered. "Yes, hi . . ." She seemed incapable of saying anything more profound.

Recalling her first meeting with Korum, Mia knew just how her sister felt. Apparently, even marriage and pregnancy could not shield a woman fully from the impact of her lover's magnetic appeal.

Turning to Connor, Korum said, "And you're Marisa's husband, right? Connor?"

Her brother-in-law politely held his hand out. "Yes, it's nice to meet you. Korum, right?" He looked far less star-struck than his wife.

Her lover accepted his hand, shaking it briefly. "Indeed. The pleasure is all mine. Can I offer you a drink while we wait for Mia's parents?"

"A beer would be great," Connor said easily. Mia had to give him kudos for his composure. Outwardly, he didn't seem intimidated at all.

Korum smiled and disappeared into the kitchen. In that moment, Marisa caught Mia's gaze. "Wow," her sister mouthed. "Just wow."

Mia grinned. She had always been jealous of her popular older sister who'd managed to have it all—good grades, great friends, and a ton of cute boys chasing after her. And now Marisa was envious of her?

Korum reappeared, carrying a tray with a beer, a glass of champagne, and a cup filled with some milky liquid. Handing the champagne to Mia and the beer to Connor, he held the cup out to her sister. "This is something that should settle your stomach," he said kindly. "At least for the rest of the evening."

Marisa gratefully accepted the cup and drank its contents, not even bothering to question the safety of the liquid. Clearly, their dad's experience had given her the confidence to trust K medicines. "Thank you," she said, and then her eyes widened. "Oh, wow, I'm already feeling much better . . ."

At that moment, the doorbell rang. Mia's parents had arrived.

After greeting them, Mia and Korum led them into the dining room, where Korum had prepared a meal that was more like a feast. Mia felt a little bad that she hadn't helped him at all, but Korum had shooed her away from the kitchen when she'd offered, explaining that she would simply be in the way. Not the least bit offended, Mia had gone to sit by the pool and catch up on the latest developments in Saret's lab, chatting with Adam via a Skype-like device that projected his image like a three-dimensional holograph.

In the meanwhile, Korum had prepared a gourmet feast consisting of five different varieties of salads, exotic sushi-like vegetable concoctions, various types of noodle dishes with delicious-smelling sauces, and fresh fruit for dessert. A bottle of Cristal was chilling in a bucket of ice, and the table was decorated with a large centerpiece of gorgeous flowers. He had really gone all out, and Mia's heart tightened at the realization that he was actually trying to impress her family.

And impressed they were.

Her mom kept asking Korum for recipes of all the dishes they were eating, and even her dad seemed to be in a much better mood, his earlier headache gone without a trace. The atmosphere at the table was surprisingly relaxed, with her family questioning Korum about life on Krina and her lover telling amusing stories about his parents and the pranks Saret used to pull on him when they were children. Watching him, Mia realized he had deliberately steered the conversation toward those topics that would be most likely to put her family at ease . . . that would humanize him in their eyes. And even though Mia knew that he was putting on a show, she couldn't help the little melting sensation she got inside when she thought of Korum as a little boy, playing in the forests of Krina and getting in trouble with his friends.

The dinner lasted until ten. Finally, replete and happy, everyone departed. On their way out, Mia's mom kissed Korum on the cheek, and her dad shook his hand. Marisa blushed and stammered a little, thanking Korum again for the anti-nausea medication, while her husband gave him a huge smile and told him they would be coming over for dinner every night, given the awesome meal they'd just had.

As soon as her family drove away, Mia wrapped her arms around Korum's waist and hugged him tightly. Still holding him, she looked up and found him regarding her with a tender look on his beautiful face. "Thank you," she told him sincerely. "This really meant a lot to me."

He stroked her cheek gently. "I would do anything to make you happy, darling," he said softly. "You know that, right?"

Mia nodded and buried her face in his chest, feeling like she couldn't contain all the emotions filling her chest right now. She loved him so much it hurt. And in that moment, she was almost certain that he loved her too.

* * *

The next morning, Mia woke up to the sound of Krinar language being spoken. A soft female voice, oddly familiar, could be heard, interspersed with Korum's deeper tones. The doctor, Mia realized. She must've already arrived to inspect Marisa.

Getting out of bed, Mia quickly dressed and washed up, checking the time. Sure enough, her sister was supposed to get there in a few minutes.

Entering the living room, Mia saw a beautiful Krinar woman sitting there, chatting with Korum about the local beaches. Tall and slim, she reminded Mia of a Brazilian supermodel, with her bronzed skin, dark brown hair streaked with golden highlights, and sparkling hazel eyes. Again, something nagged at the back on Mia's mind, some elusive memory that she couldn't quite place.

She approached them, and the K female rose and extended her hand to Mia. "Hi," she said warmly. "I'm Ellet."

Smiling, Mia shook her hand briefly, surprised at the human greeting. Other than Korum's cousin Leeta, Mia hadn't spoken to a lot of K females. All four of the other assistants in Saret's lab happened to be male, and Mia hadn't really socialized with anyone else yet.

"Thanks for coming all the way here," Mia told her. "I can't even begin to tell you how much I appreciate your help with this."

"Oh, it's my pleasure," Ellet said, beaming with a megawatt smile and causing Mia to like her immediately. "This is my first time in Florida, and I'm loving it so far. So much like Costa Rica, yet so much more developed and with so many humans!"

Mia raised her eyebrows in surprise. Developed and teeming with humans were usually negative factors for most Krinar, but Ellet seemed to be saying just the opposite.

"Ellet loves humans," Korum said dryly. "You're her specialty. I don't know why she's even bothering to stay in Lenkarda—New York would be a much better place for her."

"It's a little too cold and dirty for my taste," Ellet said, smiling. "But Florida seems much more promising . . ."

"Really?" Mia asked, staring at her. "You would move here and do what? Open a clinic?"

Ellet smiled. "I would like to, but I probably won't be able to get permission. It goes against the mandate."

"The mandate?"

"The non-interference mandate—one of the conditions under which the Elders have agreed to let us live here, on Earth," Ellet explained, shooting Korum a quick and unreadable look.

"Oh, I see," Mia said, though she didn't really. She knew that the Ks hadn't shared any of their technology and science, and she presumed it was because they wanted to see how their grand evolutionary experiment would turn out. However, she hadn't realized there was an actual mandate in place.

Before she could ask any more questions, the doorbell rang. Marisa had arrived.

Mia went to open the door.

Once again, her sister looked wan and pale, the dark color of her hair only emphasizing the unhealthy pallor of her face. The medication Korum had given her yesterday was obviously no longer working.

"Ellet is already here," Mia told her. "She's very nice—you'll like her."

Marisa nodded, looking a little green. "Mia," she whispered, "what if they find something really wrong with me or the baby? Something that our doctors haven't been able to diagnose? What if it's something bad—like truly bad?"

"What? No! I'm sure you're perfectly fine. It's probably just some weird hormonal imbalance . . . You can't start stressing about crazy what-ifs before the doctor even looks at you! Here, come here . . ." Mia pulled her in for a hug and felt her slim body shaking in her arms.

In that moment, Ellet and Korum entered the hallway, having apparently overheard something with their sharp Krinar hearing.

"You must be Marisa," Ellet said warmly, coming up to her sister and studying her with an inquisitive look on her perfect face.

Marisa pulled away from Mia, looking a little stunned to be confronted with such a gorgeous creature.

The Krinar woman gave her a wide smile. "I'm Ellet," she said gently, "and I'm an expert in human biology. Please, don't worry, you have nothing to be afraid of. Come, let's go into the living room and I'll take a look to see if there's anything wrong. And even if there is, I'm sure that we can fix it. The human body holds few mysteries for us at this point."

Marisa nodded, looking somewhat reassured, and they all walked into the living room.

"Please, can you stand still for just one minute?" Ellet requested, reaching for a small white device that was sitting on the coffee table next to the couch. Picking it up, she directed it toward Mia's sister, running it slowly over her body from head to toe, focusing especially on her stomach area.

Then, putting down the device, she said, "Did your doctor tell you that you have borderline hyperemesis gravidarum?"

Marisa blinked. "Uh, he did mention something along those lines, but I thought that was just a name for severe nausea and vomiting . . ."

"It is. It's a condition that happens when you have excessive levels of beta hCG hormone. It could be dangerous if you get severely dehydrated, and I don't think human doctors know how to treat it other than assigning you IV fluids in the more extreme cases and making sure you rest. However, I should be able to fix it for you, so the rest of your pregnancy proceeds smoothly."

Marisa gave her a desperately hopeful look. "Really? You can make it go away?"

"I can normalize the hormone levels for you. Since you're only in your first trimester, you may still experience mild nausea every now and then, so I'll give you a little something that you can take for that. But you'll be able to eat and function normally again—and start gaining weight like you're supposed to."

"And the baby? Is everything okay with the baby?" Marisa asked tremulously.

Ellet smiled. "Yes. She's going to be a beautiful girl."

"Oh my God, a girl!" Tears of happiness filled

Marisa's eyes. For as long as Mia could remember, Marisa had talked about wanting a daughter, and now it seemed like her dream would be coming true. Mia grinned at her and squeezed her hand.

"All right, ready? We'll need privacy for the next step," Ellet said.

"You can go into one of the bedrooms upstairs," Korum told her. "We'll be waiting down here."

Marisa looked a little nervous. "What are you going to do?" she asked Ellet. "Is it like an operation?"

"I won't have to cut you or anything," the K reassured her. "It's just a small device that needs to go inside you. It will take about five minutes, and then you'll be able to go home."

"Go ahead," Mia encouraged her. "It'll be okay . . ."

Marisa and Ellet went upstairs, and Mia sat down next to Korum. "Thanks again for getting Ellet to come out here," she told him. "She's wonderful."

"Yes, she's one of the nicest individuals I know," Korum admitted. "She's still relatively young, only about four hundred years old, but she's very passionate about what she does and she's made a lot of contributions to her field." He sounded admiring.

A sudden unpleasant thought occurred to Mia. "Did you and her ever . . . ?" Ellet was one of the most beautiful women Mia had ever seen, even in Lenkarda.

Korum shrugged. "It was nothing serious—just a casual fling a few years ago. It's nothing that you need to be concerned with."

Mia swallowed, the pit of her stomach suddenly burning with jealousy. "You were lovers?" A wave of nausea rolled through her as she pictured them together in bed, the K's pouty lips on Korum's body, her slender hands touching him in intimate places.

"Only briefly. You have to understand something, my sweet—sex is a fun, recreational activity for us. Unless it takes place in the context of a serious relationship, we don't assign any meaning to it."

Mia stared at him, trying to digest that for a second and to push away the unpleasant, pornographic images still lingering in her mind. "So what determines whether you're in a serious relationship or not?"

"Whether we care about the other person and to what degree."

"And you didn't care about Ellet?"

He shook his head. "No. We were too similar in some ways. It quickly became obvious that we didn't have much beyond the initial attraction—which faded within a few weeks."

"But she's so incredibly beautiful . . . How can you possibly not be attracted to her anymore? And she to you?" Mia asked quietly, feeling irrationally upset. What could Korum want with a regular human who couldn't hold a candle to one of his former lovers? If his attraction to Ellet had faded so quickly, what chance did Mia have of holding his attention longer? They had been together just over six weeks at this point. Would he get bored of her within another month?

Korum reached out and cupped her cheek in his large, warm palm. "Mia," he said softly, "what are you worrying about? I've known thousands of beautiful women, but I've never wanted one of them as much as I want you . . ."

Mia looked at him, the knot in her stomach easing.

"And you are far more appealing to me, physically, than she ever was," he continued, his eyes turning a brighter shade of gold. "How can you even have doubts about that at this point? Is it not enough that I all but keep you chained to my bed? If you were any more attractive to me, I would stay buried inside your sweet little body day and night . . . and then where would we be?"

A hot blush spread over Mia's face, and she could feel herself reacting physically to his words. At the same time, she realized that her sister and Ellet would be coming down any minute. "Korum, please," she whispered, "what if they overhear us?"

He gave her a wicked grin. "Then they'll learn something shocking—the fact that we have sex . . ."

As if on cue, Mia heard footsteps on the stairs, and Marisa entered the room, followed closely by Ellet.

Quickly pulling away from Korum, Mia jumped up and ran to her sister. "Marisa! How did it go?"

Marisa shook her head, looking like she was in a mild state of shock. "I barely felt anything when Ellet touched me, but now I'm already starting to feel less sick . . ."

"You'll feel even better in a couple of hours as the nanos gradually normalize your hormonal production," Ellet said, looking pleased. "Also, if you still have any residual traces of nausea, just take that powder I gave you and you should be fine for the rest of your pregnancy. And like I told you, I would be more than happy to come out here when it's time for you to deliver . . ."

Marisa sniffed, looking all teary-eyed, and then gave Ellet a hug, obviously surprising the K. "Thank you, Ellet, so, so much! I wish everyone knew how nice your kind can be—"

Ellet hugged her back a little awkwardly. "Thank you, Marisa, but remember what I told you. You can't go around telling people about this—or I could get in trouble. We're not supposed to interfere with humans too much—"

"Why not?" Mia asked. "What's the big deal if you

help one pregnant woman?"

Korum came up to her and wrapped his arm around her shoulders, pressing her against him. "I'll explain it to you later, my sweet," he said, and there was a warning note in his tone. "For now, why don't you and Marisa hang out for a while? I have to catch up with Ellet about a few things back in Lenkarda."

He wanted to be left alone with his former lover? The sick feeling of jealousy she thought she had under control returned in full force. Nevertheless, she nodded stiffly and asked, "Marisa, would you want to go for a walk on the beach?"

Her sister smiled. "Sure. That sounds lovely," she said, and Mia knew that the signs of tension had not escaped Marisa's sharp eye.

Korum bent down to kiss her forehead and then released her from his embrace. "Go ahead," he said. "Your morning shake is in the kitchen. I made one for Marisa as well. You can take it with you if you want."

Mia thanked him, and the two sisters left, grabbing their shakes on the way.

CHAPTER EIGHTEEN

"All right, baby sis, spill. What was up with your reaction back there?" Marisa took a sip of her shake and looked at Mia expectantly as they strolled along the water, the ocean surf pounding against the sand only a few feet away.

Mia kicked a small shell out of the way, getting sand into her flip-flop in the process. "I just learned he had a thing with Ellet in the past," she told Marisa glumly. "And now he wants to be alone with her in the house. How am I supposed to react to that?"

"Ouch."

"Yeah."

Marisa was silent for a few seconds, apparently mulling that over. "I don't think he has anything going on with her anymore . . ." she said thoughtfully. "In fact, I'm pretty sure of it. He has eyes only for you—it's almost scary, actually, how intensely he watches you all the time. Still, that wasn't a very nice thing to do. But maybe he had some business to discuss with her?"

"Probably," Mia agreed, shrugging. "He said it's been over between them for a few years and it was never serious in the first place. Still, I just can't help imagining the two of them together, you know?"

For about a minute, they walked in comfortable silence, slowly drinking their smoothies and looking out over the water.

Then Marisa spoke again. "You really love him, don't you?" she asked, sounding worried for the first time.

Mia sighed and looked down at the sand. "More than I can say," she admitted. "More than I could've ever imagined."

"Oh Mia . . ."

"I know, I know. I don't need a lecture on this. It can't possibly end well, believe me, I know."

Her sister reached out and squeezed her hand. "Well, for what it's worth, he seems crazy about you. Absolutely crazy. I've never seen anything like that. He looks at you like he wants to devour you—and like he would do anything for you at the same time. He seems obsessed with you, baby sis . . ."

Mia laughed, Marisa's words startling her out of her gloomy mood. "Oh, please, I'm sure you're exaggerating. We just have good chemistry, that's all—"

"No, Mia," Marisa shook her head, looking serious. "What you guys have is way more than that. I don't even know how to describe it. He watches your every move. It's kind of uncanny, actually. And he can't seem to go more than a couple of minutes without touching you . . ."

Mia flushed a little, wondering if her sister had overheard their earlier conversation. If so, then Ellet definitively did; the Krinar tended to have a sharper sense of hearing than most humans.

"How did you end up getting involved with him, anyway?" Marisa asked with unconcealed curiosity. "You never really told me the full story, just that BS about your lover from Dubai . . . You've always been so cautious and by the rules—I can't quite picture you jumping into an affair with a K."

Mia hesitated. She didn't want to lie to her sister anymore, but she also wasn't up to telling her family the full story. "It wasn't easy for me," she admitted. "I was pretty scared in the beginning, and Korum can be . . . intimidating at times. But I was very attracted to him, obviously, and he was very persistent . . . and, well, you know the rest of the story."

Marisa regarded her intently. "I see. I'm sure there's more to it, but you can tell me when you're ready."

"Thanks, Marisa. You're the best sister a girl can ask for," Mia told her sincerely.

"I know—and very modest, too." Her sister grinned as she said this, and Mia smiled back at her.

They walked some more, each occupied with her own thoughts, until Marisa spoke again. "Is there any way things could work out for you guys?" she asked, her face serious again. "Any way at all?"

Mia shook her head. "No, I don't see how. We are literally different species—with very different lifespans. He will ultimately leave me . . . and I don't know how I will survive that at this point."

"Oh Mia . . . Baby, I don't even know what to say . . ." There was a look of intense pity on Marisa's pretty face.

"You don't have to say anything," Mia told her calmly. "It's my own fault for falling in love with him. I could've found myself a nice, normal guy—someone like Connor—but no, I had to get involved with an alien. I'm sure I will ultimately recover . . . and maybe even meet a human man that I will grow to care about."

"Have you talked to him about any of this?"

"Not, I haven't," Mia told her honestly. "I'm too happy right now to bring this up quite yet. For once, I'm trying to seize the moment—to enjoy something without worrying about the consequences . . ."

Marisa smiled, but there was still a shadow of worry on her face. "You go, baby girl. Carpe diem and all that."

* * *

The Krinar watched the two girls walking slowly along the beach. They were both pretty, but only one held his interest.

There was no point in observing her now, rationally he knew that. He should be concentrating on his enemy, not some little human who couldn't possibly be a threat to his plans.

Yet he couldn't look away.

She laughed, turning her face up toward the sun, and he zoomed in, pausing the recording for a second. Her lips were parted, showing even white teeth, and her pale skin appeared luminous, almost glowing.

She looked happy, and he almost regretted what he had to do. If it worked tomorrow, she would be upset for a while.

At least until he had a chance to take her pain away.

* * *

That evening, Korum took the whole family out to dinner, bringing them to a gourmet restaurant that had recently opened in Hammock Beach, an exclusive private community not too far from Ormond.

To Connor's happy surprise, there was actual seafood on the menu, as well as steak and caviar. The prices for animal products were astronomical, of course, with some of the dishes costing close to what some teachers made in a week. Her parents gaped at the menu, stunned, until Korum told them firmly that the dinner was his treat and that he would not hear any protests in that regard. Initially hesitant, her family ultimately gave in, with Connor ordering himself a prime rib and her parents sharing a shrimp cocktail as an appetizer and lobster as the main course. Mia got noodles made from real egg, while Marisa had some Russian-style blinis with caviar. Korum, as usual, stuck to mostly plant-based fare, although he did allow a little butter in his hibachi vegetables. "One of the tastier human inventions," he explained wryly.

The first part of the dinner passed uneventfully, with Korum politely asking her parents about their jobs and how they came to this country as children. He seemed particularly interested in the immigrant experience and the acclimation process for humans. Her parents were more than happy to talk about that, and the conversation flowed smoothly and easily.

A few glasses of wine later, however, her brother-in-law began to venture into some less comfortable territory. "So why did you guys come to Earth, anyway?" Connor asked, looking at Korum with unconcealed curiosity.

Mia froze, remembering her lover's rather low opinion of the human race and its treatment of Earth—the planet the Ks regarded as their future home.

But she needn't have worried. Korum's parent-pleasing façade was firmly in place. "Our solar system is much older than yours," he explained casually. "And our star will begin to die long before your sun. So it made sense for us to begin preparing for that eventuality. Also, it's good to be diversified in terms of locations: if some kind of a cosmic disaster were to befall Krina or our home galaxy, at least some of the Krinar would survive."

"Oh, wow, you guys really think ahead, huh?"

Connor sounded impressed, and Korum gave him a small smile before steering the conversation to Mia's childhood and what she had been like in kindergarten.

The rest of the dinner flew by, with her family competing for a chance to tell the most amusing and embarrassing story about Mia as a baby—everything from her odd preference for purple clothes when she was three to Marisa bribing her with candy to get her to do her math homework in first grade.

"I find it hard to believe that Mia ever had to be forced to do her homework," Korum said, smiling at her warmly. "I can't get her to stop doing it now. Her work ethic is incredible—even Saret is impressed, and he's had a lot of talented and dedicated assistants over the years."

Her parents grinned, looking proud and pleased, and Mia realized yet again what a skilled manipulator Korum was. He had her family eating out of the palm of his hand, despite the fact that they should've been madly worried about their youngest daughter being in a relationship with an extraterrestrial predator. Not that she minded, of course. Her lover was doing exactly what Mia wanted—setting her parents' mind at ease—and she was grateful for that.

Finally, the dinner wrapped up around ten. Saying good-bye to her family, Mia climbed into Korum's Ferrari and they drove home, with Mia feeling happy and full from the delicious meal.

* * *

Waking up the next morning, Mia bounced out of bed full of energy. Quickly brushing her teeth, she put on the two-piece bathing suit that Korum had thoughtfully left for her and went to look for him.

She found him lounging by the pool, sunning himself like a big golden cat. Unlike a human, Korum never burned, his skin always the same lightly bronzed shade. Come to think of it, Mia had somehow managed to avoid sunburn herself thus far, despite not using any sunblock. For a second, she wondered if Korum had given her something to protect her skin without her knowing and then forgot about it, too excited to start the day.

Seeing her enter the pool area, Korum gave her a slow, sensuous smile that reminded Mia of the wicked things he'd done to her last night. Her lower belly tightened with remembered pleasure. He couldn't seem to get enough of her—and she of him—to the point that Mia was beginning to wonder whether they were addicted to each other after all. Of course, Korum had warned her of blood addiction, not sexual addiction, but she couldn't imagine craving him more than she did already.

Tall shrubs and a solid white fence surrounded the pool area, blocking it from the view of anyone passing by on the beach and providing privacy for the mansion's residents. Encouraged by that, Mia came up to him and ran her hand down his chest, reveling in the feel of his smooth, sun-warmed skin.

He grinned and caught her hand, bringing it to his mouth for a kiss. "Ah, my lady awakes," he teased, his soft lips nibbling lightly at the back of her hand.

A shiver of pleasure ran through her at his touch, and she suddenly felt much warmer. Fighting a blush, she asked, "Do you want to go to the beach this morning?"

They were supposed to meet her parents for lunch today and then drive to St. Augustine to visit the Alligator Farm, one of Mia's favorite attractions in the area. However, it was only 9 a.m. right now, so they had plenty of time to kill.

"What about breakfast?" he asked her. "You're not hungry?"

"I can eat a banana on the way," Mia told him, itching to go for a swim in the ocean. "I'm still sort of full from yesterday's dinner."

"Then let's go."

The beach in front of their house was beautiful and almost completely deserted. Although it was not a private beach, there were no hotels nearby and no easy parking for the potential beach-goers. As a result, only the wealthy residents of the beachfront houses and a few hardy souls practicing long-distance beach walking were likely to be found there.

Exiting through the gated pool area, they walked on a narrow wooden bridge that led from the house to the sand, bypassing the dunes.

As soon as they stepped off the bridge, Mia kicked off her flip-flops and ran toward the water, eager to test its temperature. At this time of year, the Atlantic was not as warm as it would be later in the summer, but she didn't care. Despite the relatively early hour, it was already hot outside, and she was looking forward to the coolness of the ocean.

They swam for a solid hour until Mia felt pleasantly tired, her muscles aching from the unusual exertion. She was surprised at her own endurance; other than swimming a little in Costa Rica in the evenings, she really hadn't done much cardio in recent months. Perhaps she was still in shape from a year ago, when Jessie had signed both of them up for a 5K charity race and Mia had gone on a mad exercise spree to prepare for it. Or maybe all that nutritious food Korum was feeding her was actually that good for her body.

When they finally came out of the water, Mia stretched out on a big towel they had brought from the house, and Korum lay down beside her. Closing her eyes, she relaxed, the hot rays of the sun beaming down on her skin. She vaguely wondered if she should put on sunblock, but she felt far too lazy to move. Just a few minutes, she promised herself, just enough to produce some vitamin D . . .

A pleasant tickling sensation woke her up from her nap some time later.

Opening her eyes, she turned her head to the side, squinting a little from the bright light. Korum was lying there beside her, propped up on one elbow. Looking down at her with a smile, he was gently stroking the side of her ribcage with one long finger. His dark hair gleamed in the sunlight, and there was a warm glow in his thickly lashed amber eyes.

"What?" Mia murmured, feeling a bit self-conscious. The bikini she was wearing left very little to the imagination, and the way he was staring at her right now made her feel absurdly shy.

"Nothing," he said softly. "Your skin just looks so delectable in this light. I never realized before how pretty such pale skin could be."

"Um, thank you . . ."

"And it blushes so prettily too," he teased, brushing his fingers against her suddenly too-warm cheeks.

Mia gave him a slightly embarrassed smile. It was still

so new to her, being in a relationship, having someone touching and admiring her body like that. And to have that someone be the gorgeous creature lying beside her—that was beyond anything Mia could've ever imagined.

"How long was I out for?" she asked, remembering her impromptu nap. "I really didn't mean to drift off . . ."

"Not all that long. About twenty minutes or so."

Mia yawned delicately, covering her mouth with the back of her hand. "Sorry about that . . . You must've been so bored—"

"I'm never bored with you," he said, still studying her. "I like watching you sleep. You always look so sweet and peaceful . . . like a dark-haired angel. I find it very relaxing, seeing you like that."

Mia grinned at him. Korum could be very strange sometimes. "That's good, I guess, considering how much I sleep."

He just smiled in response, tucking one of the curls behind her ear. "Are you getting hungry now? Or still full from last night's dinner?"

Mia considered it. "I could eat. But don't we have lunch with my parents soon?"

"In another two hours. You're probably going to starve by then."

"Hmm, okay. I want to go for another swim first, though."

"Sure. Want to go in now?"

"I actually have to run to the restroom first," Mia admitted. "Will you wait for me? I'll be back in a few minutes."

"Go ahead," Korum told her, grinning. "I'll wait."

Jumping up, Mia ran back toward the house. Entering the fenced pool area, she used one of the bathrooms on the first floor. Then she headed back to the beach, eagerly anticipating the pleasant coolness of the water on her overheated skin.

Approaching the tall fence, Mia pushed open the gate . . . and froze.

Right outside the fence, with the landscaping blocking her from the view of anyone on the beach, was Leslie—one of the Resistance fighters Mia had worked with.

And in her slim, muscular arms was a gun pointed directly at Mia's chest.

CHAPTER NINETEEN

For a few seconds, icy terror held Mia completely immobile, unable to think or react in any way. Just like a deer in the headlights, some part of her brain noted with morbid amusement. Her legs felt weak and heavy, as through she were caught in quicksand, and her vision had narrowed so that all she could see was the deadly weapon pointed at her.

And then a surge of adrenaline kicked in, clearing her head and sending her heart rate through the roof. If she didn't do something, she would die, Mia realized with utter clarity. Korum was too far away to help her if she screamed; the bullet would get her long before he got anywhere near the house.

"Hands up, bitch," Leslie ordered harshly, her delicate features so twisted with hatred that they were barely recognizable. "You fucking traitor, you're going to get exactly what you deserve—"

"What are you doing here, Leslie?" Mia interrupted, trying to keep the tremor out of her voice and slowly raising her hands. *Don't show your fear to a rabid dog. Never show your fear. Keep her talking. Buy yourself time.*

"Did you honestly think you could get away with it?" Leslie spit out, her arms shaking and her finger nervously tapping on the trigger. "Did you really think you could betray your entire race and live happily ever after, fucking that monster?"

Her clothes were ripped and dirty, Mia noted with some semi-functional part of her brain. The girl must've been on the run for quite some time.

"Leslie, listen to me," Mia said desperately, knowing that she probably only had seconds left. "If you shoot me, Korum will kill you. You won't be able to get away fast enough. He'll hear the shot, and he'll be on you—"

A mad, triumphant smile lit Leslie's face. For a second, she looked positively gleeful. "Oh, you think I'm risking my life to kill you?" she said contemptuously. "You think I'm that stupid? No, bitch, as much as I'd love to put an end to your worthless existence, my orders are to keep you alive—alive and out of the way while he deals with your lover . . ."

Horrified, Mia stared at her, sickening fear spreading through her veins. "What do you mean?" she whispered, her brain barely able to process the implications. "While who deals with him?"

Leslie laughed, clearly enjoying Mia's reaction. "I knew it. I knew you had fallen for that monster. I told John not to trust you, but he was stupidly convinced you were on our side. But I knew better. I knew you were just the type to fall for that pretty façade. Did he get you addicted too? Do you walk around now begging Ks to bite you every hour, like my brother did before they killed him?"

Mia's thoughts whirled in panic, her heart pounding

so hard she felt like it would break through her ribcage. At the same time, a fury slowly began to build deep in the pit of her stomach. "While who deals with him?" she repeated through clenched teeth, her voice low and mean.

Leslie's lips twisted into a parody of a smile. "You think the Keiths were alone?" she said mockingly. "You think they got caught and that's the end of it?"

Stunned, Mia could only stare at her in shock.

"Oh yes, there are more Ks involved," Leslie confided, and there was cruel pleasure on her face. "Your lover's being turned into particles as we speak . . ."

Mia sucked in her breath, her lungs unable to get enough air. Her vision darkened for a second, and then rage unlike anything she had ever experienced swept through her, leaving no room for fear.

And suddenly, she knew exactly what she needed to do.

For a brief moment, her gaze drifted to a point just beyond Leslie's shoulder, and she let an expression of wild joy light up her face.

Startled, Leslie turned to look behind her for a second, and Mia sprang at her, her hands closing around the gun even as the girl realized she'd been tricked.

The force of Mia's jump brought them both tumbling down on the ground, with Mia landing on top, her desperation giving her strength she didn't know she had. However, Leslie managed to maintain her grip on the weapon, her training and larger size giving her an immeasurable advantage, and they rolled, each trying to gain possession of the gun.

The heavier girl ended up on top, her weight pressing Mia into the ground. Her knee hit Mia in the stomach, and she gasped, air temporarily knocked out of her. At the same time, Leslie wrenched at the gun with both hands, nearly tearing Mia's arm out of her socket. The pain barely registered, dulled by the adrenaline coursing through her veins and the murderous fury filling her mind.

For the first time in her life, Mia knew what it felt like to truly want to kill someone, to tear them to shreds and watch them bleed. A reddish haze taking over her vision, she fought with no regard for her own safety or anything resembling fairness. Her face ended up near Leslie's shoulder, and she bit, her teeth sinking savagely into the fleshy part of her upper arm. The fighter screamed, and Mia delighted in her pain, in the metallic taste of blood filling her mouth. Her knee came up hard, smashing into Leslie's pubic bone with all the force that Mia could muster, and the girl gasped, her grip on the weapon loosening slightly.

That was all the opportunity Mia needed.

Instead of pulling at the gun, she pushed down, twisting at the same time. Leslie's index finger caught in the trigger guard, twisted with it, and the girl screamed as the digit snapped, bending unnaturally backwards.

Taking advantage of her distraction, Mia yanked at the weapon, wrenching it away from Leslie's hand.

And then, hardly cognizant of her own actions, she brought it down with savage force on top of Leslie's skull.

The girl's body went slack, blood seeping out from where the hard metal object made contact with her head. Gasping and shuddering, Mia pushed her away, her mind filled with only one thought: getting to Korum before it was too late.

Jumping up, she grabbed the gun and ran, ignoring the unconscious girl left lying on the ground.

Mia ran faster than she'd ever run in her life, her lungs burning and the rough wooden bridge floor cutting into her bare feet. The gun felt heavy in her hand, unfamiliar.

On the other end of the bridge, she could see a male Krinar standing with his back turned toward her, his right arm outstretched and pointed at Korum—who stood utterly still, his gaze glued to the object in the other K's hand.

Leslie hadn't lied. In another minute, it might be too late. Slowing slightly, Mia lifted her hand, aimed at the broad back of the K ahead of her, and squeezed the trigger.

Nothing happened except a soft snick. *Not loaded, the damn thing was not loaded.*

Throwing the weapon aside, she ran faster again. Dark spots danced in front of her eyes, interfering with her vision as her brain fought to get sufficient oxygen. Everything around her blurred, greyed out, as she sprinted toward the scene with every ounce of strength still left in her body. All she could see, all she could focus on, was the deadly scene ahead.

And then she was there, seeing the K looming in front of her, his large body shaking and sweat glistening on the back of his neck. Through the roaring of her heartbeat in her ears, Mia vaguely heard the soothing tone of Korum's voice as he tried to convince the K to put the weapon away, to just listen—and glimpsed the horror on her lover's face as he saw her running and realized her intention.

With no further thought, Mia leapt on top of the K, heedless of the futility of her attack, her fingers grabbing his hair and viciously yanking on it. Startled and screaming in sudden pain, the K flung her away from him with one powerful blow, sending her flying into the dunes nearly twelve feet away.

Her left side slamming heavily into the ground, Mia lay there for a moment, stunned, the wind completely knocked out of her. And then her lungs expanded and she drew in a gasping breath, sucking in some much needed air. Dizzy and disoriented, she tried to get up, rolling over onto her stomach and then attempting to rise up onto all fours.

As she moved, an agonizing pain shot up her left arm.

Whimpering, she glanced at her side, and her head spun at the sight of white bone sticking out through a bloody tear in her skin. Sudden hot nausea boiled up in her throat, and she retched uncontrollably, the contents of her stomach emptying onto the dry grass of the dune.

Falling onto her right side, she tried to crawl away, her limbs weak and shaking, when strong arms lifted her, cradling her against a familiar chest.

His entire body trembling, Korum knelt in the sand, holding her in his arms and rocking back and forth. His breathing was harsh and ragged, and Mia could hear his heart beating like a drum in his chest.

"Mia . . . Oh my sweet, I thought I lost you . . ." The terror in his voice was a mirror image of the fear she'd felt at the sight of him in danger. He seemed incapable of saying anything else, just holding her pressed against him as he fought to regain control of himself. Even in his panic, he seemed mindful of her injured arm, taking care not to cause her any more pain.

"Th-the K . . ." she managed to croak out. "D-did he . . . ?"

"Don't worry about it," Korum said rawly. "He's no longer a threat. You're alive and that's all that matters."

Still holding her, he got to his feet. "Don't look," he said roughly, carrying her toward the bridge.

Mia closed her eyes for a second, but it made her feel even more sick and nauseated, so she opened them right away.

And saw immediately why Korum had warned her not to look.

Lying on the sand, just a few feet away from them, was what used to be his attacker. The body was hardly recognizable as such now, with the right arm missing and a bloody hole where the head and neck used to be. Blood was everywhere, all over the place, covering the disfigured corpse, soaking into the sandy ground.

For a brief second, she thought it couldn't be real, but the metallic odor was undeniable, as was the underlying stench of something much more foul, like sewage. The scent of death, she realized with some still-rational part of her brain. She'd never smelled it before, but something primitive inside her knew and recoiled from it.

A horrified moan escaped her throat before she could suppress it.

Korum cursed, and his pace picked up until he was almost running toward the house, still taking care not to jostle her injured arm.

Closing her eyes, Mia tried to take deep breaths, to convince herself that she'd just seen a scene from a movie, that there wasn't really what used to be an intelligent being lying there dead and mangled in the sand of Ormond Beach. But the images before her eyes were too vivid and undeniable, and her stomach twisted. If she hadn't emptied it just a minute ago, she would have vomited again.

The K who held her in his arms had just literally torn apart his opponent.

CHAPTER TWENTY

Her stomach churning, she instinctively pushed against Korum's chest with her right hand, but he ignored her feeble attempt to free herself.

"Shh, my darling, it'll be all right," he whispered to her fiercely, entering the pool area and carrying her toward the house.

As they went through the gate, Mia opened her eyes again and saw that Leslie's body was still lying there, right outside the pool gate. With a strange detachment, she wondered if the Resistance fighter was dead too. She knew she should be horrified at the thought, but she simply felt numb right now—numb and cold inside.

Korum carried her up the stairs and into the large bathroom on the second floor. Placing her gently on her feet, he turned on the shower and adjusted the water settings while Mia stood there, weaving slightly and listlessly observing his actions. A kind of merciful haze had descended on her mind, partially shielding her from the brutal reality of the situation. She knew what she was seeing, but it didn't seem to touch her in any way, as though it were happening to someone else.

Korum's entire body was covered with blood and sand, his hair encrusted with it. He looked like he had been through a battle—which, actually, he had been. If she had understood that gruesome scene correctly, he had killed the other K with his bare hands.

Hot bile rose in her throat again, and she held it back with effort. Even though she knew it was self-defense, she was still horrified that her lover was capable of that level of violence.

But what frightened her even more was the fact that she was too.

Because underneath it all, she was ferociously glad that the other K was dead—that it was his body, not Korum's, lying there in pieces. If he had succeeded in his attack . . . If he had managed to kill Korum, Mia would have gladly killed him herself—either that, or died trying.

Her eyes drifted to the left, and she saw her own reflection in the large mirror hanging on the wall. Streaks of dried blood were all over her face, all around her mouth area—from when she'd bitten Leslie, she realized. Dirt, sand, and dried bits of grass covered her mostly naked body, and small twigs were stuck in her hair, adding to the overall murderous madwoman impression.

"Here, let's get you in there," Korum said softly, carefully picking her up and bringing her into the shower stall where he'd gotten the water to perfect temperature.

The hot spray felt amazing on her skin, and Mia realized that she felt chilled, frozen inside despite the hot weather. She was also trembling. Her body must've gone into shock, she thought with almost clinical objectivity. She didn't dare look at her arm for fear of embarrassing herself again; for now, the pain was somehow tolerable, as though she'd received an anesthetic of some kind. Unlike most people, Mia had never broken anything before, and she wondered if this is what it always felt like. If so, then it was truly not all that bad, definitely survivable.

"Stay here," Korum told her. "I'll be right back with something for your arm."

Mia obediently nodded, and he disappeared for a minute, returning with a small pill in his hand. Stepping into the shower, he gave it to her and told her to swallow it.

She did so, and the dull throbbing pain eased almost immediately.

"Close your eyes and don't look," he said. "I mean it, Mia. Keep them shut."

Taking a deep breath, she squeezed her lids tightly. She could feel his hands on her injured arm, manipulating it gently—and somehow, it didn't hurt at all when he straightened it, popping the bone into place.

"It's done," he told her hoarsely. "You can open your eyes now."

Mia looked at him, and the frozen shell encasing her suddenly cracked.

Harsh sobs broke out of her throat, and she sank to the floor, shaking uncontrollably. All the terror and the violence she'd just experienced came rushing to the front of her mind, completely overwhelming her. She could've lost him, they could've both died, he had brutally slaughtered another Krinar, and she might've killed Leslie . . . It was too much, all of it, and Mia brought her knees to her chest, her body shuddering with the force of her gasping sobs.

"Mia, shhh, darling, it's over. It's over, I promise you . . ." he murmured, kneeling and gathering her closer to him. Reaching up, he directed the shower head so the water cascaded over them and simply let her cry, knowing that was exactly what she needed right now.

After a few minutes, her sobs began to quiet, and he lifted her, placing her carefully on her feet and removing her swimsuit. Then, pouring soap into his palm, he washed every inch of her and shampooed her hair, removing all traces of blood and dirt from her body. Afterwards, he did the same to himself, until they were both completely clean.

Turning off the water, he stepped out of the shower stall and came back with a big fluffy towel, which he wrapped around her. Too traumatized to do anything else, Mia just stood there, accepting his ministrations.

"Is she dead?" she asked dully, thinking of the girl she'd left bleeding and unconscious by the pool gate.

Korum shook his head, toweling himself off as well. "I don't think so—I saw her breathing as we passed by. I called the guardians who were in the area watching your family. They're almost here. They'll take her into custody and clean up the rest—"

"Who was he? Did you know him?"

For a second, rage flashed in his eyes, and then Korum controlled himself with visible effort. "I did," he said, and she could hear the barely suppressed anger in his voice. "I had no idea he was involved with the Keiths, none at all. I can't believe he fooled all of us like that."

Mia continued to look at him, and he took a deep breath, trying to calm himself.

"His name was Saur," Korum explained evenly. "He worked in your lab—in Saret's lab—ever since we first came to Earth. He was the one who left a few weeks ago, creating the opening that you filled. Saret had always spoken very highly of him. Saur was his youngest and most brilliant assistant—at least until Adam had arrived. I don't know what motivated him to get involved with the Keiths; he had so much to offer our society . . . And why he came out here to kill us, I have no idea . . ."

"To kill *you*," Mia corrected him, feeling cold again at the thought. "Leslie told me her orders were to keep me alive and out of the way while he dealt with you . . ."

His eyebrows rose. "I see," he said thoughtfully, leading her out of the bathroom and into the bedroom.

He had already prepared clothes for her to wear to lunch with her parents—a pretty peach-colored sundress and a silky white thong—and he dressed her carefully, as though she were a small child, his hands particularly gentle around her broken arm.

Which didn't hurt at all now, Mia realized.

Mildly curious, she glanced down at her left side and blinked, hardly able to believe her eyes. Where there had been a bloody gash with bone sticking out just a few minutes ago, there was now perfectly smooth skin, without even a trace of any injury.

Surprised, Mia moved her arm, and it worked quite well. She lifted it, flexing her bicep, and everything appeared to be functioning normally. How did a little pill do this?

In general, she felt much better now. The shower and the medicine he'd given her had done wonders for her physical state, even if her mind was still trying to come to terms with everything they'd just been through.

"It should be all right now," Korum said, watching her testing out the arm.

He had already dressed himself as well, putting on a white T-shirt and a pair of jeans. He looked so gorgeous—and so *alive*—that Mia almost started crying again at the thought of what had almost happened.

"Now," he said softly, coming up to her and tilting her

chin up with his fingers, "tell me . . . What the fuck you were thinking, risking your life like that?"

Mia blinked at him, startled by the quiet fury in his voice. "Leslie said he was going to kill you. Sh-she said you were b-being turned into p-particles . . ." Her voice trembling with remembered horror, she could barely hold back the tears that filled her eyes again.

"So you what? Jumped an experienced fighter who held a gun on you? Tackled a Krinar who could kill you with one blow?" Korum was almost shaking with rage now, his eyes completely taken over by those dangerous yellow flecks. "Don't you realize how fragile, how delicate you are? How easily something can hurt you, snuff out your life completely?"

Mia swallowed. "I couldn't bear it if something had happened to you—"

"To me? How do you think I would've felt if something had happened to *you*?" He was almost beside himself, his teeth tightly clenched and a muscle pulsing in his jaw. She had never seen him in this state, and Mia vaguely wondered if she should be afraid. After all, he had just brutally killed an intelligent being. Yet, for some reason, she couldn't muster up even an ounce of fear. Somehow, in the last couple of weeks, she had gone from thinking he would kill her for spying on him to feeling completely safe with him. Even angry, he wouldn't hurt her; she now knew it with bone-deep certainty.

"I don't know," she told him, and watched his eyes turn even brighter. Faster than she could blink, he picked her up and sat down on the bed, cradling her on his lap. Holding her so tightly that she could barely breathe, he buried his face in her hair, and Mia could feel the fine tremors shaking his big, muscular frame.

"You don't know?" he whispered harshly. "You truly

don't know that you mean everything to me?"

Hardly daring to believe her ears, Mia pushed at his chest to put a little distance between them so she could look up at his face. "I do?"

"Of course, you do." His gaze burned into her with an intensity she had never seen before. "How could you doubt it?"

"Are . . . are you saying you love me?" she asked tremulously, afraid to even voice such a possibility. What if he said no? What if she'd misunderstood him, and he would now laugh at her silliness? Her chest tightened in anxious anticipation.

"Mia, I love you more than life itself," he said, his voice rough with emotion. "If anything happened to you . . . If you were gone, I would not want to go on living. Do you understand me?"

Mia nodded, too overcome by her own feelings to say anything. He loved her? This beautiful, amazing man loved her?

His eyes narrowed. "And if you ever, ever put your life in danger like that—"

Mia didn't let him finish. Instead, she reached up and buried her hands in his hair, bringing his head down toward her. And then she kissed him, expressing the full depth of her emotions in the way in which they had always communicated best.

At first, he froze, as if wary of hurting her, but then he groaned low in his throat and kissed her back, his hands tightening around her again and his mouth hungry and desperate on hers.

Mia clung to him with equal desperation, her earlier fear and adrenaline morphing into a frenzy of arousal. He was alive—they were both alive—and her body wanted, needed to reaffirm that fact in the most primitive, instinctual way possible.

She ended up on her back on the bed, pinned underneath his hard, muscled weight, her hands frantically tearing at his T-shirt. She felt like she was starving, like she would die without his touch, her body crying out to be filled by him. His kiss consumed her, his tongue stabbing deep into her mouth, and Mia sucked on it, craving his taste, wanting all of him. She felt unbearably hot, her skin too tight, too sensitive to contain the desire burning within her, and she arched toward him, frantically trying to get even closer.

He groaned again, her frenzied response provoking an equally passionate reaction from him. His left hand twisted in her hair, holding her head still for his mouth's ravishment, while his right hand bunched up the skirt of her dress, exposing her lower body. Now only her tiny thong and his jeans stood between them, and he made short work of that too, tearing off her underwear and unzipping his pants. And then he was inside her with one powerful thrust, his cock penetrating her in one smooth slide.

Gasping at the shock of his sudden entry, Mia dug her nails into his shoulders, both stunned and immeasurably relieved to have him inside her. He was unbelievably hot and thick, and the blunt, heavy force of him was exactly what she needed right now. Her muscles quivered, stretching around his large shaft, even as her inner core melted, liquefied at the feel of him filling her so perfectly, quenching the emptiness inside.

He began to move, each stroke pressing her deeper into the mattress, and she was screaming, the tension inside her peaking until her entire body seemed to explode with the force of her orgasm, her sheath uncontrollably pulsing and clenching around his cock.

Panting, he rose up on his elbows, staring down at her with eyes that were almost pure gold. Droplets of sweat were visible on his forehead, and his face was flushed underneath the bronzed hue of his skin. He looked magnificent and savage, and Mia couldn't look away from the blazing intensity in his gaze. He hadn't climaxed yet, and his cock was still hard inside her.

"You're mine," he told her hoarsely, and Mia couldn't dispute the truth of that, not with him lodged so deeply inside her body, inside her heart. She felt incredibly vulnerable like this, but she now knew that he was vulnerable too—that she also held power over him.

"And you're mine," she whispered back, her hands tightening on his shoulders, and felt his shaft jerk inside her as his body reacted physically to her words.

He began thrusting heavily into her again, his hips hammering and recoiling, imprinting himself on her flesh with a ferocity that she almost matched. She felt each thrust deep within her belly, the head of his cock pushing against her cervix, the pleasure so sharp it was verging on pain . . . and then she could feel him swelling up further inside her and her body tightened as another violent orgasm ripped through her. At the same time, he bucked in her arms, achieving his own climax with a hoarse cry, his semen releasing inside her in a few short, warm bursts.

For about a minute, they stayed like that, their bodies joined together as their breathing returned to normal and their heartbeats slowed. Mia had never felt so connected to another person in her life. It was as though they had ceased to be separate individuals, as though the sexual act had linked them together in some way that went beyond the physical. She could feel his heart beating in tune with her own, the heat and scent of his body surrounding her, cocooning her as he held her in his embrace, his weight pleasantly heavy on top of her.

After a while, he rolled off her and gathered her toward him, letting her lie on top of his chest. She knew that she should get up and clean herself, that they had to leave soon for the lunch with her parents, that there was still a lot they needed to discuss—but in this particular moment, she just wanted to lie there with him, shutting out the rest of the world.

She loved him, and he loved her, and that was all that mattered right now.

* * *

The guardians arrived a few minutes later, their ship landing soundlessly on the beach near the house. Zipping his still-intact jeans and dropping a kiss on her forehead, Korum went to greet them, leaving Mia to freshen up before their lunch.

Getting up, Mia noted wryly that her legs were still trembling a bit and her sex throbbing subtly in the aftermath of their passionate encounter. She had no idea what sex would be like with another man, with a human man, but she strongly suspected that what she experienced every night—and frequently during the day—was far from typical. Maybe in the future, when they'd been together longer, their insatiable desire for each other would ease a little, but for now, no amount of sex seemed enough. Was this what Korum had meant by their unusual chemistry? Had he known it would be like this from the very beginning?

Going to the bathroom, she splashed some water on her face and tried to smooth her curls into a more presentable state. Underneath the paleness of her skin, her face glowed with subtle color, and her lips were fuller, swollen a little from his kisses. She looked happy and satisfied, a far cry from the traumatized mess she'd been earlier in the day. She also looked and smelled like she'd just had sex. Another quick shower was clearly in order.

Ten minutes later, she was clean and dressed in a different outfit. It was almost time for them to drive to St. Augustine, so she went to look for Korum.

She found him in the pool area, talking to three Krinar males who were dressed in what looked like light grey uniforms. She remembered seeing similar uniforms on the Ks who had apprehended the Keiths two weeks ago.

These had to be the guardians Korum had mentioned.

One of the guardians held Leslie, who was now conscious and looked like she had a bad headache, or maybe a concussion. Mia felt hugely relieved. She hadn't killed her after all, nor did it seem like she'd caused any permanent damage. However, Leslie did look terrified to have been captured by the creatures she regarded as real-life monsters, and Mia almost felt bad for her, remembering how scared she'd been of Korum in the beginning. Almost—because she couldn't forget the fact that the girl had held her at the gun point and conspired to kill Korum.

Now that she could think again, Mia wondered why Saur wanted Leslie to keep her—Mia—alive and out of the way. Did he think she would somehow be of use to the Resistance? Or did he want something else from her? And why was Korum his target? None of it made any sense.

Suddenly, something occurred to her. The memory loss of the Keiths! If Saur had access to some of the lab's technology and enough knowledge, he might've been the one to erase their memories. In fact, Adam once mentioned that Saur had worked on mind manipulation.

Excited, Mia approached Korum and the guardians.

Giving him a huge smile, she said, "I just realized something . . . If Saur worked in Saret's lab—"

Korum nodded approvingly. He had obviously figured it out already. "Exactly. This would explain quite a bit—though I still don't really understand his motivations."

Leslie observed their exchange with a bitter expression on her pain-twisted face. "Xeno bitch," she muttered, shooting Mia a hate-filled look.

"Keep your mouth shut," Korum said coldly, staring at the girl with a contemptuous look on his face. "You should thank whatever pathetic deity you pray to that Mia didn't get hurt today—and that the gun was not loaded. If anything had happened to her, you and all your Resistance buddies would have learned the true meaning of suffering. Do you understand me?"

The fighter visibly gulped, but refused to look away. Mia reluctantly admired her courage; had Korum said that to *her*, she would've been scared out of her wits. Maybe Leslie was too, but she had a pretty good poker face.

Mia wondered what was going to happen to the girl. Did the Ks intend to let her go after embedding surveillance devices in her, as they'd done to the Resistance fighters who had attacked them? She determined to ask Korum about that later, when they were alone. Despite everything, she still hoped that Leslie wouldn't be punished too severely for her actions; the fighter didn't seem like a bad person—just very misguided in her hatred for the Ks.

Two more guardians came in through the gate. "It's done," one of them said in Krinar. "All the evidence has been recorded and removed."

"Good," Korum told them. "Thank you for coming out here so quickly."

The guardian who had just spoken nodded. "Of course. If you think of anything else relating to this attack, just contact us."

Korum promised to do so and the guardians left, taking Leslie with them.

"What are they going to do to her?" Mia asked, observing the look of panic on the girl's face as a guardian carried her away in the direction of the beach.

"She'll undergo some rehabilitation," Korum said. "She's caused too much trouble at this point, and we'll give her the same treatment that we gave the other Resistance leaders we've captured thus far."

"A rehabilitation?"

Now that Mia had spent some time in Saret's lab, she knew that influencing someone's mind to that degree was a very complex and delicate process. It was easy to cause irreparable damage, and every brain was highly unique—what worked for one person might not work for another. Mind-tampering was the most advanced branch of Krinar neuroscience—and even Saret admitted that it was still very imperfect.

"Not the same kind of rehabilitation as for the Keiths," Korum said. "A much milder version. It doesn't take as much effort with humans; she might simply walk away with a small memory loss."

Mia had thought of something else in the meanwhile. "Korum," she asked slowly, "you're not going to be in trouble, are you? Because of what happened on the beach?" Because of the Krinar he'd torn apart—but she couldn't quite bring herself to say that.

He gave her a reassuring smile. "No. It was a very clear case of self-defense, and I have recordings to prove it."

"Recordings?"

He lifted his hand, showing her his palm. "Having

embedded technology is very handy. Also, if we need to go even further, we can get some images from the satellites we have in Earth's orbit. What happens on a public beach like that is never a secret. There might be an investigation, just to follow protocol, but there won't be a trial."

Mia exhaled a sigh of relief. "I'm so glad." Stepping toward him, she wrapped her arms around his waist and hugged him tightly, inhaling his warm, familiar scent. He hugged her back, pressing her against him with one hand and stroking her hair with another. They stood like that for a minute, simply enjoying each other's nearness, letting the horror of the day dissipate in the warmth of their embrace.

CHAPTER TWENTY-ONE

Mia's parents met them for lunch in St. Augustine at a small, quaint restaurant called The Present Moment Cafe. Before K-Day, it was one of the few vegan restaurants in the area, showcasing various exotic ingredients and unusual raw dishes. These days, such places were much more common—diners and steakhouses were now the rarity—but the cafe still enjoyed the reputation of being one of the best at gourmet plant-based food.

Korum again insisted on paying for the meal, and her parents acquiesced after a few half-hearted protests. During the lunch, he entertained them with some stories about his initial visit to Earth seven hundred years ago and how different Europe was at that time. Mia could see that her parents were absolutely fascinated—and so was she, to be honest—and time passed by very quickly.

Looking at him interacting so easily with her family, Mia marveled at Korum's incredible composure—or maybe it was simply good acting skills. He laughed and joked with her parents as though nothing had happened, as though he hadn't just killed a fellow K with his bare hands. She tried not to think about that, to move past this morning's events, but she couldn't help the disturbing images that kept flashing into her mind.

Although Mia knew that violence had been a big part of Krinar history and culture, it didn't seem like it was anymore. At least, Mia hadn't run into anything of the sort during her two-week sojourn in Lenkarda. She knew that Korum's favorite sport consisted of fighting—and she knew about the Arena challenges. But that was a far cry from killing someone on the beach. Was Korum bothered by his actions at all, or did he not care? Was the man she loved—and who apparently loved her back—a remorseless killer? And if he was, did *she* care?

After a couple of hours, they said goodbye to her parents and drove to the Alligator Farm, one of St. Augustine's most popular attractions. Korum seemed very interested in seeing the cold-blooded creatures, explaining that they were quite different from anything they had on Krina.

As they wandered through the paths, studying the various species of alligators and crocodiles, Mia decided to bring up something that had been on her mind since this morning.

"Have you killed before?" she asked, trying to sound nonchalant about the whole thing.

Korum stopped and looked at her. "I was wondering when you'd get around to that," he said softly, and there was an unreadable expression on his face. "What would you like me to tell you, my sweet? That I've never been in any other situation where I've had to defend myself and others? That I've managed to live for two thousand years without ever having to take a life?"

Mia swallowed, staring up at him. "I see."

"Do you?" His mouth twisted slightly. "Do you really? I know you've lived a very sheltered life, my darling, and I'm glad for you. If I could've spared you what you saw this morning, believe me, I would have."

"How many?" Mia knew she should stop, but she couldn't help herself. "How many people—Krinar or human—have you killed in your life?"

He sighed. "Not as many as you're probably thinking right now. When I was young, I was very hot-headed and got into a few fights over matters that now seem quite trivial. Several of my opponents challenged me to the Arena, and I accepted their challenge. And once we were in the Arena . . . Well, you might not understand this, but it's very hard for us to stop once the first blood gets spilled. In the heat of battle, we operate purely on instinct—and our instinct is to destroy the enemy at all costs. That's why the Arena fights are so dangerous and so rare these days, because the outcome is often quite deadly—"

"Why hasn't your government outlawed it, then?" Mia interrupted, trying to understand this peculiar quirk of Krinar culture. "Why not get rid of such a barbaric custom? Your society is so advanced in every other way . . ."

"Because the violence is more contained this way—better controlled, if you will," he explained calmly, watching her with those amber eyes. "If someone has a problem with me, they can just challenge me in the Arena instead of going after my family. Vendettas still happen occasionally, but they're much more rare than in the past—and our society is much more peaceful as a result. Technically, it's illegal to kill someone in the Arena, but nobody has ever been prosecuted for getting carried away in a fair fight."

"Is that what happened today? You got carried away during the fight?"

He nodded, his mouth tightening. "I did . . . but my only regret is that I didn't get a chance to question him, to find out why he did what he did. He hurt you—he could've easily killed you—and he deserved exactly what he got."

Mia looked away, not really knowing what to say. He had killed to protect her—and she probably would've done the same for him—but she still found it frightening, knowing that he was capable of taking someone's life with so little compunction.

"What about humans?" she asked as they walked further, thinking of all the rumors she'd heard about K brutality during the Great Panic months. "Have you killed many humans?"

He didn't answer for a few moments. "Why are you doing this, Mia?" he said quietly as they stopped in front of a large alligator pen. "Why do you ask questions to which you don't want to know the answer?"

"I don't know," Mia told him honestly. "In some ways, you're still such a mystery to me. I love you, yet I feel like I barely know you . . ."

He gazed down into the water with seeming fascination, watching the alligators gliding smoothly through the water. The tourists gave the spot where they were standing a wide berth; like most humans, they had correctly deduced that the K among them was by far the most dangerous creature in the vicinity. Mia was now so used to this that she barely paid attention. Whenever they went somewhere in public, Korum's presence inevitably attracted frightened stares and whispers among the human population.

After a while, he turned to look at her. "Yes, Mia," he

said wearily. "I've killed humans. Some in self-defense, some for other reasons. I've had many interactions with your kind over the centuries, and not all of them have been good. Is there anything else you would like to know?"

Mia moistened her lips, staring at him. "Would you have killed Peter that night? In the club? If I hadn't stopped you?"

"You didn't stop me, Mia," Korum said coolly. "I had already made up my mind to let him go with a warning. His offense was not grave enough to warrant anything more."

A breath she hadn't realized she'd been holding escaped her lips in relief. "I see."

"Of course," he added, his eyes glittering, "if he had touched you more—if he had slept with you—the outcome would've been different."

Mia's heart skipped a beat. "You would've killed him for that?" she whispered, a shiver running down her spine.

Korum didn't answer, just looked at her evenly . . . and she knew that what she had always sensed about him was true.

He *was* dangerous—not to her, but to everyone else. As civilized as he appeared on the outside, as advanced as the Ks were with their science and technology, at the core, he was a predator. A predator with a violent nature and a deeply ingrained territorial instinct.

A predator who apparently loved her as much as she loved him.

* * *

That evening, Marisa and Connor came over for dinner

again, and Korum prepared a smaller version of the feast he'd made the previous day. Her sister was positively glowing, her skin flushed with healthy color and her eyes sparkling. Her appetite was back to normal, and she was again eating all her favorite foods. Whatever procedure Ellet had performed on her seemed to be having the promised effect.

Connor was beyond grateful. "I finally have my wife back," he confided to them when Marisa went to use the restroom. "The last few weeks have been hell—I was so afraid she would need to be hospitalized for the rest of the pregnancy. The horror stories we'd heard about women with her type of condition . . ."

Korum smiled at him. "I'm glad everything worked out. Ellet is quite skilled—"

Mia felt a pang of jealousy at his praise of the woman who had been his lover, but she did her best to ignore it.

"—and she was more than happy to help in this situation."

After the dinner was over, the four of them decided to go see a movie—the latest James Bond thriller featuring a K villain. Korum was highly amused by the premise, particularly the parts where the human agent managed to outwit the evil K and use the Krinar's own technology to thwart his plan of exterminating all humans. The villain was played by a human actor who actually did a fairly decent job of imitating a K with the aid of computer graphics, but Mia still found his performance inadequate. Marisa and Connor really enjoyed it, however, and peppered Korum with tons of questions on their way back to the house.

As Mia observed their interactions, she realized that her family was completely enthralled with her lover. They'd never seen his truly intimidating side, and they'd never had a reason to fear him—the way Mia did in the beginning. Instead, to them, he was a fascinating foreigner who could entertain them with endless interesting facts and stories, a generous benefactor who had already given them the priceless gift of improved health, and a kind boyfriend who treated Mia like a princess.

And Mia loved it. Never in her wildest dreams would she have expected her family to get on so well with her alien lover. She'd thought they would be frightened and worried sick about her—and they probably would've been if Korum hadn't put in the effort to win them over. That, more than anything, showed her how deeply he cared. He'd known that her family was important to her, and he'd made sure that they would be comfortable with their relationship—or at least as comfortable as they could be knowing that their daughter's boyfriend was not human.

Her thoughts turned to the future again, and she felt a familiar ache in her chest—the same sensation she always got when she thought about the inevitable end of their relationship. He loved her, but surely that couldn't last forever. How long would she remain young and pretty? Ten years, twenty if she was lucky? Granted, some of the actresses these days looked amazing even into their late forties and fifties. Maybe Mia would as well, particularly if Krinar medical prowess extended to cosmetic procedures as well. She pictured Ellet giving her a facelift and almost shuddered at the thought of the beautiful K seeing her when she was old and wrinkled.

Finally, they arrived back at the house and said goodbye to Marisa and Connor, who picked up their car and drove away.

Smiling, Mia waved to them and came into the house,

where Korum was already sitting on the couch, studying something in his palm.

Hearing Mia come in, he looked up and gave her a smile. "You were very quiet on the way back," he said, regarding her inquisitively. "You didn't like the movie?"

She approached and sat down next to him. "It was entertaining," she answered, shrugging.

"Then what's the matter? Are you still upset about what happened earlier today?" He reached out and took her hand, lightly massaging her palm in a way that made her melt a little inside.

"No." Mia stared at the large hand cradling hers so tenderly. Her fingers appeared tiny and delicate in his grasp, the pale color of her skin contrasting erotically with his darker hue. "Well, maybe. I don't know. I'm trying not to think about it too much. The movie was a good distraction, actually . . ."

"So then what?" He clearly had no intention of letting it go.

Mia raised her eyes to meet his gaze. "I was just wondering about the future, that's all. I know I should focus on the present and enjoy what we have right now, but I just can't help it sometimes—"

He leaned toward her and kissed her lightly, his lips stopping her next words. "We'll talk about this when we're back in Lenkarda," he murmured, pulling back and looking at her with a rather enigmatic expression on his face. "Don't worry about anything right now. It will all work out, I promise."

Surprised, Mia blinked at him, and then she remembered that he'd mentioned something similar a few weeks ago, when they were still in New York. Unbearably curious, she opened her mouth to ask him another question, but Korum kissed her again and all rational thought left her head.

Picking her up, he carried her upstairs to their bed, and Mia didn't have a chance to think for the rest of the night.

CHAPTER TWENTY-TWO

The next morning, Mia woke up in Korum's arms. It was such an unusual occurrence that her eyes flew open as soon as she realized what was happening.

She was lying on her side, cradled against his body. They were both naked, and she could feel his semi-hard erection prodding at the curve of her buttocks. Startled, Mia turned around to look at his face and saw that he was wide awake.

At her sudden movements, he smiled and brushed his lips against her forehead. "You're awake, I see."

She nodded, blinking at him sleepily. "What are you doing here? You're usually up much earlier . . ."

"I didn't want to leave you alone," Korum explained softly, caressing her cheek. "You seemed to be sleeping restlessly, crying out every couple of hours, and I wanted to make sure you were okay."

Touched, Mia burrowed against him, holding him tightly. "Thank you," she mumbled into his shoulder. "I think I must've had nightmares after yesterday." She vaguely remembered some dreams involving guns and blood, and she was surprised that she'd actually been able to sleep through the night. Undoubtedly, Korum's presence beside her had helped in that regard.

He slowly stroked her hair. "Of course, my darling. It's entirely understandable."

"Do you ever have nightmares?" she asked, pulling back, the psychology student in her suddenly curious about the topic.

"Not typically," Korum admitted, his hand now playing with her long curls. "I usually sleep very deeply for a couple of hours, and then I wake up. I can't remember the last time I had a dream of any kind. It can happen for us, but it's rarer than for humans. Our sleep cycle is somewhat different."

"Oh, I see."

"What do you want to do today?" he asked. "We don't have any plans right now."

"I was thinking we could have dinner with my parents again tonight, but I don't know about the day . . . No beach, though—I don't think I'm ready to go back there yet."

"Of course." His body tensed for a moment. "Why don't we do something else entirely? How about a trip to Orlando? We could visit one of those theme parks with roller coasters and all—"

"What, like Disney World?" Mia gave him an incredulous look.

"Sure," he said seriously. "Or maybe Universal. That's the more adult one, right?"

Unable to help herself, Mia burst out laughing. "Really? You want to go to Universal Studios?" She pictured the two of them standing in line for the

Incredible Hulk, and all the tourists freaking out at the sight of a K near their children.

"Yeah, why not?"

Why not indeed. Still giggling, Mia said, "Okay, I'm game. We can go to Islands of Adventure—that's the part of Universal that has more roller coasters. How are we getting to Orlando? Driving?"

"Might as well. I don't mind driving—it gives me a chance to see more of the area." He grinned at her, looking so charming and carefree that she couldn't help but kiss the dimple on his left cheek.

When her lips touched his face, however, she could feel his mood shifting. By now, she was so attuned to him that she realized immediately what he wanted. Sure enough, when she pulled back, he was regarding her with a heavy-lidded golden gaze. "This is why I don't normally stay in bed with you," he muttered before his lips descended on hers and his hand ventured lower between her thighs.

And for the next hour, they forgot all about Orlando, caught up in their own wild ride.

* * *

Two hours later, they were whizzing down the highway at over a hundred miles per hour. With anyone else at the wheel, Mia would've been scared out of her mind, but Korum's reflexes were better than any race car driver's and she felt utterly safe with him. For the first twenty minutes of the ride, he drove with the top down, but Mia's hair kept blowing into her face, and they had to pull over to put the top up.

"I should really cut this mess," Mia grumbled as they got back on the highway, trying to smooth down the curly explosion on her head. It was futile. Wind and her hair didn't mix.

"Don't even think about it," Korum said seriously. "I love your hair long."

Mia sighed. "Fine. Maybe I'll just get it straightened . . ."

"Why? Your curls are beautiful. Leave them just as they are."

"You're weird," Mia told him. "Most men like straight, silky hair, not this rat's nest I've got going on here—"

"I don't care what most men like. Leave the hair as it is." His tone was utterly uncompromising.

Mia smiled to herself, mentally shaking her head. Even in this small matter, he had to be in control. It was strange that she didn't mind it quite as much anymore, though nothing had really changed. She was still his charl, and he still had way too much power over her life. The difference was that now she knew that he loved her, that she wasn't just a human toy to him.

A little tidbit from her encounter with Leslie nagged at the back of her mind. "Korum," she said tentatively, "what exactly is this blood addiction you've warned me about before? Leslie said something about it yesterday . . ."

Keeping his eyes on the road, Korum asked, "What did she say?"

Mia struggled to remember the girl's exact words. "It was something like her brother was addicted and he was walking around begging Ks to bite him every hour until they killed him . . ."

For a few seconds, Korum remained silent. "That sounds like a particularly unfortunate case," he said after some time. "It must've happened not long after we first arrived here."

"What do you mean?"

"Do you remember how I told you that we no longer require blood to survive? That it's now basically a pleasure drug for us?"

"Yes, of course."

"Well, it turns out that there's a side effect to getting too much of this drug. The pleasure is so intense that it's addictive for us—and for the humans we're drinking from. However, for a Krinar to become physically addicted, he or she has to drink from the same human more frequently than a couple of times a week. Essentially, the Krinar gets addicted to the specific DNA signature in that human's blood. It's a peculiar side effect of the genetic fix that allows us to survive without blood. Some of our best scientists are currently studying this phenomenon and trying to figure out why it's happening and how it can be stopped."

Mia stared at him in fascination. "So what happens when you get addicted? Is it physically painful?"

"When the Krinar is separated from their human for whatever reason, yes. They can't go longer than a few hours without getting their fix—and that's a problem both for the human and the Krinar."

"So is that what happened to Leslie's brother? I'm not sure I fully get it . . ."

"No, it works differently for humans. Your species gets addicted to the substance in our saliva, but any Krinar's saliva would work. I don't exactly know what happened to Leslie's brother, but I can venture a guess. It sounds like he might've been involved in some of the early x-clubs—"

"X-clubs?"

"X-clubs, xeno-clubs—that's your slang term for

nightclubs where humans go to interact with our kind."

Mia blinked. "I've never heard of this before. Is it like the websites where humans advertise to have sex with Ks?"

He looked vaguely amused. "Pretty much. The websites are usually for those who are just curious. Very few people posting there would consider actually going through with their fantasy. The ones who are serious about it go to x-clubs."

"Really?" Mia was amazed that she'd never come across this before. "Where are these clubs located? Are there some in New York City?"

"No, they're actually close to our Centers—we generally don't like going to major cities. That's probably why you don't know about them. There are a few in Costa Rica, some in New Mexico and Arizona, some in Thailand and the Philippines . . ."

"And Ks actually go to these places?"

Korum nodded. "Some do, especially those who are otherwise reluctant to venture outside of the Centers. I've never gone myself, because I don't have a problem spending time in human cities and towns. Many Krinar do, though; they can't stand the crowds or the pollution, so the clubs are a convenient way for them to enter into sexual relations with humans."

"So you think Leslie's brother might've gone to an x-club?"

"It's a likely possibility. In the last couple of years, these places have become more strictly regulated. Now a particular human is only allowed in twice a week, and the Krinar who go there are warned against sharing that human for the night. However, in the early days, everything was much more disorganized, and some humans got carried away. They would hook up with one or more Krinar per night and have their blood taken much too frequently."

Mia wrinkled her nose, disturbed at the thought. When Korum took her blood, it was such a transcendent experience that she couldn't imagine sharing it with anyone else. Of course, she couldn't imagine having sex with anyone else either, so it probably wasn't a fair comparison. "I see."

"My guess is that Leslie's brother became seriously addicted. Why he died, I have no idea. Perhaps he became violent and tried to force one of the Krinar women—that's been known to happen and could be one reason why he would've been killed—"

"A human forcing a Krinar?"

"I didn't say he would've succeeded. Our women are much weaker than Krinar men, but they are still stronger than humans. However, an attempt would've been sufficient to earn him a death sentence. No sane human would try such a thing, of course, but some of these addicts are not rational, particularly when they've been deprived for a while."

Mia shuddered. The whole thing sounded awful. "Is there a cure?" she asked, trying to imagine how desperate those poor people must be.

"Not yet. As far as I know, it's still in the experimental stages."

"When did you learn about this? The addiction, I mean? Was it before or after you came here?"

"We've known about it for a few thousand years, but it wasn't regarded as a real problem until we came here. It mostly happened with charl and their cheren, and it was considered to be part of the bond between the couple. And since those relationships were exceedingly rare, nobody really thought anything of it. Of course, now that we're living among humans, it's very different."

"I see . . ." Mia looked out the window, trying to understand the implications. Something didn't quite make sense to her, but she couldn't place her finger on it right now.

And then it hit her.

Turning back to look at him, she frowned in puzzlement. "Korum, what would happen when the charl passed away? To the Krinar, I mean? If they were addicted to that specific human, how did they go on?"

For a second, Korum didn't answer. Then he said softly, "The charl wouldn't pass away, Mia."

Stunned, Mia stared at him. "What do you mean?" she whispered, unsure if she had heard him right.

He was silent again, and she could see the tightening of the muscles in his jaw. All of a sudden, he swerved into the right lane and headed for the exit, disregarding the sound of screeching brakes and the outraged honking from the drivers he cut off. Startled, Mia gripped the door handle with her right hand, trying to hang on. A minute later, he pulled into the parking lot of Comfort Inn and put the car into "park" mode.

Turning to her, he said quietly, "We don't let the humans we love die, my sweet. You, Maria, Delia—you're all as close to immortal as a biological being can get. You won't age, you won't get sick, and any injuries you get—as long as they're not beyond repair—will heal quickly, as they do for me."

CHAPTER TWENTY-THREE

For a few seconds, Mia could only gape at him in shock. Was this a joke? "B-but h-how?" she stammered. "I'm not Krinar—"

"No, you're definitely not Krinar," Korum agreed. "You're human, just as you've always been."

"So then how?" Mia could barely process what he was telling her. "How is this possible?"

"Have you noticed that you've been healing quicker? Maybe feeling better, more energetic?"

Mia nodded, her heart galloping in her chest.

"And you've never wondered how that's possible? How your arm healed so quickly yesterday?"

"I thought you gave me something," Mia whispered. "That pill yesterday . . ."

"The pill was a painkiller; it didn't have the ability to heal you like that. For that, I would've needed specialized equipment similar to the devices I've used on you before. No, my darling, your arm mended so well because there are now millions of highly advanced and complex nanocytes in your body, and their sole function is to keep you healthy by repairing any damage—whether it's on a cellular or DNA level."

"What?" Dark spots swam in front of her vision, and she inhaled deeply, realizing that she'd stopped breathing for a second. "What do you mean? How would they have gotten into my body?"

"Ellet implanted them at my request the first night after you arrived in Lenkarda," he explained, studying her with a watchful amber gaze. "I brought you to her lab, and she performed the procedure."

Mia's head was spinning, and she couldn't seem to wrap her brain around what he'd just told her. "Y-you brought me to Ellet's lab? While I was sleeping? You did this to me over t-two weeks ago?"

"Yes," he said, his eyes slowly turning more golden. "I didn't want to chance something happening to you by delaying it any further."

She stared at him, utterly bewildered. "Why didn't you tell me? Why didn't you ask me before you did it?"

"I couldn't take a chance that you'd refuse," he said simply. "You were still too angry, too resentful when I had first brought you there. And frankly, my darling, I was too angry with you—too hurt and angry to offer this to you at the time and have an entire discussion on this topic. Your betrayal wounded me, Mia. Logically, I understood why you did it, but it still hurt me more than anything anyone had ever done . . ."

Mia swallowed, tears welling up in her eyes. "I'm sorry . . . I really am so sorry about that—"

"And later on," Korum continued, his gaze holding hers, "after the procedure was done, I delayed telling you because I wanted to see how our relationship would develop, whether you would grow to feel as strongly about me as I felt about you . . ."

"You were testing me?"

He nodded. "In a way. I know how much immortality would mean to most humans. I wanted you to love *me*—and not just the long life I could give you. I was going to tell you when we came back to Lenkarda, but the topic kept coming up, and I didn't want to lie to you."

Her thoughts racing a mile a minute, Mia reached for the door, her hand scrambling to find the handle in the unfamiliar vehicle.

"What are you doing?" he asked sharply, his eyes narrowing.

"I . . . I need a minute," she said tremulously, her arm shaking as she pushed open the door. She felt violated and invaded, and the realization that the man she loved had done that to her was making her sick. "I just need a minute—"

Before she could get out of the car, he was already there, looming over the passenger side. "Stop it, Mia. You're not going anywhere."

Feeling like she was hyperventilating, Mia scrambled out of the car, ignoring his order. She needed some distance between them right now, needed to find a way to come to terms with everything she'd just learned.

He grabbed her arm as she tried to slide past him. "Stop acting like this. You said you loved me—you even risked your life yesterday to save me—and you're upset about the fact that we can be together long term?"

Mia frantically shook her head, trying to yank her arm away—a futile attempt, of course. "No, of course not!" She could hear the edge of hysteria in her own voice. "But you didn't even ask me! How could you do something this big without asking me?"

"Do what?" His tone was ice-cold, and his expression hard. "Give you perfect health? A long life?"

Mia felt like her head would explode. "Implant something into my body! Perform a medical procedure on me without my knowledge or consent!"

"I gave you a gift, Mia." His eyes were almost purely yellow at this point. "It's not like I stole your kidney—"

"You stole my free will!" Mia was vaguely aware that she was yelling, but she didn't care right now. Her vision was hazy with rage, and she could feel herself trembling with the force of her emotions. All the frustration of the past few weeks boiled to the surface. "You stole my ability to make any decisions in my life! Yes, I love you, but that doesn't give you the right to treat me like a possession. Don't you understand, Korum? Don't you realize how that makes me feel, knowing that you can do something like that to me?"

He stared at her, and she could see the muscle pulsing in his tightly clenched jaw. "I did what was best for you. I gave you immortality, Mia. Wasn't that what you were worrying about? Our future together?"

"The future where I'm treated like a slave for centuries to come? The future where I don't have any say over my own body, my own life? That kind of future?" Mia asked bitterly, too furious to think about what she was saying.

She heard him inhale sharply. "Get in the car, Mia," he ordered, his voice low and cold. "You're being irrational."

"Or what?" she said defiantly. "You're going to force me in? You're going to make me?"

"If I have to. Now get in."

Shaking with helpless anger, Mia got in and watched as he shut the passenger door and walked over to the driver's side.

"We're going back to the house," he said, pulling out

of the parking lot with the sound of squealing tires. "I don't think a theme park is the best idea right now."

* * *

The ride home passed in tense silence, with Mia looking out the window and Korum concentrating on driving. It took less than thirty minutes to make the drive back, with the speedometer pushing a hundred-and-thirty. Thankfully, they weren't stopped by the police. Mia had a strong suspicion that any state trooper unfortunate enough to confront Korum in this mood wouldn't have fared well.

As much as she'd wanted to have some time to herself, the silent drive accomplished nearly the same thing, giving her time to think. With her temper slowly cooling, the full implications of what he'd just told her dawned on her. He'd made her immortal—or at least as close to immortal as a biological being could get, she mentally corrected herself. She could still die if her body was damaged beyond repair, just as Korum could—but not from aging or disease, like the rest of humanity.

Did that mean that she would now live for thousands of years? She couldn't begin to comprehend that length of time. She was only twenty-one now, and even thirty seemed far away. A thousand years? It was like something out of a fairy tale. Never aging, never getting sick . . . He was right; it was every human's dream come true. It was *her* dream come true.

But the way he'd done it . . . Mia stared at her palms, where she still had tracking devices implanted from the time he'd shined her. Why had she been so surprised that he would do something else to her? He obviously regarded her as "his"—his charl, his to do with as he pleased. Yes, he'd given her an impossible, priceless gift, but he had also taken from her any semblance of an illusion about the true nature of their relationship. He wasn't her boyfriend or her lover; he was her master. She didn't have any say when it came to her own body, her own life, and he clearly saw nothing wrong with doing whatever he wanted to her.

For the past couple of weeks, she'd lived in a dream world, reveling in being with him, in the phenomenal opportunity he'd given her, in the way he'd interacted so well with her family . . . And all this time, she hadn't known that he had fundamentally changed her, that she was no longer the same Mia she had always been.

Immortality. It seemed so crazy, so impossible . . . For millennia, people had searched for that elusive fountain of youth, and yet the Ks had had it all along. A shiver ran through her as she fully understood what that meant: the Krinar had the power to indefinitely extend human lifespan, and they chose not to.

The non-interference mandate.

That had to be the only explanation. The Krinar had created her kind, and they continued playing God with them. Humans were nothing more than an experiment to them, and Mia realized how foolish she'd been to hope that Korum would ever see her as an equal. He might love her in his own way, but he didn't see her as a person, as someone who had the same basic rights as he did. How could he when his species regarded humans as nothing more than their creations, the result of their grand evolutionary design?

The car pulled into the driveway, and Mia got out as soon as it stopped, rushing into the house. She couldn't look at Korum right now, couldn't talk about this rationally. Not yet, not until she'd had a chance to digest this further.

To her relief, he didn't follow her, giving her some much needed space.

She ran upstairs and locked herself in one of the guest bedrooms. The lock was beyond flimsy, of course; it probably wouldn't deter a human man, much less a Krinar. But it still made her feel a tiny bit better, having that barrier between them.

Sitting down on the bed, Mia looked down at her hands, clenched so tightly on her lap. On her right thumb, there had always been a tiny scar; she'd cut herself with a kitchen knife when she was seven, trying to peel an apple. The scar was now gone. Why hadn't she noticed that before?

Getting up, she walked over to the large mirror hanging on the wall near the entrance. The image reflecting back at her looked remarkably normal. Same pale face, same unruly dark curls. Yet upon closer inspection, she could see the subtle differences. Her skin, usually lightly freckled, was completely smooth and white, without even a hint of any blemish. The minor sun damage she'd accumulated in her twenty-one years seemed to have disappeared. Her hair looked healthier as well, without any split ends—yet she hadn't seen the inside of a salon in over six months.

Lifting her arm, she flexed it slightly, watching the small muscle moving beneath her skin. Even her body had changed slightly; she'd always been thin, but now she looked a little more toned, as though she'd been exercising regularly. She remembered how she'd been able to swim for an hour, how she'd fought Leslie and won . . . It appeared that improved fitness was one of the benefits of this procedure.

No wonder Ellet had seemed so familiar to her. Mia

recalled the dream she'd had when she first arrived in Lenkarda—a dream where a beautiful woman was touching her with her elegant fingers. Ellet. It had been Ellet. Korum had brought Mia to her lab for the procedure, and Mia must've been semi-awake for at least part of it.

Walking back to the bed, Mia lay down and curled up into a little ball, bringing her knees to her chest. She felt nauseous, and she knew that it was all in her head. She couldn't get sick now; it was a physical impossibility. But the unpleasant sensation in her stomach lingered, her insides twisting as she imagined Korum drugging her and bringing her to his former lover. She pictured Ellet performing the procedure on her unconscious body and shuddered.

How could he have done this to her? How could he have given her something so precious, something she hadn't even dared to hope for, while at the same time destroying her trust? And how could she be with someone who could do something like that, who could completely disregard her will?

Yet how could she not?

Mia tried to imagine a future without Korum, and the years stretched in front of her, grey and empty. If she'd never met him—if she'd never experienced his passion, his caring—she would've been content, but now . . . Now he was as necessary to her as air. Even though they'd only been separated for a few minutes, she felt his absence so acutely it was as if a part of her was missing. If he ever left her, she wouldn't be just devastated; she would simply cease to exist, to function as a person. She would be nothing more than a broken empty shell, a mere shadow of her former self.

Was that how he felt about her too?

Tears burned in her eyes at the thought. Was that why he'd done this, because he couldn't wait, couldn't bear the possibility of any harm befalling her if he delayed the procedure by even a couple of weeks? Had he taken away her freedom of choice because of the strength of his feelings for her?

She tried to imagine how she would've felt if someone she loved was weak and fragile, prone to illness and injury. Korum had always been so strong, so invulnerable; other than that time on the beach—and before, when she'd been working with the Resistance—she'd never really had to worry about his health and wellbeing.

But he worried about her constantly. She knew that.

He went out of his way to take care of her, to make sure she was warm and well-fed, to heal all her injuries, no matter how minor. Knowing how important school and career were to her, he hadn't tried to limit her in that regard. Instead, he'd provided her with an incredible opportunity, giving her a chance to feel happy and fulfilled in that part of her life. He'd even made sure that her family was comfortable with their relationship. He'd given her everything—except the ability to make her own decisions.

No, she couldn't imagine a life without him—and now she didn't need to. For better or for worse, they could be together forever, and her foolish heart filled with joy at the thought. She didn't know if she could forgive him for doing the procedure without her consent—not quite yet, at least—but she could try. She would have to try. She loved him too much not to.

After all, they now had centuries to figure it all out.

CHAPTER TWENTY-FOUR

Ten minutes later, Mia headed downstairs, ready to talk. She had a million questions for Korum, and she couldn't wait to get the answers.

To her surprise, she found him standing in the living room, staring out the window at the ocean beyond. Hearing her footsteps, he turned around to face her, and Mia froze on the stairs, shocked by the remote look on his face.

His eyes seemed empty, as though he was looking straight through her, and the expression on his face was hard and shuttered, giving nothing away.

"Korum?" Mia was aware that her voice trembled slightly, but she couldn't help herself. She'd seen him cold and mocking, she'd seen him angry and passionate, but she'd never seen him like this before. It was as though a stranger was looking at her right now, a stranger with the familiar features of the man she loved.

"The car keys are over there," he said, gesturing at the

coffee table. His voice was flat and unemotional. "I'll make sure that Roger sends all your things to your parents' house. For now, I transferred money into your bank account, so you can buy some basic necessities until your luggage arrives."

"What?" Mia whispered inaudibly, feeling like all air had left the room. Her chest felt like it was getting squeezed in a giant vise, and she couldn't seem to get her lungs to work.

"The guardians will continue to watch over you and your family for now, until we're sure that Saur was acting alone. You should be safe enough now that he and Leslie have been caught."

Her brain couldn't seem to process what he was telling her. "K-Korum? What are you talking about?"

He turned away then, looking out the window again. "That's all, Mia. You can go."

Hardly aware of her actions, Mia slowly walked down the stairs, a cold sensation spreading throughout her body. "Go where?" she asked, unable, unwilling to understand. Pausing a few feet away from him, she stood there trembling, desperately needing him to turn around, to look at her with that warm smile of his.

But he didn't. He was like a statue, completely still and unmoving. "I assume to your parents' house," he finally said. "Isn't that where you usually spend your summers?"

"You want m-me to leave?" Mia could barely choke out the words through the constriction in her throat. A black pit of despair seemed to yawn underneath her, ready to engulf her at any moment. Surely he couldn't mean that, surely he didn't really want her to go . . .

"Take the car," he said, still looking out the window. "You know how to drive, right?"

"I don't have my driver's license with me," she said

numbly, staring at his back.

"If any cops stop you, I'll take care of your ticket. Your license and the rest of your things will be delivered to you this week."

Her throat closing up, Mia wrapped her arms around herself, trying to contain the agony within. "Why?" she whispered hoarsely. "Why do you want me to leave?"

"Isn't that what you wanted?" he asked coldly, turning around to look at her. His face was completely expressionless; only the faint yellow flecks in his irises gave away any hint of emotion. "Isn't that what you've been fighting for all these weeks? Your freedom? Well, you have it." He turned away again, effectively dismissing her.

Feeling like she was suffocating, Mia desperately sucked in air. "Korum, please, I don't understand—"

"Is my English not clear enough for you?" His words lashed at her like a whip. "You're free to go. Leave, get out of here."

Almost choking on the sob rising in her throat, Mia backed away, the pain of his rejection nearly unbearable. The back of her knees touched the coffee table, and her hand automatically closed around the car keys lying there. Grabbing them, Mia turned and ran out of the house, her vision blurred by tears streaming down her face.

She got as far as the car before sinking down to the ground. Her entire body was shaking, and she could barely draw in enough air through the compression in her chest. For some reason, Korum didn't want her anymore. He wanted her to leave. After everything, he was letting her go.

It didn't make sense; none of it made sense. Leaning

against the car, Mia sat on the hard ground, hugging her knees and rocking back and forth. After a couple of minutes, when the initial shock of agony had subsided, she tried to gather her thoughts, to attempt to understand what had just happened. Surely, there had to be a logical explanation for this. Why would he bother making her immortal if he was planning to walk away from her all along? Why would he have gone so far as to make her family like him if he didn't care about her? Why would he have told her that he loved her? Had it all been a lie? Had he been toying with her all along? The thought was so excruciating that Mia had to push it away for the sake of her sanity.

Or was it all her fault? Did her reaction to his revelation make him change his mind about their relationship? Perhaps he was beginning to tire of her already, and this had been the last straw for him. Mia raised her fist to her mouth, biting down hard to contain a moan of pain. She couldn't imagine her life without him, and he didn't want her anymore. She'd lost him; for whatever reason, she'd lost him . . .

She should get in the car and leave, try to salvage some pride instead of crying in his driveway, but she couldn't make herself move. If she left now, she might never see him again. He had no reason to be in New York anymore, and there was no guarantee she would ever be allowed in Lenkarda again. If she drove away, the person she loved more than anything would be gone from her life.

She couldn't allow that to happen.

Her face wet with tears, Mia resolutely got up, brushing the dust and gravel off her dress. If Korum truly didn't want her, she needed to hear him say so. He would have to explain himself because she wasn't leaving without a fight. He had forced his way into her life, into her heart, and now he thought he could walk away without an explanation? She might have been too afraid to question him in the beginning, but she wasn't anymore. If he wanted to get rid of her, he would have to physically remove her from the premises. She wasn't leaving until they talked about everything.

And wiping her cheeks with the back of her wrist, Mia headed back into the house to confront the only man she'd ever loved.

* * *

Korum was standing in the same spot, still looking out the window. Hearing her approach, he turned around. For a second, a flash of something appeared on his face before it smoothed into its expressionless mask again.

"You didn't leave," he said quietly, studying her dispassionately. She knew his sharp gaze didn't miss the remnants of tears on her face or traces of dirt on her legs.

"No," she said, her voice rougher than usual. "I didn't leave."

"Why not?" He inquired, looking mildly curious, as though they were talking about nothing more important than a movie she didn't enjoy.

Mia's eyes narrowed. "Why do you want me to go?" she countered, her chin lifting. "Yesterday, you said you loved me, and now you don't want to be with me?"

His expression darkened, and his eyes turned that dangerous shade of gold again. "Mia, if you don't walk away right now, you won't be able to. Ever. Do you understand me?"

Her heart hammering in her chest, Mia stared defiantly at him. "No, I don't. I don't understand you at all." And instead of walking away, she took a step in his direction.

In the blink of an eye, he was next to her, moving so fast that she jumped in surprise. His hand flashed toward her and closed around the front of her dress, holding her in place as he loomed over her. "What don't you understand?" he said softly, and she heard the barely controlled rage in the velvety smoothness of his voice. "You want me to beg you to stay? To tell you how much I love you again?"

Her chest rapidly rising and falling with every breath, Mia swallowed to get rid of the obstruction in her throat. She'd never seen him in this kind of mood before, and she was almost frightened. Almost—because she now knew that he would never hurt her. Not physically, at least.

"Why didn't you leave when I gave you a chance, Mia?" he whispered harshly, jerking her toward him until she was pressed against his body, feeling the heat radiating from him and the hard bulge growing in his jeans. "Don't you know how much it cost me to let you go?"

He wasn't trying to get rid of her. He was giving her freedom because he thought that's what she wanted.

The truth dawned on her, and Mia almost burst into tears again. Korum loved her; he loved her enough to let her walk away, to overcome his own need to keep her with him.

For the first time, he was giving her a choice.

Her heart filling with incandescent joy, Mia stared up at him, seeing the signs of strain on his beautiful face. He loved her, and he was letting her walk away. The magnitude of his gesture didn't escape her. This gorgeous, powerful man had never been denied anything he truly wanted before—and she now knew beyond a shadow of doubt that he wanted her. His intellect and ambition had propelled Korum to the top of Krinar society, and he was used to having an extraordinary amount of influence and control. Here on Earth, his power was even greater; as a member of the race that conquered her planet, he could do almost anything without consequences. Among humans, he was like a god.

What would it be like, to wield that kind of power? Would she have been able to restrain herself if she knew that she could take anything she wanted? Have anyone she wanted? Mia had never asked herself that question before, and she wondered if she would like her own answer.

The fact that he was giving her a choice now . . . She knew how difficult it was for him, how much it went against his nature. He considered her his, and by Krinar law, she belonged to him. For Korum to relinquish that power, to let her leave him—that, more than anything, showed her how much she now meant to him.

So instead of flinching away in fear of his temper, she slid her hands up his chest, gripping his face between her palms. Holding his gaze with her own, she whispered, "I don't want to go. I don't ever want to go . . ."

His eyes flared brighter, and she could see his pupils expanding even as his mouth descended on hers, his lips hard and almost bruising. His tongue invaded her mouth, his kiss all-consuming, and she met him eagerly, reveling in the frantic hunger she could taste in his kiss. His hands migrated to her back, tightened until she could barely breathe, and she could feel his large body trembling with the intensity of his emotions.

Pulling back for a second, he growled, "You're staying," and Mia nodded, even though it wasn't a question. Standing up on tiptoes, she kissed him again, and felt the room tilt as he swung her up into his arms, carrying her to the couch.

The control he exerted over himself earlier was completely gone, and she could feel the primitive need driving him now. He wasn't gentle, and she didn't want him to be, not right now, not when she so desperately craved his passion. His hands ripped off her dress, her underwear, and then he was plunging into her, wild with the urge to get inside, to claim her in the most basic way possible.

At the force of his entry, Mia cried out and arched toward him, her fingers curving into claws, digging into the back of his neck. He felt impossibly hard and thick, stretching her, filling her until she forgot all about the agony of nearly losing him, lost in the driving power of his thrusts.

His right hand fisted in her hair, pulled her head to the side, exposing her neck, and then he bit her, the sharp edges of his teeth slicing across her skin. Mia gasped at the sudden pain, and then his mouth latched onto the wound and the world around her dissolved as ecstasy rushed through her veins.

For the next several hours, all she knew was the dark rapture of his embrace.

CHAPTER TWENTY-FIVE

"So tell me more about this immortality thing," Mia said lazily, watching as he lifted one long curl and traced a circle with it on his own shoulder.

They were lying in bed side by side, having sated themselves yet again this morning.

Mia could hardly remember the rest of the day yesterday. After he'd bitten her, she didn't regain her senses until late in the evening, when he'd woken her up from exhausted sleep in order to feed her dinner. Then he brought her back to bed, and she passed out again, opening her eyes this morning only to find him watching her with a hungry look on his face. "Finally," he'd muttered before stripping away the blanket and crawling down her body, his skilled mouth bringing her to orgasm before she was even fully awake. Afterwards, he'd taken her again, as though he couldn't bear to be physically separated from her for even a few hours.

Now he turned his head to look at her, a warm glow in his eyes. "What do you want to know?" he asked, smiling.

"Everything," Mia told him. "Have you always known how to do that—to make humans immortal? And how does it work, exactly? Am I still human, or am I some weird hybrid? Do I also have enhanced speed and strength? And will I ever change physically, or is this how I'm going to look for the rest of my life?"

He laughed, rising up on his elbow. "That's quite a few questions. Let me start with the easy ones. Yes, you're still human. No, you're not really that much stronger or quicker than you were, although you're in somewhat better shape. However, you do heal very fast. If you wanted to get stronger, it would be easy for you; all you'd need to do is start lifting weights and doing exercise. Your body regenerates so rapidly now that you won't need any downtime, and you could become as fit as any of your top athletes in a matter of weeks.

"You have more endurance now too, again because of your body's rapid healing properties. And no, you're definitely not a hybrid of any kind. The nanocytes mimic the natural functions of your body and repair all damage; that's really all they do. They restore your body to its optimal state, so yes, you won't really change physically going forward. You're going to remain young and beautiful for years and centuries to come."

Mia listened to his explanation, her pulse beginning to pound with excitement. "Wow," she whispered in amazement. "I don't even know what to say. Just . . . wow."

Korum grinned at her, and then his expression became more serious. "As to the first part of your question, this is a relatively new technology for us. We've only had it for the last few thousand years."

"A few thousand years? That's a really long time . . ." They could've given humans immortality at any point in the last few thousand years?

He sighed. "If you say so."

"Korum," Mia said tentatively, "what exactly is this non-interference mandate? Is that the reason why you haven't shared any of your technology with us?"

He nodded. "Yes. The non-interference mandate was set by the Elders, and it supersedes any laws that the Council can pass—"

"The Elders?"

"The oldest Krinar in existence. There are nine who are known as the Elders; they're the ones who have been around for millions of years. Lahur is the oldest among them, and it's said that he's been alive for over ten million years."

Stupefied, Mia stared at him. "Ten million years?" Ten million years ago, humans didn't even exist as a species. And there were Krinar around who were that old?

"It's unimaginable for me as well," Korum said, understanding her awe. "They had to have seen so much, learned so much throughout their lives. There's nothing that can compare to the wisdom of the Elders."

"Where are they?" Mia asked, goosebumps springing up all over her body as she tried to picture someone that ancient. "Did any of them come to Earth?"

"No, they're on Krina. For the most part, they're very reclusive; few Krinar have ever met them, and that's how they like it. I've seen Lahur from a distance, but I'm one of the few who has."

Mia frowned, perplexed. "So how did they set the mandate? How do they enforce it?"

"They don't have to enforce it, Mia. The Elders are revered in our society; to go against them is an offense punishable by death."

"But why did they do it? Why set that mandate in the

first place?"

"I don't know their exact motivations," Korum admitted. "But I do know that two of them were part of the team of scientists that guided human evolution. They were the original creators of your species. If I had to venture a guess, I would say that they are still overseeing that project."

Mia's frown deepened. "So why did they let you come to Earth in the first place?"

"Because the Council—specifically, myself, Saret, and a few others—was able to convince them that it was necessary for the ultimate survival of the Krinar. Your weapons, your technology were evolving so rapidly and in such a destructive direction that you were endangering your planet. And since we will ultimately need to call Earth home—when our star dies in a hundred million years or so—we couldn't allow you to make this planet uninhabitable."

Mia digested that quietly. She still didn't fully understand this Elder situation. "So how is it that you were able to make me immortal despite this mandate?"

"By claiming you as my charl." His eyes glittered at her. "We're allowed to make exceptions for our charl."

"I see." Mia looked at him, remembering his assertion that being a charl was an honor. Now she could understand why he thought so. Yes, the charl may have few rights in the K society, but they had something no other humans could achieve—perfect health and an incredibly long lifespan. Even in modern-day United States, there were probably many who would gladly trade whatever rights and freedoms they enjoyed for a chance to live even a few extra decades, much less hundreds or even thousands of years.

"What about my parents and my sister?" Mia asked,

holding her breath. “Does the mandate make exceptions for them?”

A look of genuine regret appeared on Korum’s handsome face. “No, Mia, I’m sorry. It doesn’t. I’ll do everything I can to keep them healthy and maximize their natural lifespan, but I can’t give them what I gave you.”

Painfully biting her lip, Mia looked away. She’d suspected that might be the case, but it still hurt to hear him confirm it. She would remain young and healthy, while everyone around her would age and pass away. The thought was unbearably depressing.

“My darling, come here,” he murmured, pulling her into his arms. “I’m sorry, I really am. For what it’s worth, I will petition the Elders on your behalf. I just don’t know if it will do anything.”

“Thank you,” Mia whispered, staring him in the eyes. “Thank you for that, for everything.”

“I love you,” he said softly, his hand stroking her back. “And I’ll do anything for you. You know that, right?”

Mia smiled, her heart overflowing with emotion. “I love you more . . .”

“That would be impossible,” he told her, and the intensity in his voice startled her. “I love you so much it hurts. If you had left me yesterday . . .”

Swallowing against a sudden surge of tears, Mia hugged him tighter. “I wouldn’t have,” she said thickly. “I don’t ever want to leave you. I thought you didn’t want me anymore . . .”

“I’ll always want you.” He sounded utterly convinced of that fact.

“How do you know that?” Mia asked curiously. “We’ve known each other less than two months. How do you know how you’ll feel in a few years?”

His lips curved into a tender smile. “That’s where

experience comes in handy, my sweet. I know how I feel—I've known almost from the very beginning. The first time I held you in my arms, the first time we made love, I knew this was unlike anything I've ever felt before. I couldn't think of anything but you—the way you tasted, the way you smelled, the stubborn tilt to your chin . . . I thought I was losing my mind because I was becoming so obsessed with a human girl—a girl who didn't want to be with me, no less. I wanted to fuck you, yes, but I also wanted to keep you safe, to take you with me and never let you go . . ."

"Why didn't you tell me?" Mia asked, her heart skipping a beat at his words. "Why didn't you tell me how you felt earlier?"

The smile left his face, his expression turning serious. "Because I was frightened," he admitted darkly. "Because I had never felt like that before, and I didn't know how to cope with it. For the first time in centuries, I was driven by emotion, instead of reason, and I didn't always make the wisest choices when it came to you. I wanted to have you, and I couldn't think of anything beyond that need, that craving. I wasn't sufficiently patient, and I ended up scaring you . . . and then you got involved with the Resistance as a result. I loved you, and all you seemed to want is to have me permanently out of your life. Even later, when you told me you loved me, I wasn't sure if you truly felt that way, or if you were just playing along, giving me what I wanted—"

Mia shook her head, unable to believe her ears. He'd always seemed so invulnerable, and the realization that she'd had the power to hurt him all along was truly humbling. "No, Korum," she murmured, raising her hand to stroke his face. "I fell in love with you back in New York. Even though I thought you wanted to harm my kind, even though I was afraid of ending up as your sex slave, I still fell for you . . . And I can't live without you now—"

He drew in a deep breath and pressed her tighter against him, burying his face in her hair. "And I can't live without you, my darling," he whispered, "I don't think I can ever let you go, not anymore . . ."

"Then why did you? Why did you try to let me go yesterday?"

He pulled back, looking at her again. "Because I realized I couldn't force you to love me, to want to be with me." A bitter smile appeared on his lips. "I could keep you with me until the end of time, but I couldn't make you love me. It was no longer enough, you see, just to have you. I wanted more—I wanted you to love me freely. I thought you would rejoice at being made immortal, but you were upset instead . . . And I knew then that I couldn't do that to you, couldn't make you stay with me against your will—"

"Oh Korum," Mia whispered, "it's not against my will. It hasn't been against my will for a long time . . ."

His expression softened again. "I'm glad," he said quietly, brushing some hair off her face. "I want you to be happy with me. I never meant to make you feel like a slave. I just couldn't bear the thought of anything happening to you if I put off the procedure until you'd had a chance to acclimate to Lenkarda and get used to being with me. I thought I was giving you something you would want . . ."

"I do. I do want it," Mia told him sincerely. "How could you even doubt it? You've given me a priceless gift, and I didn't mean to imply otherwise . . . But, Korum, can you please promise me one thing?"

He studied her with a watchful gaze. "What?"

"Can you please never do anything to me without my consent again? Even if you think it's for the best, even if you're not sure I'll agree to it?"

He hesitated for a second, and then nodded reluctantly. She could see how much it cost him to make that concession, the extent to which it went against his nature. But he had now given her his word, and she knew that he would keep it.

"Thank you," she told him, caressing his shoulder. "This means a lot to me."

He smiled and leaned toward her, giving her a gentle kiss.

When he pulled away, Mia made a serious face and asked him, "Do you know what else would mean a lot to me right now?"

He looked a little wary. "What?"

"Some yummy breakfast," she told him, and watched his face light up with a dazzling smile.

* * *

On Friday morning, they left to go back to Lenkarda.

The rest of their visit to Florida had been uneventful, and her family had been sad to see them leave. Korum promised to bring Mia back for a couple of days before the end of summer, which earned him a tearful hug from her mom and a sincere thank-you from her dad. Marisa had been particularly emotional, thanking Korum again for everything he'd done for them and then blushing fiercely when he gave her a kiss on the cheek as goodbye.

"I'm going to miss them," Mia told him as they drove toward the airport where he was planning to create their ship. "I really wish I could see them more often."

"You'll be able to," Korum said, keeping his eyes on

the road. "Once I'm sure that it's completely safe, there's no reason why you can't drop in every couple of weeks or so. It doesn't take that long to get here from Lenkarda—"

"From Lenkarda?" Mia inquired delicately. "I thought we were going back to New York in the fall . . ."

Korum sighed. "If you still want that, then yes."

"Why wouldn't I?"

He shrugged. "You don't really need the degree if you're going to continue working at Saret's lab. It's not like you'll learn anything more in school than you would staying in Lenkarda—"

"Is that what you're hoping?" Mia asked. "That I would decide not to go back to school?"

"I prefer Lenkarda to New York," he admitted, "but I don't mind if you decide to finish college. I know it's still important to you, and I promised that I would bring you back for the school year. Nine months—that's nothing in the grand scheme of things, and if it gives you peace of mind . . ."

For the first time, Mia thought seriously about the possibility of not finishing school. Korum was right: what she was learning at her apprenticeship was head and shoulders above anything the university had to teach her. And if Lenkarda were to be her home, a college degree was meaningless. Would Saret allow her to return to the lab after such a long absence? She would hate to lose this opportunity in order to write a few more papers and study for a few more exams. She needed to discuss this with her boss and soon, Mia decided.

They arrived at the Daytona Beach International Airport, and Korum assembled the ship in a far-off section there, out of sight of any other humans. As the aircraft quietly took off, Mia remembered how frightened she'd been when she'd left New York, flying to Lenkarda for the very first time. Was it only three weeks ago? It seemed like a lifetime had passed between now and then.

The girl who had left New York had been frightened and traumatized, uncertain about her fate and unsure whether she could trust the man she loved—the one she had regarded as an enemy, the one she had betrayed.

She was no longer that girl.

This Mia felt utterly secure in Korum's love.

Over the past few days, their relationship had undergone yet another subtle shift. There was an openness to it now that had been missing before. Until they'd had that discussion—until he'd given her a choice—Mia had still had doubts about their relationship. It had been an uncomfortable feeling, knowing that he held all the power and had no qualms about using it—and she now realized that she'd held a part of herself back as a result, that she had still subconsciously resisted him.

Now, however, it was different—it felt different. Yes, she was still his charl, but she no longer felt like he owned her. He loved her enough to let her walk away, to relinquish his control over her, and that knowledge was like a balm to her soul, soothing the scars left by the tumultuous beginning of their affair.

Every evening, after dinner with her family, they had gone for a long walk on the beach and just talked. She'd learned about some of Korum's past relationships (there had been many) and about the fact that he had never been in love before. He'd actually thought himself incapable of it. "It really caught me by surprise, the depth of my feelings for you," he'd confessed, and she realized yet again how difficult it had been for him to let her go. The fact that he'd done it proved to her that his feelings were real—that their sexual liaison could ultimately become the genuine partnership she'd always hoped it would be.

And now, as their ship flew to Costa Rica, Mia reached over and squeezed Korum's hand. "I love you," she said, and watched as a warm smile appeared on his beautiful face.

Her life couldn't possibly get any better.

EPILOGUE

They were returning.

Saur had failed, but the Krinar had suspected he would. Korum was too good of a fighter to be killed so easily. Of course, he hadn't counted on Mia getting hurt. That part had been unacceptable. If his enemy hadn't killed Saur, the K would've done so himself.

Soon she would be near him again. The Krinar raised his hand and stared at it, imagining himself touching her delicate flesh, stroking that silky skin. She would be so small, so fragile in his arms. So vulnerable. He could do anything he wanted to her, and she wouldn't be able to resist.

His cock stirred at that thought, and he cursed his apparent inability to control himself. In anticipation of her arrival, he'd ventured out to a nearby x-club and gorged himself on human girls. All three of them had been pretty, with ambitions of a career in Hollywood. One had even had curly hair, though it was more of a dirty blond shade that hadn't appealed to him nearly as much. He'd fucked them for hours, yet he'd left the place still unsatisfied.

He wanted *her*.

And soon he would be able to have her—and anything else he wanted. His week had been quite productive.

Another few days, and he'd be all set.

FROM THE AUTHOR

Thank you for reading *Close Obsession*, the second book in the *Krinar Chronicles* series! I hope you enjoyed it. If you did, please help other people find this book by leaving a review or mentioning this series to a friend.

Mia & Korum's story concludes in *Close Remembrance*, which is now available. There will also be other novels with different characters set in the Krinar world, as well as books in contemporary settings. Please visit my website at www.annazaires.com and sign up for my newsletter to be notified when new books become available.

You can also connect with me on Facebook, Twitter, Goodreads, and LinkedIn.

Thank you for your support! I truly appreciate it.

ABOUT THE AUTHOR

Anna Zaires fell in love with books at the age of five, when her grandmother taught her to read. She wrote her first story shortly thereafter. Since then, she has always lived partially in a fantasy world where the only limits were those of her imagination. Currently residing in Florida, Anna is happily married to Dima Zales and closely collaborates with him in the writing of the Krinar Chronicles.

To learn more, please visit www.annazaires.com.

CPSIA information can be obtained at www.ICGtesting.com
Printed in the USA
LVOW04s1511030415

433204LV00014B/306/P